ONE-WAY TICKET TO RYDE

James London has had a home on the Island for over twenty years, having been a regular visitor since the 1980s. He loves its quiet pace, its history, and the gems of English life that unexpectedly reveal themselves there.

The Island is a microcosm of the world, capable of revealing good and evil that is everywhere, which he shows through the activities of Detective Inspector Bruno Peach – The Island's Murder Squad detective, with a sharp eye for a clue.

By the same author:
The Folks That Live On The Hill
The Island Murders

One-Way Ticket To Ryde

James London

Discript

First published in the United Kingdom by
Discript Limited
67 Fishbourne Road West
Chichester, West Sussex
PO19 3JJ

www.discript.com

A catalogue record for this book is available from the British Library

ISBN 978-1-9163613-0-0

Designed and typeset in Minion Pro
Printed in Scotland by Bell & Bain Ltd

To Pie

For whom I have always been pleased
to purchase a return ticket.

With my love and thanks.

CHAPTER 1

Saturday 9 June

It was 8.30 a.m. on a bright sunny summer Saturday morning when Detective Inspector Bruno Peach and his partner Janet drove into Morrisons Supermarket car park in the centre of Newport, Isle of Wight, to do the weekly food shop and relax over breakfast in the superstore restaurant.

It was a task that Bruno enjoyed. He was still in the honeymoon phase of their house-sharing relationship; having a fridge full of good solid food to select from was a step up from his thirty-five-year-old bachelor routine of a choice between Lancashire hotpot or a lasagne from the ready-made meals counter. Janet was an excellent cook, so in his new life he was eager to please. They went early before queues formed at the checkouts.

Janet with a well-prepared shopping list knew the layout of the store intimately, so her list was compiled accordingly, which reduced the shopping time to a minimum.

While Bruno pushed the trolley alongside her, weaving past stationary shoppers browsing beside their half-filled trolleys, she selected from the shelves against her list passing the items to Bruno to arrange neatly in the trolley.

At the checkout he unloaded onto the conveyor while Janet sorted into Morrison bags the veg, the fruit, separating the fridge items from the bakery and dry goods. It was a very efficient exercise, and they were finished and the car loaded in 40 minutes, leaving time for a full English in Morrisons restaurant, before their two-hour free parking slot ran out.

However, this Saturday morning's relaxed breakfast was interrupted by a call from Newport Police station's Desk Sergeant, Jack Tripper, asking Inspector Peach to report in

1

to the station immediately. Jack would not have crashed into his free time unless it was urgent, so within 10 minutes Janet had delivered Bruno to the station and was on her way home to unload the shopping.

Jack Tripper greeted him in a serious manner.

"Sorry, sir, to encroach on your Saturday, but very glad you were nearby. We have what appears to be a murder on our hands. A cleaning lady found a body in the gentlemen's lavatory at the Isle of Wight Steam Railway Havenstreet Station. She discovered the body just after 8.00 a.m., when she went to clean the lavatory. A pool of blood had seeped under the door and congealed. Too frightened to go in, she showed the manager who called us. The uniforms are already there, they've sealed off the scene and are waiting for the SOCOs and yourself, sir."

Bruno had been appointed head of the murder squad because of his success in solving recent murder cases. The parts of the job he particularly disliked were the tasks involved in every case of murder, namely examining the corpse, and the gruesomeness of the killing, then witnessing the reaction of relatives identifying the corpse in the mortuary, sometimes brutally beaten, emaciated or decomposed.

Nevertheless, he reacted immediately to the brief report from Jack jumping into a patrol car with a driver to take him to Havenstreet station. En-route he called Janet with his whereabouts, and telling her what he'd be doing for the rest of the day.

Havenstreet lay 4 miles due east of Newport on a decent road, and as traffic was moderate, the journey time was under 10 minutes.

Waiting for him was the railway manager, John Jenkins, and the chairman of the committee who oversaw the running of the business, Bill Crouch. After introductions they adjourned to The Station Master's office, a 1920s constructed detached building alongside Platform A with a printed white sign above an original Southern Railway green painted wooden entrance door.

At the end of Platform A was located the gentlemen's lavatory, in which lay an undisturbed body awaiting the SOCO's arrival.

Two uniformed police stood guard over the entrance together with a young officer known to Bruno, newly-promoted Sergeant Andy Bowen, who had worked with him recently. The arrival of two SOCOs, within minutes, enabled Bruno to leave them to search the scene and examine everything connected to the crime, whilst he and Andy Bowen talked to the Isle of Wight Steam Railway representatives to find out what they knew.

John Jenkins, the Station Manager, said it was routine practice to clean the lavatory before 9.00 a.m. each morning prior to the passengers arriving in time for the first train departure at 10.05 a.m.

Vera Beckett, the cleaning lady, had reported the pool of blood at 8.10 a.m. outside of the toilet cubicle door, and sensibly had left the lavatory undisturbed.

She had reported this to John Jenkins who, likewise, did not enter the cubicle, concluding that a body lay inside. He had locked the entrance door to the lavatory, returned to his desk, and called the police. He then called Bill Crouch, who came immediately. They closed the booking hall and cancelled the 10.05 a.m. departure.

"That is all we have done so far, although I think I shall cancel the 11.22 a.m. and the 12.34 p.m.," Jenkins said to Bruno.

The SOCOs took their time before telling Bruno that the victim was a male in his fifties, who had been stabbed twice from behind, while standing at the urinal, resulting in instant death from multiple organ failure. No weapon was found in the toilet. The SOCOs' work took two hours to gather forensic evidence, after which they released the body to the waiting ambulance for further examination by technicians at the mortuary.

Before he departed, the senior SOCO, Tom Mulligan, gave his opinion of how he died. The killer had followed the victim into the lavatory, who, whilst standing with his back to the assailant, in full flow into the urinal, had been stabbed with considerable force, twice, with a long-bladed knife that had penetrated his heart, lungs and liver. Tom Mulligan provided Bruno with the identity of the victim from items in the pockets of his clothing which he later handed to the Desk Sergeant in Newport who would record and retain these personal items for the detectives in preparation for a visit to the victim's home address later in the day. Before the SOCOs departed Havenstreet Station they conducted an hour-long search in the close proximity of the murder site in search of a weapon. Nothing was found.

Whilst the SOCOs examined the crime scene, John Jenkins ran through the entire previous day to Bruno and Andy Bowen. The weather had been hot and it had been very busy. Platform A, where the restaurant and gents' lavatory were situated, had had a continuous flow of customers until closing at 6.00 p.m. He showed Bruno the manifest of Friday's passengers and the train time departures throughout the day. It was list of names of mainly people who could not be contacted, although Bruno's experience had taught him to value everything at the start of an investigation.

Once the SOCOs and the ambulance departed with the body, Bruno and Andy Bowen examined the toilet where the victim had been stabbed to death and repeated the search of the area around the gents' lavatory. It did not require a great deal of imagination to understand what happened in that tiny enclosed space. The toilet, like the station itself, had been preserved with 1940s fixtures and fittings. The cistern above the pan was flushed by pulling a chain. The brass coat hook had S.R. engraved into it. Andy Bowen noted the shoulder-height lavatory window was broken. When he enquired, he was told that it wasn't broken on Friday morning and for health and safety reasons it would have been repaired within the hour.

The SOCOs' report was available to them by the time they had returned to the station, and provided the details of the murder required by Bruno to begin his investigation and make his first visit to the address of the victim and speak to next of kin, and try to answer the who, what and where questions of this grisly murder.

The victim's name was Geoffrey Klinker. He was fifty-four and lived permanently in London. He was also one of the wealthiest landowners on the Island, having inherited his father's estate of more than 10,000 acres of farmland and its main house, Clive Hall, several years previously.

He had been stabbed with a long blade knife twice, the first penetrated his left lung and the second split the casing of his heart killing him instantly, whilst he stood relieving himself with his back to the assailant. The killer was a right-handed person, according to the SOCO, who had followed the victim into the toilet, weapon at the ready, sprung forward and administered the two stabbings in just a few seconds. He had then pulled the body into the cubicle leaving him astride the pedestal, remaining in the toilet for a very short time leaving no prints or evidence. The hands and finger nails of the victim showed no sign of a struggle, suggesting that the knife thrusts were accurately administered through light summer clothing, causing instant death.

The farmhouse, Clive Hall, was imposing. Stone built in the late nineteenth century, it was situated on the edge of Tennyson Down, east of Chale. It had not stood empty since the death of his father, Tom Klinker, because his will had provided that Geoffrey Klinker's mother, Madeline, could continue to occupy the house for so long as she wished, even until she died, which she had 2 months previously.

Bruno, accompanied by Andy Bowen, drove to the

Klinker farmhouse to meet Mrs Galloway, Geoff Klinker's housekeeper, who had been informed of their arrival. She was a neat and tidy attractive woman, who showed them into a well appointed, stylishly furnished country house lounge. She explained that Dr Klinker was unmarried and he lived in London, although until his mother passed away two months previously, he had visited her regularly since his father's death five years before. She explained that Dr Klinker's half-brother, Mr Arnold Harris, was Mrs Klinker's son from her first marriage and had stayed with her on and off for a number of years, and he had arranged her funeral which Dr Klinker had attended.

"Inspector, I should state that I was Geoffrey's aunt and Madeline Klinker, Geoffrey's mother, was my sister. When Tom died five years ago she needed a live in companion so she asked me to housekeep for her, and as my husband died six years ago, I accepted. I had not noticed that Geoff had not returned the previous evening as he often came and went unannounced."

The news of his murder was an immense shock to her, and she demonstrated a great deal of distress at the news and reluctantly agreed to visit the mortuary to identify his body later that evening, and if she could contact Arnold Harris, she would bring him with her.

Mrs Galloway was an efficient, experienced housekeeper. Without outside help she managed the five-bedroom farm-house Clive Hall that had been the Klinker family home for over 100 years and where his father had been born and brought up.

The house throughout revealed a woman's touch. It had patterned cushions and well-hung curtains, well-polished old-fashioned furniture of no antique value, pictures of the Isle of Wight and many framed photographs that showed Tom Klinker's interest in sailing. While they looked around the house, she recovered from her distress at the news of her nephew's murder and made them tea and answered questions about him in a straightforward way. There were no deviations in her answers, no gossip or tales that might reveal anything unusual about Geoff Klinker. She had no knowledge of his personal life in London.

"He was a little superior, like I imagine all hospital consultants to be," she said. "He was not the sort to get his hands dirty, hence farming had never appealed to him as a job. He had no friends, least not on the Island. After his father died, I think he regarded the farm as a millstone round his neck."

"Why did he come here?"

"Because it was home. I think he loved this place, but he couldn't look after it doing what he did in London.

When his father and mother were alive, he used to come for the day and go back the same day."

"Was he married?"

"I am not sure, Inspector, he was very attractive to women."

"What was he doing here on this occasion?"

"He came for his old school reunion, forty years since they all started at Ryde School. They were the Class of '78. That is what he was doing on the Havenstreet Express. They all went on it and had lunch to celebrate."

"Can you show us any personal effects he brought with him or that he keeps here?"

"I will show you his study and his bedroom. Most of the pictures and ornaments were Mrs Klinker's, but you can regard them as Geoffrey's now," she said.

With that she left Bruno and Andy to examine the contents of his two rooms and to wander freely about the house.

Leaving her privately to come to terms with the awful news, at their request the two detectives examined his personal effects, which were scattered around his library, for clues that might lead to suspects. There was nothing of interest amongst his personal possessions to the two detectives.

Bills relating to the house and correspondence from local solicitors concerning boundaries and land registry documents lay on his desk.

In the bedroom there was nothing of a personal nature. One almost expected to find a copy of the Gideons' hotel bible in the bedside cabinet. His study had been his father's office. On the desk was an A5 notebook containing short profiles of his fellow classmates, to remind him of their personal characteristics, which appeared to date from his school days. There were 20 names giving some typical schoolboy assessments. Against some of the names were ticks, presumably indicating they were turning up for the fortieth anniversary reunion.

It was obvious from his travelling bag, that Klinker had planned a short visit, and nothing to indicate any contact with anyone living on the Island.

Before departing, Bruno asked Mrs Galloway if she planned to stay in the farmhouse. She replied that she didn't know, but she as owned her house in Ryde, she would leave when they wanted her to go.

Bruno left her with his private number should she be able to contact Arnold Harris to arrange an identification visit which, after speaking to Harris, she confirmed for 6.30 p.m.

Bruno had requested a uniformed officer be present who took charge of escorting Mrs Galloway and Arnold Harris to the body, which lay in the hospital mortuary. Neither spoke a word as the technician exposed Klinker's face. Mrs Galloway kept hold of Harris's arm during those 20 seconds and both turned towards Bruno and Harris spoke quietly to him that it was Geoffrey Klinker. Bruno thanked them for attending and the two shocked, confused family members departed. From their quiet sad demeanour, Bruno saw nothing that would aid his investigations.

As yet there were no suspects. The murderer could be anybody, a member the railway staff, or a passenger on the train. A list of passengers, in as complete a form as possible, had been emailed by John Jenkins and was sitting on Bruno's desk at the Newport Police HQ, a detailed examination of which he would start Sunday morning.

Janet was in a state of heightened curiosity waiting for his arrival home.

She loved her job as the head of a local primary school, but envied Bruno's life as a sleuth, and the excitement that often presented him with a new puzzle to solve. However, she understood for a policeman not every day was crammed full of excitement, police work was mostly dull plodding and laborious to write up, but this was not one of those days.

Over supper he told her of his day's activity, hoping that with her thoughtful input she might help him plan his investigation into the murder of Geoff Klinker.

When he mentioned the name of the victim, Geoff Klinker, she knew something about him.

"I know he is an eminent surgeon who lives in London, owns a large farm on the edge of St Catherine's Down. Who would want to kill him down here?" she said.

"He doesn't live on the Island so how could he have enemies here?" she said. "And a stranger to the Island would not choose an obscure location like the public gents' lavatory at a tourist spot to stab him to death. The killer must have been familiar with Havenstreet station."

Bruno hadn't yet had time to consider the motive for his killing.

"But assume it was a stranger from London on his tail who struck when the opportunity presented itself?" he said.

She thought about his suggestion for a short while.

Janet always made valid observations that could set him on the track of finding the killer.

"You mustn't start with that in mind. Begin with the school group and the few people he had contact with on the Island, like his half-brother, Arnold Harris."

CHAPTER 2

Sunday 10 June

Bruno Peach and Andy Bowen met in the police station to plan a course of action, and examine the email from John Jenkins, listing the staff that were on duty on Friday 8 June: those working on the train, the platform, booking hall, and catering staff, a total of 16; and the 91 passengers on the 11.05 a.m. departing Havenstreet station on the E5022 express. From the ticket purchases on the day, 26 had paid by credit card, whose names could be eventually identified and supplied by the card issuers; while the 24 names of those who'd booked in advance and paid by credit card were listed by John Jenkins. The identities of the 10 men on a school reunion could be obtained from the Ryde School secretary, which would confirm that the victim, Dr Geoffrey Klinker, was one of that party, which left 31 cash paying passengers who could not be identified.

The time of his murder was given by the medical officer at between 3.00 p.m. and 4.00 p.m. on the afternoon of 8 June, after the school party had travelled on the train for lunch at Wootton at noon lasting until 1.45 p.m.

With Jenkins's list to hand they returned to the scene of the crime at the Isle of Wight Steam Railway at Havenstreet station and caught the 11.05 a.m. steam train travelling to Wootton. Bruno believed there was relevance in the train journey, to understand how a murderer might conceal a large knife if in fact he had made the journey on the train.

"Had the killer planned to kill Dr Klinker in the lavatory after the school outing had ended mid-afternoon, or had the opportunity just presented itself? If it was the latter then the killer could have chosen anywhere," said Andy.

The lavatory suggested it was an Islander with local

knowledge which made Jenkins list of visitors to the Island less important.

The journey to Wootton was short, approximately 8 minutes. At Wootton the engine ran around the train recoupling after Smallbrook Junction via Havenstreet before recoupling for the return journey to Havenstreet. On arrival back at Havenstreet they made a more careful examination of the restaurant, the gift shop, and the scene of the murder, re-enacting the actions of the killer up to stabbing, and his likely movements thereafter.

Their Sunday morning train had carried roughly the same number of passengers as it had two days previously. On the journey Bruno had been struck by the great and varied amount of wildlife to be seen. Rabbits, game birds, farm livestock of every variety and sometimes deer were spotted running away from the track.

Having gained all possible information about the carriages and re-examined the scene of crime, they mingled with the visitors and came to the conclusion that amongst a group of 90 passengers awaiting to board and non-travelling visitors, who were spectators on a sunny June day, it was easily possible to get lost in the crowd.

Although desirable to interview the passengers on the Friday afternoon journey and the Havenstreet railway staff as soon as possible, it was only the school party that could be contacted immediately through the school secretary. The day-trippers would have to wait, and the cash payers would remain unidentified, although TV cameras might identify some, and the credit card payers would be identified with help from the card issuers, but that would take time. Circumstances indicated that the killer and his motive was close to home. The school party, together with a list of names and addresses, would be supplied by the school secretary, Marion Hislop, who made the ticket reservation. The other persons of interest were the train staff and Havenstreet volunteers who worked on Friday 8 June, consisting of the train driver; a footplate assistant stoker/driver; and a guard on rear carriage: a total of three persons on the train.

At Havenstreet Station, the staff on duty were 5 catering staff, located in the restaurant on Platform A; 3 Gift Shop staff; 1 ticket office; 1 platform porter; 1 signalman; a second platform guard; plus John Jenkins, who was present throughout the day, and acted as a reserve for all jobs: a total of 16.

Each of the volunteer staff had been employed for at least one year. They wore uniforms of the period and were part of a team of thirty who reported for shifts when required. They were respected members of a select social club. Bruno skipped through the names, addresses and ages of those working on Friday but decided not to speak to any of them before examining the school party passenger list. This they obtained from the school first thing Monday morning.

To interview the former pupils who had attended the reunion was the most urgent task. The ten of them the school secretary had booked for the trip, in the opinion of Marion Hislop, had little in common with each other apart from the fact they had attended Ryde School together in the late 1970s. They had followed different professions after leaving school.

CHAPTER 3

Monday 11 June

Promptly at school opening, the detectives arrived at the school to interview Marion Hislop, the school secretary, who had arranged the Class of '78 reunion on the Havenstreet Express.

Ryde School had an excellent reputation as a minor public school founded in 1921 by a husband and wife team, William and Constance McIsaac. It took boarders and dayboys and since the late 1970s it had become co-educational, admitting girls, and merging with Upper Chine boarding school for girls, which had been located in Shanklin.

Marion Hislop was upset to hear the news of Geoff Klinker's murder at the Havenstreet train station during the school reunion the previous Friday. After a prolonged silence she shed a tear and expressed her disbelief that this could have happened to such a nice gentleman.

She could provide very little information on the day or on the group of pupils who had attended the reunion except their names email and home addresses and the dates they had joined the school and the list of those attending which she had provided to the station ticket office when she reserved their places.

Bruno noted that Jenkins, the station manager, had not given him the list of school attendees.

"Do you arrange many school reunions, Miss Hislop?"

"Not many," she said. "The Class of '78 have one every ten years. They are a special year because 1978 was the year the school helped with restoration work on The Needles Battery and all the new boys in that year were involved. It became their project for the time they were here. It created a bond between them. It was a focus and it bound them together

13

like no other year at the school. The Old Battery, situated
on the western tip of the Island, was built in 1861 to protect
the recently constructed Needles Lighthouse from attack
from the sea. It was surrounded by steep cliffs and a sunken
ditch, which acted as a moat from the landward slide. It was
heavily armed and defended the approaches to Portsmouth
during the First and Second World Wars. Bruno had visited
this isolated outpost now maintained by the National Trust
and understood the sense of achievement of those involved
in its restoration. When the project was completed in 1982
the Prince of Wales came and the '78-ers were introduced
to him, together with the National Trust volunteers who led
the restoration.

"A reunion at the Battery ten years ago had meant a great
deal to the Class of '78."

Marion Hislop gave Bruno and Andy Bowen copies of the
paperwork connected with the '78-ers reunion, namely, the
invitation to 25 former pupils and the names and addresses
of the 10 who attended, together with a brief biography of
each attendee.

Instructions and timetable for the day started with:

> Meet at Havenstreet Isle of Wight Steam Railway
>   restaurant at 10.30 a.m. for coffee.
> Departure on the Havenstreet Express at
>   approximately 11.30 a.m.
> Lunch Wootton station. Private caterers.
> Depart for Smallbrook 1.45 p.m.
> Returning to Havenstreet at approximately
>   3.00 p.m. for afternoon tea in the station
>   restaurant prior to departure.

Attendees:–
Dr Walter Mullion – Consultant Urologist at
    St Mary's hospital, Newport.

Kaz Ali – Manufacturer and Importer of heavy
machinery to Mumbai, living in Paris.
Edward Hawkins – Maritime artist, living in
Portsmouth.
Dr Geoff Klinker – Consultant Urologist –
London Hospitals.
George Lewis – Pharmacist, living in Cowes.
James Tennant – Farmer, living in Winchester.
Kevin Billings – Owner of Billings Artisan Bakers,
Ryde, I.o.W.
Lieutenant Colonel Phillip Masters – retired,
living in Cowes.
Professor Ian Walters – lives in Oxford. Professor
of Criminology at St John's College, part of
Oxford University.
Roger Beale – Isle of Wight farmer, Newberry
Farm, Freshwater.

◆

Bruno hoped that from the school group he would find a
clue to the identity of the killer, and a motive for the murder,
which with nine potential suspects would be an exhausting
exercise.

He began his series of interviews with Roger Beale, whose
5,000-acre Newberry farm was situated in the west of the
Island off the B3399, the Newport to Freshwater road on the
eastern edge of Freshwater, a few hundred yards before a
right turn into Wilmingham Road.

The entrance to Beale's farm was through recently restored
brick pillars along a 200-metre gravel drive that led to an
immaculately preserved Georgian style house. Its presentation suggested a higher than usual degree of farm wealth and
prompted a comment from Andy Bowen.

"I suppose all these names will be from well off families?"

"Not necessarily Andy," said Bruno. "Money doesn't
always stick with those who inherit, and not all the pupils at

Ryde School have wealthy parents. They award scholarships to bright children from state schools who sit an entrance exam, and their fees are covered one hundred per cent."

Sheep, dairy and vegetable farming were Rogers Beale's business, boosting his farm income from a terrace of former farm workers' cottages converted for holiday lettings.

A smartly dressed, tanned, middle-aged farmer greeted the two detectives and led them through to a comfortable sitting-room where a tray of coffee was laid out.

Beale was fifty-three, like most of the pupils in Ryde Class of '78 who attended the reunion. He did not show the weather-beaten features and large scarred hands and fingers, of a hands-on working farmer. He was a gentleman farmer and ran his farm through an experienced manager.

"Thank you for the sad news about Geoff Klinker. I am at a loss to know what to say to you," he said.

"How well did you know him?" said Bruno.

"I didn't know him at all. In the last three or four years we've met twice. He didn't live on the Island."

"Can you describe the day to us, and what you talked about?"

"I'll try, Inspector, but for me it was my first time seeing any of them, apart from Klinker, since leaving school 35 years ago.

"We all met for coffee before we boarded the train. Everyone arrived on time at 10.30 a.m. I think half the group came from the mainland. Although this reunion took place every ten years, only some of the boys had attended before.

"It was hot but we all wore a jacket and a school tie. I bought a tie when I was in Ryde a couple of weeks ago."

"So, what was it like meeting school mates you've not seen for so long?" said Andy.

"It was a very pleasant day. Although we were all strangers, I was able facially and physically to match them with the eighteen year-olds I remembered. Over coffee I spoke to three or four of them, and at lunch I had a longer chat with Geoff Klinker. He said he had travelled down from London for the reunion, and that he'd also spent a couple of days on farm business."

"You said you had met him a couple of times in the past, what was that about?"

"I knew Geoff was a London-based hospital consultant, not a farmer, although he owned one of the biggest farms on the Island, twice the size of Newberry, so I was interested to see if there was any opportunity to co-operate.

"I asked him if he intended to make a permanent move to the Island, he said he had a brilliant farm manager, so that wasn't necessary, although he might retire from medicine soon and then he might want something else to do.

"He said he was fortunate to have such a good, experienced farm manager to run his business, or he'd have to make a choice between farming and remaining in London. I said if he were ever interested in selling his farm would he tell me, and he said he would."

"Why would you have bought it?"

"It's twice the size of what I have here in West Wight, and it is in a far better location and I would like to scale up my farming operation using plant and machinery that he doesn't use, change the crop rotation, and develop the Island as the garden of England. The Island is the sunniest place in the UK and is capable of much more. It has untapped potential."

"Was that the conversation you had with him last Friday?"

"Not quite, Inspector, if you look at my background you will discover that for twenty years, I was professor of farm economics at the University of Cape Town, probably explains my slight South African accent. I am experienced at improving farming methods, especially on larger farms, and that was my interest in talking to Geoff.

"After coffee we boarded the train and with a great deal of

steam and noise we set off for Wootton, where we had lunch – poached salmon salad, with ample Premier-Cru Chablis. It was an enjoyable meal. I didn't sit near Geoff at lunch; I sat with Ali, who'd come over from Paris where he now lives.

"As a boy I remembered he came from Mumbai, or Bombay as it was called when he was at school.

"Ali said he operated an import/export business from Paris, which I thought was ambitious for an Indian, but his English was very good."

"Whom did Klinker sit with on the train?"

"We occupied two carriages and he was with Wally Mullion as far as Wootton. He is another Island surgeon. Really he is a GP who does minor surgery, vasectomies and wart removal for extra cash. On the stage of the journey to Smallbrook we occupied a different carriage."

"How long was the return journey?"

"It was slow, just under an hour, we'd all drunk a lot of wine and lunch took an hour and a half."

"Did anything strange happen on the return journey?"

"Not that I noticed. I sat next to Jack Tennant, who has a garden centre business near Winchester. We were neighbours when his father farmed on the Island until the late 80s before the bank closed him down. We bought his farm at an auction in Winchester. It was 1,000 acres and it adjoined our southern pastures so it was a natural addition.

"We bought it for a song, but the Tennants made enough to clear the bank and they moved to the mainland. Basically, Jack Tennant got old, farmed all the wrong things, ended up doing Christmas trees, which nobody bought."

"When you all arrived back at Havenstreet what happened then?"

"We had tea and cakes in the restaurant, which was busy. They had set aside a couple of tables for us. It was mid-afternoon on a beautiful day, you couldn't move in the restaurant, and the passengers on the platform were preparing to board the train. After tea we said our goodbyes, handshakes all round, making promises to get together again next year."

"Did any of you use the lavatory on the platform?"

"After we returned from Smallbrook most of us did. We'd had a very liquid lunch and as you know there are no toilets on those steam trains. Corridors on trains with toilets front and back did not come into service until after the First World War, and that version of carriage could not run on the Island because the railway track bends were too sharp. That is why from the beginning of Isle of Wight rail every station had a Ladies and Gents lavatory on every platform. When trains stopped one could jump out and go to the toilet and the train would wait."

"Did you notice Klinker leave?"

Beale thought for a moment before answering.

"Come to think of it, no," he said. "When you walk around shaking everyone's hand saying goodbye you can't be certain you don't miss someone, I don't specifically remember seeing Klinker when I left."

"Everyone went in different directions. Some had called their wives to collect them. I strolled off to the car park to see if my taxi had arrived."

"Had it?"

"It was waiting in the car park."

"And that was it?"

"Yes, Inspector, that was our reunion over."

"Did you speak to everyone at some time during the day?"

"I think so, over coffee and in small groups before we sat for lunch, and of course in the carriage on the journey. It was a warm friendly get-together, I didn't notice anything strange throughout the day."

"Your farm is quite a large business, as is Klinker's, did you compete with him?"

"Yes, we did, the Island is a small place, Inspector, and we are two of the most profitable farms on the Island."

"So, does Klinker's murder end your interest in acquiring his farm?"

"On the contrary, it will probably come up for sale after probate, and I will try to buy it when it does."

"Possibly to run it as a theme park?"

"That was an idea three or four years ago. Things change and 15,000 acres create new economies of scale, let's see."

Bruno had gotten from Roger Beale all he could expect from someone who had attended the reunion. His previous contacts with Klinker did not imply there was anything between them that might cause Beale to kill him, nor in Beale's nature anything that suggested he was capable of such an act.

"Thank you for your account of the day," said Bruno.

"I'm sorry I could not be more helpful, Inspector."

On their journey to see Walter Mullion at St Mary's hospital in Newport, Bruno and Andy Bowen discussed his version of the reunion.

"He had reported seeing Klinker lunching with Mullion so we might get something from him," said Andy. "What are we looking for, sir?"

"Someone at Havenstreet Station on that day, and possibly on that journey, had a reason to kill Klinker, who doesn't seem to be the most obnoxious person on earth. The reason could be petty, obscure and long forgotten, or something sinister we don't yet know about."

"What else did we learn about him from Beale?" said Andy.

"Very little," said Bruno. "But we know exactly how the day proceeded, and that Beale has a reason to be pleased that Klinker's farm might come up for sale."

He highlighted the crowded restaurant where they took afternoon tea and that Platform A, where the restaurant and lavatory are located, was teeming with visitors waiting to board the train at the time murder was committed.

"Would they be using the gents' lavatory before boarding the train?"

"Maybe, but I think they'd be more interested in a window seat on the train. His view was that the platform was crowded, suggesting that the murder could have been anybody on the station and not just the school party."

"Yes, and so we should not just focus on the school group."

"For now let's see it as a helpful comment, until we find out more from the others."

Hospital reception was crowded with people sitting waiting as the two detectives identified themselves at the reception desk.

"Dr Mullion is expecting you," said a smiling uniformed receptionist.

After a few minutes they were shown into a small consulting room to meet Dr Walter Mullion, a big man with an ego to match, living up to that portrayal of a hospital consultant portrayed by James Robertson Justice in the *Doctor in the House* film series.

"Gentlemen, I cannot convey my sadness to you about the murder of Dr Klinker," were Dr Mullion's opening words.

"What can you tell us about the day, Doctor?" said Bruno.

"We all met for coffee at 10.30 a.m., and introduced ourselves to each other, as strangers would. Everybody was enthusiastic and friendly saying what a great idea it was to ride a steam train. The train was full. We occupied 2 compartments, 8 seats in each, 4 passengers each side, very comfortable seats."

"Inspector, I don't think anyone of the Class of '78 would kill Klinker."

"That's as it may be Doctor, but I am sure you would not be surprised to learn that murderers come in all shapes and sizes and from every conceivable background, and we are starting with Dr Klinker's friends, hopefully to obtain a lead for our investigation."

"We shall speak to every passenger who was on the train, but of the Ryde School party half are Island residents who knew the victim, so that is the logical place to begin our investigation."

"Beale says you had a lengthy chat with Dr Klinker. He said you lunched together?"

"That's true," he said, somewhat irritated that somebody should have reported on him. "We talked about the cottage hospital in Shanklin, which closed fifteen years ago, and has since been demolished, and what happened to the staff who worked there, mutual friends. In medical terms Klinker was bang up-to-date and suggested some treatments I might want to introduce to the Island.

"Why would anyone kill him?" said Bruno.

"It has to be something personal. He was a secretive man, and I'll bet the killer is not from the Isle of Wight," he said. "Except for his school friends, he didn't know anybody."

"In what way was he a secretive man? You don't know any more about your other school chums?"

Mullion struggled with that question.

"He was one of the wealthiest landowners on the Island, but he stayed away in London, seldom came here, was not married, as far as I know. He didn't know what went on here."

Mullion spoke as if the Island was the centre of the universe.

"You mean no gossip, Doctor?"

"If you like, Inspector."

"Would you say you were all pals?"

"Not buddies, but we were probably the only people on the Island he had anything in common with."

"Can I ask why you went on this reunion Doctor?"

"Inspector, on the Island I am considered to be the pillar of the community so it's my duty to attend, like the village fête, or the literary festival in Cowes. There were lots of passengers on that train on Friday, anyone who was on the trip could have killed him," he said.

"It could not have been carried out by a stranger," said Bruno. "Time and place were important."

"But the place could have been new to him and the killer grasped the opportunity amongst a crowd," said Mullion. "For certain the killer was not a stranger to him and he could have chosen a popular tourist attraction to create anonymity."

"The location suggests it was someone with an intimate knowledge of Havenstreet station therefore an Island person, and as Klinker did not live on the Island and seldom visited, his old school mates were probably the only people he knew," said Andy Bowen.

"That's exactly why the killer is not from the Island," insisted Mullion.

"We shall speak to passengers, the train crew and the station staff in due course, but the visitors are more difficult to find. Did you notice anything strange on the journey on Friday?"

"Nothing. The children were young, pre-school age, so the parents were all hustle and bustle, and moving around. It was crowded. You could have gotten lost on the station platform. I'll think through that day very carefully this evening, and if anything comes to mind, I'll call you immediately, Inspector. Let me repeat how sad I am that Klinker has been murdered. I don't think the Class of '78 will attend another school reunion."

Bruno and Andy agreed that Walter Mullion lived in his own world but nothing in his manner suggested he might be a murderer and contrary to his opinion that no one in the Class of '78 could have murdered Klinker, his comments had helped to sow the seeds that one of the school group was a killer.

Back at the station an email from John Jenkins, the

Havenstreet station manager, offered to make all members of the staff who were working on the previous Friday available for questioning the following morning.

Also a copy of the SOCOs' report found no prints in the lavatory or on the lavatory window that had been broken that day. It was assumed the murderer wore gloves.

The 6-inch by 4-inch window pane could have been smashed noiselessly, at the time of the murder. There was nothing to suggest it had been broken during a struggle or a fight. The autopsy confirmed that the weapon was a knife with a solid grip handle with a seven-inch blade, capable with a firm thrust of penetrating vital organs. The entry point of the knife had a clean edge and had pierced the heart and the spinal cord from the victim's back. Since the exact time of the killing mid-afternoon a small amount of decomposition had taken place and there was no discolouration of the skin.

A knife of that specification would require a sheath to conceal it on the body, a point that the SOCOs noted.

"Quite a hefty weapon," said Andy.

To maintain momentum Bruno accepted Jenkins invitation to speak to the train staff regarding any unusual behaviour during that afternoon and if they had remembered any person or persons behaving strangely.

CHAPTER 4

Tuesday 12 June

The staff on duty at Havenstreet on 8 June consisted of 16 employees, including John Jenkins the manager, the train driver and his stoker in the cab. There were the 2 platform guards (each alternatively serving on the train as carriage staff), the signaller, the ticket seller, the platform porter and the 5 catering and 3 gift shop staff, all of whom Bruno considered as 'persons of interest'. All had an opportunity to commit the murder on the Havenstreet premises.

Dan McCain and Graham Wood were platform guards in their sixties and Ed Thompson and Ian Wright were the carriage staff, and were both twenty. Dan and Graham lived in Wroxall. They came to work together and did the same shifts twice a week, taking turns to drive to the Havenstreet car park.

Ed lived in Shanklin and Ian in Sandown. They worked as a team twice each week at times confirmed by Jenkins.

Both were engineering students at Portsmouth University. At Havenstreet one acted as a station porter and the other in the signal box. They had occasional opportunities to ride in the cab with the driver as stoker, and understood the way steam engines work. None of the four had any connection with the group from Ryde School.

Ed and Ian did not recall anything strange that took place on that afternoon. They reported that throughout the year there are many enthusiasts that come and spend hours looking at the rolling stock in various places around the station yard. They enter any unused carriages and they know the layout of the station very well, there is also the museum. Ed and Ian were full of opinions and keen to air them.

"This is an opportunist killing. If Klinker had not used this lavatory he might still be alive, or have been murdered else-where," Ed said.

They thought the murderer could have waited for Klinker to return to Havenstreet, and took the opportunity in the lavatory, but did not have to be part of the school group.

"Did you notice anything unusual or anyone behaving strangely?" Bruno asked everyone.

"Truth is, Inspector, we don't get a second when we work here, it's frantic from start to finish."

No one could add to the little they had said about the day. They were busy answering questions from the passengers and ensuring they did not behave dangerously. They provid-ed a clear picture of how the Havenstreet Railway operated day to day.

All of the five catering staff were female, as was the ticket seller who remained in the ticket office at the entrance to the station. Ian, the signaller, was in the signal box throughout the period the train was in the station. The role of Ed, the platform porter, was to patrol the platform throughout the day, and to help passengers step up to the train when board-ing. At the estimated time of Klinker's murder the platform was very crowded with passengers waiting to board the 3.30 p.m. departure.

Jenkins had sat in on all the interviews between the detec-tives and his staff, ensuring they were relaxed and were as co-operative as they were able. However, there was nothing much to assist Bruno in his search for a meaningful clue to the identity of the killer.

After Havenstreet Bruno and Andy visited another of the Class of '78, George Lewis, a dispensing chemist with a busi-ness in Sandown High Street next to the Public Library.

They met in a newly refurbished shop consulting room, which pharmacists had recently been encouraged to create to comply with a government directive that as they were qualified to dispense medication and were also qualified to give advice to patients. It would relieve some pressure on the National Health Service general practitioners for them to do this.

George Lewis had inherited the business from his father, the first Sandown-based chemist. His first job after University at Southampton was in the hospital pharmacy at St Mary's Hospital in Newport until his father retired.

"Mr Lewis, one of your group at the Ryde School reunion last Friday, namely Dr Geoffrey Klinker, was found brutally murdered in the Gents' lavatory on Platform A at the Isle of Wight Steam Railway Havenstreet station. We are investigating his murder by interviewing all the former pupils who attended the reunion."

George Lewis was not brimming with personality. He was a pharmacist immersed in the exact task of getting patients' prescriptions right and the mundane detail of retail, such as not overstocking on lavender hair grease and Palmolive shaving soap, for loyal old male customers regular twice-yearly visits, many of whom pass away between visits.

"So far we've spoken to two of your school friends who were on the trip and would like you to run through the day from your perspective."

"Who were they?" said Lewis.

"Roger Beale and Walter Mullion."

Bruno's mention of Mullion surprisingly made Lewis screw his face up and slip into a silent rage.

"And were they any help?"

"They reported the day as they saw it."

"If you'd have told me it was Walter Mullion who'd been murdered, I'd have hung the flags out. I wouldn't have gone if I'd known he was turning up but once I was there, I couldn't leave. Mullion is a terrible man. I am surprised somebody hasn't bumped him off by now," he said.

"Can you give us a bit more on that?" said Andy Bowen.

"Dr Mullion is a sexual predator and I would not be

surprised if he ended up in prison or murdered. I'd hate to think of what he gets up to with some of his female patients in his consulting rooms! After I qualified my first job was as a pharmacist at Newport hospital. My then-wife Caroline was a very pretty young woman and he was a young hospital doctor. Once he'd set eyes on her she couldn't get away from him. All over her he was, she was a lovely woman, she still is, in spite of that bastard. She fell for him and I couldn't stop her leaving me. He stole my wife. She got custody of our daughter, and the courts awarded her the house I had bought with my grandmother's inheritance and I had to pay her maintenance for my daughter.

"I used to drive past that house on my way to work and see his car parked outside. He divorced his wife Anna to marry Caroline. That was twenty-five years ago. After seven years he divorced Caroline, or she divorced him because he was having it off with one of the hospital matrons. Caroline wasn't having any of that, so she took him for everything she could, their house, a share of his pension and money to keep her and my daughter Lillian, at Upper Chine Girls School. He married the matron who is now a drunk, a falling-over drunk. He drove her to drink. We all knew she liked a drink in the beginning, but she wasn't an alcoholic. Serves him right because she too was happily married until he got his hands on her. I don't know what he's got because it's obvious to anyone he's full of bullshit. Now he's penniless, look at his clothes, twenty years old, threadbare on the cuffs. I'd never let him treat me or anyone I know."

"Did you ask Mullion about Klinker?"

"Mullion hated him because he was a top surgeon in London."

"Tell us what you know about Klinker."

"He was a Consultant Surgeon at Guy's Hospital in London. After he qualified in London, he worked at the Charing Cross Hospital as a registrar, all work and no money.

He fell in love with a woman called Maisie Longmore. Her father was Longmore's the optician in Ryde High Street. She was a clever woman, the hospital administrator at Queen Alexandra's Hospital in Portsmouth until she moved to a big hospital in London to live with him. I think they were married, and he worked his way up to become a consultant, and now he is at the top of his profession. I heard there was a big row between Tom Klinker and his son because he turned up with a foreign woman. The old man said to him, Go back to Maisie or you'll be disinherited. It was no idle threat. So, Geoff crept off back to London and that was the last anyone heard of the foreign woman. They're all the same, Inspector, hospital consultants, I hear it all the time."

"And Maisie Longmore?"

"I never heard any more about her."

"You know a lot about his personal life!" said Andy Bowen.

"I am a pharmacist and I listen to gossip all day long. I am a Father Confessor to the females in Sandown who use my shop. I know about the personal lives of many people on the Island. Who the drug addicts are, those with cancer who have a short time to live, who has the pox, the depressed, the scroungers and the layabouts on income support. If you want to know something intimate about anyone, Inspector, ask a local chemist."

"I'll bear that in mind," said Bruno.

"So, you are the right person to help us find this murderer?" he said.

"I pick up Island gossip in the shop. There's lots of poor people on the Island. Not sleeping rough, but just making ends meet and in the know about the people on the Island who own everything. They all knew who Klinker was and nobody will have liked him."

"So, who would have killed him?"

"None of those and none of the school friends would have a reason to do that. You've got to look into his personal relationships in London. It would have to be someone who knew he was coming to a school reunion on the Havenstreet train wouldn't it?"

"Of course," said Lewis.

"Are you married Mr Lewis?"

"I live with Annie Atkins who runs the shop, we are partners in the business."

Through the glass-fronted consulting room wall Bruno noticed a trim attractive middle-aged lady dressed in the white pharmacy uniform.

"My daughter, Linda, who has just qualified as a pharmacist, also works in the shop."

"Did you speak to Klinker on Friday?"

"Yes, I asked him how his work was going up in London. He said it was very demanding but he enjoyed working in a university teaching hospital. I asked him about the farm, he said he was not sure of his plans for the future, because his mother had only recently died. He asked me about pharmacy and how delivering prescriptions to people's homes was good business on the mainland, a captive market he called it, people who take pills take them regularly for the rest of their lives. I disagreed because when visiting the shop, they bought things, and talked about their problems. We provide a social service too, Inspector."

"Did he seem anxious about anything?"

"Not at all, he was friendly, relaxed, mixed with everybody. He said to me he was also on the Island to meet his farm manager. He talked to everybody and I did not witness an incident that was unusual. We had a jolly good lunch and a bumpy but interesting afternoon on the Havenstreet Express. At the end of the train ride we all had tea in the restaurant, and then we all left."

"What did you do afterwards?"

"Annie met me in the Havenstreet station car park at 3.45 p.m."

"Did you say goodbye to everyone?"

"I said farewell to most of my fellow '78-ers but not everyone and obviously not Klinker. Poor chap," he said. "Inspector, I always get a little rush at this time of day and I can see a few people waiting with their prescriptions in hand. Leave your card and I'll call you if I remember anything about last Friday. Is that okay, Inspector?"

"Of course," said Bruno.

They thanked George Lewis for his help while he rushed off with a bunch of prescriptions he grabbed from an in-box on the counter.

It was opening time in the Falcon Pub opposite the pharmacy so the two detectives sat in a corner with two lemonade shandies to talk through the day's work.

"Well we know who to talk to if Dr Mullion is found dead," said Andy. "George would have killed him twenty years ago if he was a killer, but not then or now."

"They are very similar, those three," said Bruno, referring to Beale, Mullion and Lewis.

"You mean the Island is their world?" said Andy Bowen.

"Did you like any of them?" said Bruno.

"Roger Beale is creepy and has an agenda. Walter Mullion repulsive, many hospital consultants are like him, they are god's gift to women. Surrounded by female staff and patients who would do anything to be first in line. You need high moral principles to resist the temptations of your profession. Most medical consultants have high standards and do, Mullion doesn't."

George Lewis is ordinary and boring, I can understand why his wife left him, but he is honest, and Caroline his wife was swept off her feet and didn't know she was jumping from the frying pan into the fire. He built her up but she was a simple pretty face who was flattered."

"Could any of them have murdered Klinker?" said Andy.

"All of them could have done," said Bruno. "But none of them had a reason."

"What about Beale?"

"Except Beale. We need to know about his background. But I'm not excluding any of them yet," said Bruno.

"What about Maisie Longmore? If she married Klinker she'd be his next of kin and due to inherit his estate. We must find her."

"Only if she is still married to him!"

"That's a job for Kevin, in addition to a background résumé of Beale."

Having unwound from a long day, Bruno left Andy at Newport Police Station to instruct Kevin, and drove home to enjoy dinner with Janet, who'd want to go over the details of his day with him. His old habit after work of winding down with a beer to watch the early evening news and forget the events of the day had long gone. Janet brought clarity to some of his activities. Explaining his actions to anyone made him anxious and sowed the seeds of self-doubt. However, her independent, disciplined mind placed the results of his investigation in a logical sequence exposing areas that should be re-examined, which more than once had led him to the culprit.

A murder on the Island was a rare occurrence and remained the main topic of conversation and interest at every level of policing which called upon Bruno to be discreet, methodical and accurate with his reporting.

Janet saw nothing in Walter Mullion or George Lewis's recall of the events as unusual or suspicious or needed re-examining, but his report on Roger Beale suggested otherwise.

"George Lewis bears a grudge and has not moved on after twenty-five years. It must have ruined his life in the confines of a small pharmacy business.

"Beale might be up to something else. But whether that adds up to murdering Klinker, you don't know. His ambition to buy out Klinker is to improve his farming output on the Island. He sees the Island as one big agricultural business, and Klinker's gives him the economy of scale he needs to do it. But I am sure there are other farms for sale on the Island."

She was right: he should look more closely at Beale. There was something inconsistent with where he was and what he was doing. Having modernised his own farm his ambition was driving him and Klinker was the obvious target. Of the remaining six Ryde School reunion attendees he had to see, two lived on the Island, three were resident on the mainland and Kaz Ali was from Mumbai and living in Paris somewhere.

Edward Hawkins, a marine artist, lived in Portsmouth. James Tennant, a businessman farmer, lived near Winchester. And Professor Ian Walters, a University lecturer, was living in Oxford.

Back at the station Andy Bowen had set Kevin to work finding out more about Beale, and arranged to travel to Winchester the following morning to interview James Tennant.

CHAPTER 5

Wednesday 13 June

Tennant's substantial business lay back from the main road just to north of Winchester on the A34. It was a flourishing garden centre and a farm shop, covering several acres and much more than a farm. The car park was capable of parking at least two hundred cars. Large modern permanent greenhouses were situated on several acres growing bedding plants, pot plants and vegetables. Alongside the main entrance was a drive-in centre stacked with sacks of compost, topsoil and garden pebbles, with two men dedicated to sales and loading them into the boots of customers' cars. Inside the main shop was what one would regard as a garden centre department store selling fruit and vegetables, gardening equipment of every kind, gardening gloves and garden clothing. Seeds and bulbs and weed killer stood before a display of garden furniture and lawn mowing machines. The place was busy with every appearance of being a successful, profitable business employing, at a guess, two hundred staff.

James Tennant, undistinguishable from his employees, wearing a green three-quarter-length coat, spotted them straight away and introduced himself, then ushered them to a quiet table in the café restaurant section of the garden centre where a young waitress served them coffee.

"Inspector, we could have covered this by telephone to save the journey, but I am happy to answer any questions about the day, if I can," he said, in an I'm-too-busy-lets-get-this-over-with manner.

"Thank you," said Bruno. "Firstly, can you account for your movements on Friday 8 June, in as much detail as you can remember," said Bruno firmly.

"At 7.00 a.m. a member of my staff drove me to Winchester

railway station, where I caught the 7.31 a.m. to Portsmouth Harbour.

"Then I caught the ferry to Ryde Pier head arriving at 9 a.m. I was early and as it takes less than 30 minutes to Havenstreet I sat in the cafeteria with a coffee and a newspaper until just before 10.00 a.m. Then I took a taxi to Havenstreet where Marion Hislop had arranged coffee for our group on arrival at 10.30 a.m. in a private part of the station restaurant where we greeted each other and introduced ourselves. I think the last time I attended a reunion was twenty years ago, so it was like meeting strangers. After coffee we boarded the steam train to Wootton, where a splendid lunch had been laid on for us. Plenty to drink, good food, it was enjoyable and time passed quickly. The talk at lunch varied between those who wanted to tell their life stories to anyone who would listen, and those who wanted to talk about the antics we got up to at school. I was in the latter group. My life story is not that interesting."

"We understand that Roger Beale bought your family farm on the Island after you left?"

"His father bought it after the bank shut us down. My family farmed on the Island for 100 years, livestock and apples and pears in orchards. The Beales controlled the upper reaches of a stream that watered our animals, we had an irrigation system that had served the farm for centuries, like an ancient Roman aqueduct, which was fed from the rain that fell on Beale's higher ground. They diverted the input to our system to create a trout fishery, which required a fresh, free-flowing clean water input, so we lost our supply of fresh water that ultimately dried us out. That was the reason for our demise. It was a perfectly legal thing to do, but old man Beale knew it would eventually dry us out and ruin us and, without the water, it did. Once the Beales bought our farm they reconnected the water flow to our farm."

"Beale said that when Klinker's farm comes onto the

market he will buy it," said Andy. "He wants to build a theme park, bigger than anything on the mainland, like Disney World. He thinks it could make the Island."

"So, he had a vested interest in Klinker's death?" said Jack Tennant thoughtfully.

"You might put it that way," said Bruno.

"Is he one of your suspects?"

"We have no suspects yet, he is just a person of interest."

Tennant nodded, wondering if there was anything, he could say that might edge him towards becoming a suspect.

"A theme park would never work on the Island, I don't think he is a fairground operator, or that it is a serious idea?" he said. "He is a farmer, an excellent farmer, not a gambler who'd take that kind of risk. This was a smallholding when Dad rented it, run down, but he started it. We grew all kinds of things and expanded the crop acreage, now we have 122 acres on this site."

"What else can you tell us about the day?"

"After lunch we boarded the train and chugged our way to Smallbrook at the other end of the line. It was beautiful, through little copses, farms, and lots of livestock to see. Incidentally, old man Beale did us a favour. My dad is still alive and we earn more money here than we ever did farming. We've opened two more centres like this. Both are doing well. Although we were all at school together, we are all different people. A bunch of strangers might have had more in common. Ours was the school nothing else. If I never saw any of them again, I wouldn't give a toss. I can't tell you much about any of the others, I spoke to them, but just chatter."

"Did you talk to Kaz Ali?"

"A few words. I asked him if he had come from India and he said, 'No I live in Paris now'." He did not have much to say. At school he used to go back to India on all school holidays."

Bruno had all he was going to get about the Ryde School reunion from Tennant so it was time to go.

As they shook hands to leave Tennant said, "Take another look at Beale, Inspector. He's been all over Klinker's land since he returned from South Africa, and that was five years ago. Even if you've discounted him as a suspect, he might give you a clue that helps you to find who killed Klinker."

It was obvious that Tennant bore a grudge against Beale and if he could persuade the police to focus on him it would please him. However, details of the historic feud between them did nothing to advance Bruno's investigation. It was interesting that Tennant had full knowledge of Beale's interest in acquiring Klinker's farm. How did he come by that information without some connection with the Island? It suggested that he had an interest too. If his business was as successful as he had implied he could certainly be a contender to buy Klinker's, and Tennant had revealed knowledge of the connection between Beale and the Klinker estate that Beale had not mentioned.

"Should he have?" questioned Andy Bowen as they drove to Portsmouth to see Edward Hawkins, RA, the seascape painter. The purchase of Tennant's 1,000 acres by Beale's father a couple of decades earlier, and the skulduggery that initiated the departure of the Tennant's from the Island after over 100 years, with their tails between their legs, festered seriously with James Tennant, so that if he could prevent the Beale family from securing another coup he would do so. And if that meant using his resources to acquire the Klinker farm, he would. He knew the benefit to him of a big acreage on the Island producing livestock, fruit and vegetables, poultry, milk, in fact everything he already had an outlet for, and which he could expand rapidly. The thought of it became increasingly attractive to him whilst he contemplated the pleasure the Tennant family would enjoy knocking Beale out of a deal. James Tennant was certainly up for that.

"We'll not cross Tennant off our persons of interest yet, he certainly has not let go of the Island."

◈

Edward Hawkins lived in an apartment overlooking the harbour entrance on the south-eastern side, adjacent to a terrace of several houses east of the Spice Island Inn. Hawkins's four-bedroomed apartment served also as his studio. A plaque on the wall at the main entrance to the apartment block described that in the time of the Napoleonic wars men who drank in the Spice Island Inn were often cornered by press gangs and taken to sea against their wishes. They would be taken to the islands of the West Indies to load up with spices and on their return rewarded with a handsome sum to encourage them to sign up for future voyages.

The view of Portsmouth Harbour from Edward Hawkins's lounge was spectacular. The entire scene across to Gosport stretched before him. One of the busiest harbour entrances in the whole world, and the paintings of every kind of ship that hung from the studio walls, accurately depicted the high level of activity throughout the year.

Hawkins was nationally known as a marine artist. He sold paintings through a local gallery, and in a London gallery. He exhibited at the annual Royal Society of Marine Artists summer exhibition in the Mall Gallery, having achieved the distinction as a Royal Academician of using the initials RA after his name.

He supported Ryde School, appearing at school functions, and when invited taking a master class in drawing for pupils studying art.

"I am in continual contact with the school and I accept every invitation for support," he told Bruno and Andy.

"Do you know whose idea it was to go on the Havenstreet Express for this reunion?"

"It would have been Marion's suggestion."

"It's been done several times with other groups from the

school. It begins with coffee, a short trip to Wootton, where a local caterer puts on a very good lunch. We all get to know each other and then we all get back on the train and experience what it was like in the late nineteenth century to travel around the Island by train."

"Did you know Klinker well?"

"No, I didn't. I remembered him from school. He was a quiet, professional, likeable person, but he wasn't an Island person, he lived in London. At the reunion, we talked about painting. He is an art collector. Supports the Camberwell College of Art, and buys new artists. He was telling me about his collection of pictures. Said he'd come to the next Marine Art Exhibition on the Mall in September. Didn't mention the Island, he seemed happy enough, and said he wasn't going back to London until next week because he had business to attend to on the farm, but it was just a reference, no details. He also said he'd call me and come to my gallery when he was next in Pompey."

"Any idea why he should be stabbed to death on a visit to the Island if he had so little contact with Island people?"

"I would not agree that he had little contact with Island people."

"I've heard it said that Klinker owned half the Island, obviously an exaggeration, but its true he owned a considerable parcel of Island land and he didn't live here, so I imagine that's reason enough for someone on the Island to want to bump him off, don't you Inspector? But I am not the person to ask about the Island, I don't live there either."

Hawkins had provided Bruno with the first suggestion that an Island person could have a reason to murder Klinker, and Tennant had pointed the finger at Beale to the extent they should investigate his involvement in the destiny of Klinker's farm. Bruno suspected that was no more than an enquiry from a competitive neighbouring business looking for a bargain.

After thinking his way through the two interviews with Tennant and Hawkins, Bruno was tempted to return to Newport and pursue a less exacting line of investigation, and see if John Jenkins had put together a list of traceable passengers on the Friday express. However, from Portsmouth it was only a two-hour drive to meet Professor Ian Walters in North Oxford. As any trip to the mainland from the Island can be inconvenient, he decided to let Andy Bowen drive him to see the professor. That would complete their interviews of the former Ryde pupils living on the mainland during the afternoon, all except for Kaz Ali who they had yet to locate in France. A nap on the journey revived him and as they parked in the front of a pleasant country cottage in Park Town, North Oxford, Bruno was again ready to search for a clue that would help him discover who killed Klinker in the Havenstreet Station Gents' lavatory.

Their meeting with Walker had been arranged by the desk sergeant at Newport Police Station, and he was expecting them. He greeted them with light refreshments and, unlike Bruno's former interviewees, was looking forward to meeting the two detectives hunting Klinker's killer.

He looked older than his fifty-three years, but astute and focused, and like many clever people a man with a wide range of interests was keen to help to solve the riddle challenging the Isle of Wight murder detectives. He seemed almost excited to be questioned about his attendance at the reunion of the Class of '78 the previous Friday. Professor Walters was an Oxford University lecturer in Criminal Jurisprudence, an appointment he had held for eight years. It was his professional knowledge of the criminal mind Bruno believed could help them find Klinker's killer, or point them in the right direction, which they so far had been unable to find. This murder was presenting Bruno with a challenge as to motive and personality. Time and place were also confusing. As an expert in the workings of the criminal mind perhaps an academic could help, and this interview might provide a lead? Bruno wanted him to analyse what they had discovered so far and cast a light into a dark corner.

He assured them that he would help with any participation they sought beginning with his observations on their progress so far.

"Tell us why you decided to attend this year's reunion, Professor?" said Bruno.

"I like to maintain past relationships with schools and universities that I have attended. I enjoyed school and it has been a long time since I visited the Island, so it was a long-delayed return and, although I met a bunch of strangers, I enjoyed the day very much.

"When I learned of Dr Klinker's murder and since I knew you were calling, I have returned to that day to see if I could remember anything that happened that might help you. Everyone who attended has become reasonably successful, including Walter Mullion, who is a hospital consultant at St Mary's in Newport, working in a similar field to Dr Klinker. I did not see that any of them had any connection with each other and although most lived on the Island, none had any recent connection with Klinker, whom many hadn't seen for decades. The train was full of people on day trips and it could have easily been one of them that murdered Klinker. However, that person would not have been a stranger to him. It would have been possible for the murder to be committed by a casual visitor, coming specifically to kill Klinker, although I think he'd have chosen an easier, more certain location.

"The facts are that Klinker lived in London. If someone in his London social circle wanted to kill him, would he plan to do it this way? I would say not. It has to be a person who was familiar with the Havenstreet station, which almost certainly points to an Island resident. The venue is important to the killer because it provided the opportunity amongst a crowd of untraceable strangers, namely day visitors, and family groups, which amounted to 90 per cent of the passengers. Have you seen everyone in our group?"

"Not quite," Bruno admitted, and they had yet to get a list of the other passengers, which Jenkins was assembling from credit card companies.

"As you still have plenty to do why don't you see the rest and then come back and talk to me? After all it is suspects you need," he said, eliminating himself as a suspect. "I am even available to travel to the Island, help with an interview, and view the crime scene with you, if that helps."

Over smoked salmon sandwiches and lemonade, Walters ran through what he saw as motives to look out for, based on his own research and experience as a prison visitor where he had listened to the criminal mind.

It was very interesting and, as Bruno had nothing more he was prepared to tell him about their investigation so far, he graciously accepted his offer of another meeting on the Island and they left his cottage on a very friendly note.

On the way back to the Red Funnel ferry in Southampton they summarised the progress they had so far made.

"Walters sees Klinker's murder as part of an academic exercise, at which I am not surprised, and maybe he can help us. But let's get as far as we can with seeing the others before we talk to him again, unless we run up against something we can't understand or we solve this crime before we need help from him. Although he ruled himself out as a suspect to us, he remains a person of interest," said Bruno.

"Agreed," said Andy.

"He didn't give us anything that we don't already know. Let's see Billings the Island baker and the Colonel tomorrow and examine the train manifest from Jenkins."

CHAPTER 6

Thursday 14 June

Colonel Masters was waiting to meet the detectives punctually at 9.00 a.m. He lived with Mrs Masters in Cowes, in a waterfront apartment that in Cowes week he could have let out for a fortune which, as he was not a yachtsman, he and his wife did, but they didn't tell anyone. His father had been a sailor, and that explained why he chose to live in Cowes. They had inherited this magnificent apartment when his parents had passed away and since retiring from the army, they had lived in it.

"What a magnificent view of the sea, Colonel," said Andy, in his usual friendly, introductory manner.

"Yes, my father was a yachtsman, and a life president of the Royal Cowes until he died two years ago. From here you can view the water along the entire esplanade, opened by the Prince of Wales in 1926. I could never have afforded to buy it. A Colonel does not earn a fortune, he gets a good pension, but no one can live in style on a pension, so I am looking for appropriate employment, hopefully on the Island so we can continue to live here. I tried the school but their bursar is younger than I am, so no joy there. But something will turn up for a retired Colonel, it always does, because we are considered honest, reliable and punctual, and can be employed on the cheap. That's my CV," he said, in a friendly way.

"I expected you'd want to quiz me about last Friday, so I've written a report for you on the day as I saw it, from my arrival at 10.30 a.m. for coffee through until we arrived back at Havenstreet for tea at 3.15 p.m."

"Thank you, Colonel. I will read it and keep it on file. Meanwhile, can you tell us your account of the day?"

"It was my first reunion since I left the school for Sandhurst in 1984. At school the CCF – the Combined Cadet Force – was my first love. In my final year I was Cadet Sergeant Major, the senior cadet. I passed the entrance exam for Sandhurst and served for thirty-five years in Germany, Northern Ireland, one tour in Afghanistan, Aldershot and the MOD in London. I've had a very interesting life, and my wife and I loved Army life.

"Our reunion train journey started with a short steam ride to Wootton, where we had lunch. I had ridden on the railway three weeks ago. It was one of my job applications along with several other tourist attractions on the Island. Osborne House was another. I even approached the Yacht Club and applied for club secretary, bursar, and chairman non-exec. I am on their lists. Nothing so far."

"When you arrived at Havenstreet station who did you meet?"

"Jenkins, the manager. I am on his list, but I fear he will offer a non-paid position, if any at all. Many of the people at Havenstreet are volunteers. So, the reunion was my second journey on the train."

The Colonel was not a listener and explained why he had not progressed beyond the rank of Lieutenant Colonel during thirty-five years army service, in which his final three were at Ministry of Defence desk jobs, where writing reports for army high ups, like the one he'd given Bruno, was a daily task.

"What do you think the effect of this murder will be on the Havenstreet business?"

"It won't be negative, Inspector. What do you think Agatha Christie's *Murder on the Orient Express* has done for the train company that operate the Pullman journeys to Venice from Paris?"

"Interesting," said Bruno. "Colonel, as a man who has experience of many types of person at all levels, do you think any of your party killed Klinker?"

"Inspector, I hadn't seen any of them for over thirty-five years, didn't recognise a soul. There was no display of hostility towards each other amongst the old boys. Most of them were men who had done well."

"Yes, I do have a lot of experience of many types but murderers come in all ages, sexes, and are indistinguishable from the rest of us, so I couldn't give you an opinion of our school group."

"Did you see Klinker leave the group to go to the toilet on Platform A?"

"When would that have been, Inspector?"

"Any time, particularly when your train journey ended and you all went for tea.

"When we arrived back at Havenstreet the platform was packed with people waiting to grab seats in the carriages. So, it was a mêlée. The café where we had tea was busy, except for our reserved little corner. We alighted from the train with all the other passengers and we regrouped for tea in the restaurant. At the station most of us popped into the Gents' for a pee. I know I did."

"Who do you think killed Klinker, Colonel?"

"I can't point the finger, Inspector, but my guess is that it's an Island person who knew the station pretty well with a long-held personal grudge."

"Going all the way back to school days?"

"I doubt it," said the Colonel. "I'd look for something that's happened since, and the murderer surely has to gain from killing Klinker, it's not a trivial grudge."

"Do you think more than one person could be involved?"

"Could be, but not two of the old boys."

"They were not buddies, the Class of '78, nor are they distinguished, they are just a bunch of privileged public schoolboys who've inherited the family businesses and traditions. To kill someone, you need a pretty strong motive, and this lot do not have that."

"What do you think the motive could be?"

"Money. Klinker was rich, so I'd look at business partners. I don't think he was married, so a woman could be involved."

"Really?" said Bruno.

"Hospital consultants get themselves into all sorts of tangles with women, it is a peril and a perk of that profession."

The Colonel had presented himself as a typical retired middle-rank Army officer and a pretty straight guy. He had served loyally in the Army and was searching for that same sense of purpose as a civilian. He was confident he would soon find a niche and carry on serving in whatever organisation that took him on and Bruno hoped he would soon slot into a niche.

"Thank you, Colonel. Please contact me if you recall anything else of interest, and the best of luck finding a suitable appointment on the Island, I will read your report on the day."

◈

Their final interview of the Island-based Ryde School reunion party was with Kevin Billings, the proprietor and managing director of Billings the Island Bakers, established by great grandfather Billings in 1908. Man and boy Billings had lived in Ryde. At school he had walked the one mile from home to school.

He had become Billings' master baker by default. After school he'd attended Birmingham University and graduated with a first-class degree in Architecture.

Returning to the Island he had found it difficult to establish himself, and there was not a large firm on the Island he could attach himself to. The kind of work on offer was repetitive and for developers always to a price. The family business supplied bread and cakes throughout the Island, and was successful and very profitable. He was persuaded by his father to become a director and then non-executive chairman, but when his father became sick and retired there was no suitable candidate in the company so he took over as managing director. He had agreed to work for a year until the company solved its management vacancy so he could return to architecture. It never found a recruit and he knew deep down it never would. So, in the past twenty years he had designed and rebuilt the bakery on the existing site, managing to continue the business during the rebuild in an extraordinary and efficient way.

He transformed the bakery increasing its output and profit several-fold by installing Europe's best new equipment, including energy-efficient ovens from Germany.

Ten years ago, he invited the baking industry to see his new bakery, and received commissions from several other English bakeries to redesign their bakeries which, as an architect, he accepted. Very soon he was recognised as the UK's expert in bakery production, design and management.

When asked to relive his day on the Havenstreet Express he said he'd not spoken to Klinker apart from the formal round of handshaking and name recognition over coffee at the start of the day. He had sat next to James Tennant over lunch and enjoyed his company comparing running a bakery to running a garden centre, finding a number of similarities, and persuading him to stock Billings Bakery products.

He was sad that their trip should end in the way it had, and it probably signalled the end of school class reunions.

"I do not believe that any member of the Class of '78 would have committed a murder, even though we had little in common with each other, except attendance at the school. It points to an outsider probably someone who knew Klinker from London. That would be my starting point, Inspector."

"Don't you think a local knowledge of the layout of Havenstreet would be necessary? Where the lavatory is for example?"

"I think he was only killed in the lavatory because the

opportunity suddenly presented itself. Trapped in a very small place, no witness and Klinker with his back to the assailant, concentrating on peeing into a urinal."

"The killer could have been following him all day, waiting to pounce and a chance to stab him to death suddenly presented itself. Or, knowing he was on the train, perhaps he waited for him to return to Havenstreet from Smallbrook.

"During a high-profile career as a hospital consultant you will make enemies. Your patients lose trust in what you say and do, that is why you get second opinions. He has your life in his hands.

"I would examine his patient list. It cannot remain confidential following a murder, and that may lead to the killer."

Kevin Billings was chairman of the Isle of Wight Chamber of Commerce, and concerned that somebody was murdered at the Havenstreet Steam Railway Station, a prominent Island tourist attraction. None of the Island's much-visited attractions could afford damaging news, like a knife killing.

"Inspector, anyone is capable of murder. Would you like my opinion of those who came?"

"It might be helpful," said Bruno.

These were sought-after words from an amateur sleuth that often led detectives to the murderer. Billings was clever and his observations might shine a light on things they had missed.

"Dr Klinker was a nice man, he did not make enemies, and he was successful in a caring profession. He was not an Islander so he had no friends here, but he could have had enemies. These could be his employees, other Island farmers, jealous of the doctor, who'd not done a day's manual work in his life, but ended up with the spoils.

"Walter Mullion, a hospital consultant, full of himself, unpleasant, a womaniser, disliked intensely by most men, but not capable of murder, perhaps only if someone put his back against the wall, but Klinker was not that man.

"George Lewis, a pharmacist, nit-pickingly dull, unim-aginative, he had more reason to kill Wally Mullion. But he would never go so far as murdering anybody. He'd not have the bottle to carry it out.

"Masters lives in Cowes, is a newish resident on the Island, does know people here, is a highly disciplined, toffee-nosed soldier. I don't think he retired to the Island to go around killing people.

"Tennant is a successful businessman, doesn't live on the Island or come here, but a nice level-headed man. As I've said, someone I can work with to expand both our businesses."

"Would Tennant he interested in buying the Klinker farm when it is sold?"

"It's an idea," said Billings after some thought. "He has an emotional attachment to the Island, and as a produc-tion centre it could compliment his successful mainland operation.

"Edward Hawkins the artist is very involved with the school, generous and kind. He holds painting workshops at the school, and acts as a mentor to serious pupils. Never in a million years would he murder anyone. I would definitely seek his opinion on who he thinks could have committed this crime.

"Professor Walters, he's in the crime business. Don't know anything about him, but I would not rule him out. That's it Inspector."

"You've forgotten Kaz Ali and Beale?"

"The Indian? Don't know anything about him either, but he doesn't live in England, I don't think he ever has, so I'd rule him out. Klinker would be a complete stranger to him."

"And Beale?"

"He should be of interest because we know little about him, I didn't remember anything about him and this was our first meeting with him since we were at school. I found him to be aloof, self-centred, status-conscious, gave me the impression of being a big fish in a small pond. A closed shop."

"Would a patient in London, who had probably never heard of the Isle of Wight, choose to kill Klinker on the Isle of Wight?" said Bruno.

"I can think of circumstances where a bitter and twisted person, a relative or a person who had missed out because of a premature death might choose a distant location to exact revenge."

Billings was insightful and would have made a good detective, thought Bruno. However, he was keen to limit the scope of his investigation focusing on the local residents because that is where he believed the killer would be. The motive for the murder was connected to something that was happening or had happened on the Island.

"It makes sense to eliminate the locals first," said Bruno. "They live near to the crime scene and we can get to them quickly, and we believe the killer's motive is to do with something that's taken place here."

Nevertheless, Klinker's patient fatalities, if there were any, were not to be ignored. On the journey back to the station Andy Bowen requested Kevin Bell call Klinker's London secretary, Brenda Frampton, and obtain a list of any treatments carried out by Klinker during the previous five years that had resulted in the death of the patient.

"That leaves me, Inspector, which I will leave you to make up your mind," said Billings.

His lack of any association with Klinker seemed to rule him out as a suspect or a person of interest.

Was his opinion that it could have been one of Klinker's patients a new line of investigation, or an attempt to dissuade him from his belief that the killer was an Island person? If it was, Bruno didn't buy it.

"Who's left then, sir?" said Andy, after leaving Billings Bakery.

"Beale, Mullins, Lewis, Tennant, Masters, Edward Hawkins the artist, Walters and lastly Billings, that's everyone except Ali."

"They didn't give us much."

"We need to go back to Clive Hall. It starts from there."

After one week without finding a clue or a suspect, it was time to increase their effort. Each day the job of finding the killer becomes harder, accentuated by the concealing mist of memory. Rather than eliminating, they were creating more pathways to explore. The cash paying passengers were untraceable, while those who had paid by credit card, many online in advance, were not immediately traceable because their receipt for payment did not record their name and address at the time.

Following up information about Klinker's patients would take time and take them away from the Island.

"What do we do about Kaz Ali?" said Andy Bowen.

"No address for him in France as yet?" said Bruno.

"The school secretary said he lives in Mumbai, but works in France."

"What does he do?"

"He's in import/export."

"Didn't one of those attendees say he lived in Paris and taught English?"

"Yes, they did."

"That's not import/export. They must have misheard him?"

"Do you think he's returned to Mumbai?"

Andy shrugged his shoulders.

"Paris is a long way to come for a school reunion, and then return the same day," he said.

"If it was important for him to travel from Paris it is important to speak to him."

"How do we do that?" said Andy.

"Marion Hislop invited and corresponded with him, so

she must know how to contact him. He probably stayed on the Island the night before the reunion."

After a visit to Ryde School, Andy reported back that Marion Hislop had emailed an invitation to every one she had contact details for. Although she had not received an email reply from Ali, he had phoned her to check on the arrangements for the reunion.

He had said that he was going to be in France throughout June and would like to attend, saying something about using Eurostar. She remembers him saying he would send a money order for payment from Paris, which she received, and that was it.

"Not many reported having spoken to him," said Bruno.

"That's true, but some did, and nobody mentioned anything unusual," said Andy.

"Did you get his address in Mumbai?"

"It's a mailbox address. That's normal in big cities in India, they don't have a postal system like ours."

"We have to find out what happened to him after the train arrived back at Havenstreet, so give those we have interviewed a call and see if they can help."

Back at the station Andy started to call the Class of '78, and enquire if they could add to what little they knew about Kaz Ali. He started with Beale, who said he had a short conversation with Ali early on in the trip.

"I sat next to him on the journey to Wootton and I told him I'd visited Mumbai in 2013 to watch India play England at cricket. Told him I had stayed at the Cricket Club of India because it was very easy to get to the ground, just 200 metres. I also said I had stayed at the Taj Mahal Palace Hotel on a previous visit. The Taj Mahal Palace sits in front of the Gateway to India, a monument to Queen Victoria. He was friendly and I said I would tell him if I make another visit and we'd meet up. He said he didn't live in the city but an hour's drive in a small town, I can't recall the name of it. He said he had an office in the city and that he imported machinery, mostly from Europe, where he spent a great deal of time.

"I asked him where he was staying. He said he was leaving immediately after the trip as he was catching an evening flight to Paris," said Beale, then rang off.

"Did Beale say when he arrived on the Island?" said Bruno.

Andy replied, "He didn't, but he said he gave Ali a wave as he saw him jump into a cab in the Havenstreet car park, probably at about 3.30 p.m. If you check the Ryde hovercraft you should see him leave the Island," he said. "It should not be difficult to spot him."

It was a simple task for Andy to check the CCTV tapes at Ryde hovercraft terminal as it was just a few days back where he confirmed that Ali had left the Island on the 4.00 p.m. hovercraft on Friday 8 June. To trace his movements on leaving the hovercraft Bruno and Andy took a 15-minute hovercraft ride to the Clarence Pier terminal in Southsea, where a review of the concourse CCTV saw him get into a local taxi at 4.25 p.m.

The registration number of the taxi was visible as it encircled the roundabout, for which the DVLA gave the police name and address details of the car owner.

NT13 BJW was owned by Billy Wilson, who lived one mile from the terminal.

He was as helpful as he could be. He remembered taking Ali from the terminal off the 4.30 p.m. arrival on 8 June to Portsmouth Harbour station where station CCTV showed he boarded the 4.50 p.m. train to Victoria Station in London. CCTV checks at stopping stations all the way to Victoria did not show a turbaned Indian gentleman alight from the train, although at Barnham there was no CCTV, and at Clapham Junction and Victoria the camera did not cover the entire platform," said Andy.

"You can't disappear dressed as he was," said Bruno. "We just lost him."

"Do you think he has gone to France?"

"That is what he said."

"Perhaps he got off at a point where he was not picked up by cameras," Bruno said. "If he was returning to Paris from Heathrow he'd have gone to Victoria, and Heathrow is totally covered with cameras so we should spot him. Heathrow airport police reported back the following day that there were several gentlemen of Bruno's description, but no one boarded an aircraft to Paris."

"Are we sure he was flying from Heathrow? Beale did not say that."

To Bruno this seemed as far as they could go with Ali who had not caught a flight to Orly from Heathrow that evening. Further checks revealed that his name was not on any flight or any airline manifest to Paris from Heathrow on the evening of Friday 8 June .

That could have been an excuse for wanting to leave promptly: "I have to go I have a plane to catch".

He could have flown from Gatwick or a Heathrow departure could have been a story that suited his purpose when talking to Beale. Trying to find him in England would be searching for a needle in a haystack.

"Who else haven't we spoken to from the passenger and staff at Havenstreet?"

Andy took it upon himself to compile a work list for the following morning's meeting at 8.00 a.m. at Newport Police HQ.

When they called the station the name and address details of the persons on the train who'd paid by credit card had been received. It was something to start working on in the morning. It was Friday evening by the time they returned to the Island and Bruno got home to enjoy a beer in the sun with Janet. She was relaxed listening to Bruno relate the progress he was making.

The mysterious Maisie Longmore, who Lewis claimed

married Klinker in the late 80s or early 90s, was an avenue
that needed exploring.

"We are getting down to the hard work," he said. "There
are areas to investigate that should show a fuller picture of
some of the Class of '78. Although so far we've picked up
nothing that might suggest that the killer is one of the Class
of '78.

"Go back to Beale. He is the only one where there is even
a sniff of a motive. He's up to something and he's back in the
race to buy the Klinker estate, which will go on to the open
market, once probate has been granted. It will go to auction.
That's probably the law, isn't it?" she said. "Then it will go to
the highest bidder. You've got to work on that one, Bruno.
There are other potential buyers for the Klinker estate, like
James Tennant, who'd go the extra mile to stop Beale if he
could."

Bruno wasn't convinced.

"One of the passengers could have been working with the
murderer," she said. "This is much more a two-person killing than one single murderer. Think of the moment: Klinker
goes into the station platform lavatory. Whilst he is there
somebody enters the small space and knifes him twice.
Someone could have seen him enter the lavatory. Someone
could have heard a scream or a scuffle or just loud voices.
Then the killer has to exit the lavatory and lock it. Other passengers could have been waiting to go in, the accomplice
would have blocked that passenger and sent him off to find
somewhere else."

Her analysis was correct and timing and patience would
have avoided detection.

To find an accomplice you have to identify the single passengers, who live on the Island. Bruno knew that with the
information the company gathered on passengers it would
be nigh on impossible. However, the possibility that two persons were involved broadened Bruno's thinking.

"Forget Ali for the time being. My guess is that he lives in a town with a large Indian population in the UK and he's proud of being an ex-English public school boy."

It didn't persuade Bruno to believe that was a good reason to attend a reunion with strangers.

"You say strangers, but were they strangers? It might be an error to think they were strangers, two of them knew each other very well."

Janet revealed a new take on Bruno's progress confirming what he had said to Andy that it was time to get to grips with the other passengers on the train.

CHAPTER 7

Friday 15 June

The Isle of Wight Steam Railway was established to preserve the romantic age of the steam railway and designed to show young families what it was like to travel by steam train fifty years ago, before the rail lines were electrified. It closed on 21 February 1966, but reopened in 1971. Havenstreet Station has been its headquarters since then.

Of the passenger list of 91, seven were travelling alone, five had paid by credit card, of which four lived on the Island: one lady and three men. The address details were provided to the UK police authorities.

The sole lady, Mrs Idle, was a widow who lived in Wroxall, a short drive from the station and she was at home. She was seventy and had taken the trip to repeat the one she and her husband had often done on their wedding anniversary on 8 June. She was a lifelong Island resident and as a young woman had travelled to school on the train that ran through Wroxall. She had driven to Havenstreet in her Volkswagen UP!, and during the train journey had shared a carriage with a family, a man, a woman and three young boys. She had not noticed anything strange or sinister about the day, but did remember seeing a group of noisy middle-aged men board the train at Wootton about 2.00 p.m. From then on the train chugged its way through the Isle of Wight fields watched by rabbits, pheasants and every conceivable form of wildlife alarmed in that moment by a noisy whistle hauling a mass of ancient metal hurtling through their habitat.

"The steam train was wonderful, where else can you see so much wildlife in their natural habitat?" said Mrs Idle. "Jimmy loved every minute of our anniversary, it never changed," she said.

She was a nice lady who added nothing to their investigation, so Bruno and Andy moved on to Colin Pearce, one of the three men who lived in Ryde.

The men were in their late fifties and all remembered the last of the Island steam trains. As boys they had collected engine numbers from standing on bridges that crossed the lines in various parts of the Island beside country lanes. They were the last of the anoraks.

They did not know each other and individually agreed to be interviewed in connection with the murder at Havenstreet Station. Colin Pearce was a bachelor, owned the family home left to him by his mother, and worked as the night manager of the Ryde Hotel where he had worked for 18 years. He liked his job, he said he always got a couple of hours of kip before the breakfast staff relieved him at 6.00 a.m., when he returned home and slept until noon, giving him the rest of the day to make models in daylight. He had made replicas of most of the old trains and carriages, and together with models of boats and planes and cars took up every space in his house. The planes hung from the ceilings, the boats stood on shelves and the track of a model train set was fixed to the walls of the ground floor rooms where Colin had made tunnels through the walls so the toy trains chugged their way around the entire ground floor of the house. He was a man whose life was clearly mapped out by him, he was happy and in control of every minute of his every day. The fact that he was a loner did not itself absolve him of the possibility that he could be a murderer. His personality did. He was totally absorbed in his hobby pastime, and his job facilitated his lifestyle. His need to generate an income to live on prevented him working as a volunteer at Havenstreet. So, he was crossed off their list of potential suspects and they moved on to Sammy Lloyd.

Sammy Lloyd was a hovercraft engineer and lived and worked in East Cowes. He was used to hands-on physical work. After school he had served his time as an engineering apprentice at Saunders Roe and now led the engineering team as Chief Engineer. He was interested in the way the Havenstreet workshop had rebuilt the trains and desperately wanted to become a volunteer when he retired. But retirement was some way off, and like Colin Pearce he was happy in his own world, without any thoughts that might conceivably make him into a murderer. Neither Colin nor Sammy claimed to have seen anything during their visit to Havenstreet station that had any connection with the circumstances surrounding the murder. They were railway enthusiasts soaking up every visible aspect of the Isle of Wight Steam Railway.

The third male traveller was Ian Harrison who had at one time been a volunteer, but the shifts that he had been allocated always seemed to clash with his other activities, namely his work as a printer where he had deadlines to meet with customers who wanted their jobs delivered, as he said, 'yesterday'. His business was located on an industrial unit on the outskirts of Ryde. They were in luck when they called. He was there and available to be interviewed. He was the kind of person who wanted the railway to schedule their timetable around his printing deadlines. He had taken the trip on the 8th because his mate, Harry Wilshire, was driving the train that day, and wanted him to be the third man in the cab. He could not resist the invitation, because he loved steam trains so he had jumped at the chance.

"Were you riding in the cab for the whole trip?" said Andy Bowen.

"No, it got very hot in the cab after Smallbrook so I went back into the guard's cab for a break. I had stoked up to Wootton and on the haul back to Smallbrook. I ate my lunch in the guard's cab and remained there for the final stage back to Havenstreet. It was great fun, very exciting to ride in the engine and feel the steam drive the pistons."

"Whilst you were having your lunch did you notice anything unusual?"

"No, I was out of sight, sitting in the guard's seat in the luggage compartment at the end of the train. It's where passengers used to put their luggage in the old days. There is only room for hand luggage in the passenger carriages. Steam trains had a man who carried a green flag, and when the train was ready to leave he would signal the driver from the platform. He was in charge of the train then.

"I think a guard still carries a green flag. The platform staff might be a lot more helpful than I have been. The porter and guards might have noticed something. I was also dirty after stoking, so when we finished, I went home to clean up."

Bruno asked if he knew Dr Klinker.

"I've never heard of him, Inspector. I read who he was, but he didn't mean a thing to me. In fact, I didn't connect his murder with my being on the train that day."

"One last question," said Andy. "You bought a ticket when you were working?"

"I always do because I am not officially employed, or a volunteer and it's my charity donation. The ticket guarantees that in the event of an accident I am insured, and not a casual unauthorised visitor. I could have gained access to the train by calling Mr Jenkins but the lady in the ticket office would have had to call him and he was busy."

Bruno resisted asking him more questions, as he knew he'd be back to see him once he'd found out more from Harry Wilshire.

"Harrison doesn't seem the type you'd go out of your way for as a friend does he?" said Andy. "Let's talk to Wilshire. Perhaps a different Havenstreet railway employee is involved."

Harrison had suggested that the train staff might know something about the murder.

"We have time, let's go and see Harry Wilshire if he is

working today, and see why he invited his friend in the cab last Friday."

"Harry was a long-standing employee of the Havenstreet Steam Company. He had been employed for twenty years, first as a volunteer. Since he was the only person who could drive all the engines, having retired from full time work as an accountant they had put him on the paid staff. He was an essential employee and he earned a living playing his hobby."

As Harry was out on one of his engine manoeuvres he arranged to see them when he had finished on the track, enabling Bruno and Andy to nose around the premises. John Jenkins, the manager, was about and agreed to come and chat about progress with them once they had spoken to Harry.

Bruno was open minded that someone who worked at Havenstreet might be involved in the murder of Klinker although there did not seem to be a connection, socially or in any other sense between Klinker and the railway.

Harry joined them in the café just yards from the Gents' lavatory on Platform A where Klinker died once he'd finished positioning an engine on the track ready to be hitched up to carriages for that afternoon's schedule. Bruno's friendly introduction was to say that they were speaking to everyone who was working on the day of Klinker's murder and, as he was driving the train on that day, he was someone of importance. Like a captain on a ship, he might know something that could help the police in their investigations.

"It was a normal day, Inspector. Perfect weather, we steamed up quickly and were away on time. I see a lot of the passengers because they all bunch around the engine when we stop. They are all interested in the rolling stock, and are very knowledgeable about steam engines."

"You wouldn't have recognised Klinker on the train, I suppose?" said Bruno.

"I wouldn't know him from Adam," said Wilshire.

"And the other members of staff on the train?"

"It's more or less the same team today as last week. They are all here."

"Ian Harrison said you invited him to ride in the cab with you last week. Is that right?" said Andy Bowen.

"It was more that he invited himself. He did a lovely print-ing job for a family wedding in a rush, didn't charge me for his time, in return I said when I had a chance, I'd take him in the driver's cab as a fireman-stoker. Well he called me on Tuesday of last week and asked if he could come last Friday. I saw no problem. We often have a third person in the cab. He did a long stretch in the cab, which included stoking up at the beginning. Then a young man joined us for the final stage. It's usually someone important like the Mayor or a journalist who gets a ride in the cab. I've even had the Duke of Edinburgh in the cab. Last Friday afternoon it was a young man from Ryde Tech."

"I understand that Harrison then took over as the guard?"

"Yes, it was very hot, and I could see he was whacked. He joined the guard in the luggage car. It was full of children's buggies. I saw him again when our trip ended. He enjoyed his day and thanked me."

"Was it a coincidence that he should ask to come on a day that a prominent Island person was murdered?"

"It must have been, Inspector. It's food for thought," though he added, "but I've known Ian for twenty years, he's not a murderer. I'd be surprised if he had heard of Klinker."

Harry had opened up a line of investigation connected with the discrepancy between whose invitation it was for Ian Harrison to ride in the cab on that particular day.

"A slip of the tongue," said Andy Bowen later.

However, Bruno couldn't see either man killing Klinker even though they had the perfect opportunity. They were both working on the railway on that day, which gave them an alibi, yet put them at the centre of the crime. There was something more about these two that he had to find out, but for now he couldn't put his finger on it.

If the killer had an accomplice, he had cover whilst stabbing Klinker to death in the lavatory, preventing any unconnected person gaining access during the killing.

And Wilshire and Harrison were together there at the critical time, between 3.00 and 3.15 p.m. while the train stood on Platform A waiting for the next group of passengers to board the train.

"Jenkins will know that Harrison was in the cab last Friday with Harry. They must fill in a log recording things like that."

When Bruno raised the matter with Jenkins, he said he knew, but only after the event, he added. When Harrison first became interested in Havenstreet he was taken on as a volunteer. Then he stopped volunteering because of the demands in his printing job. A self-employed person has to work hard, all hours in some businesses, and printing was one of those businesses.

"Maybe that's true, or maybe they are up to something?" said Andy.

John Jenkins had become the focus of their attention before the week ended. They'd expected a contact from him during the week, an offer of help, a lead or just a how are you getting on? It was after all on his premises at a peak time of the day that Klinker had been knifed to death, and as the business head of the Havenstreet enterprise he should be all over it. Bruno had earlier sensed an air of detachment, almost irritation at the presence of two detectives asking questions about the business. Jenkins obviously did not like police officers prowling about Havenstreet station. He had served in the Royal Air Force for 32 years, retiring with the rank of Squadron Leader, and liked to be addressed by his service rank, which explained why Colonel Masters did not get beyond the interview stage with his job application. Jenkins could not accept being outranked by a senior Army officer. In the RAF he did not fly planes. He was admin and payroll. He must have been one of the most boring persons in any officer's mess; however, for Havenstreet he was just right. The murder of Geoff Klinker was a situation that unnerved him, and he had shut his eyes to its implications for the overall business.

"However, failing to disclose Ian Harrison's presence in the driving cab was an obstruction, given that he knew about it and it should have shown up on the manifest. Just like not giving us the names of the school party," said Andy. "As with Wilshire and Harrison there is something Jenkins knows about the afternoon of 8 June that is not forthcoming. Where shall we go from here?"

"Ease him into the conversation about his staff and we will hit him with this non-disclosure later."

"Tell us about your staff," was Andy's opening gambit.

"I have spoken to those who were working on the day of the murder, which resulted in a description of their job-related activities on that day. None had anything unusual to tell me, or saw any incident connected with the murder."

"Okay," said Andy. "Assume that Klinker was killed by a railway staff member or members, who in your opinion might be capable of killing him and can you hazard a guess as to why someone might kill a person who was almost unknown on the Island?"

"Obviously they would have known each other?"

"That is the difficulty we are having – connecting the victim to the killer."

Jenkins was unsure how to respond to a police officer without being offensive.

Andy, realising his discomfort, said, "John it is in the interests of your steam railway that this killer is found quickly! While he is roaming free, he could strike again at any time. Now, can you tell me about Harry Wilshire and Ian Harrison?"

"They are friends, just friends. I don't think there is anything. Harry and Ian have a small business side-line, they sell game to people on the Island who like to eat game."

That was a new piece of information about them.

"Why didn't you tell us that Ian Harrison was riding in the cab on June 8th?"

"I thought you eliminated the driver and his mate, Inspector, from your list of interviewees."

"Nevertheless, don't you think an extra person on the train was information that you should have highlighted to us?"

"You were aware of that at the time but didn't draw it to our attention?"

Jenkins remained silent to the implication that there was something behind his non-disclosure.

"So please tell us all you know about these two gentlemen."

"What sort of game do they sell?" said Andy.

"All sorts, they are quite skilled at it. Ian has a cold store at his printing business premises."

"Where do they get their game from?"

"They'll tell you they have arrangements with farmers to shoot over their land, but they're really poachers, they are out all hours. If you want pheasants, rabbit or venison, they can provide it. When you travel on the steam train the birds fly up from the verges bordering the track. What Harry and Ian do is return to those habitats and trap or shoot the animals, which they prepare for the table and sell them. There are wild deer all over the Island so at times venison is quite plentiful. That's what Harry and Ian do in their spare time."

"So, what they see from the train they go off and hunt?"

"That's about it, Inspector."

"Do they have a game licence?"

"I can't help you with that, Inspector."

"Harrison said he had to stop volunteering his time here because of pressures of work."

"Yes, but not printing letterheads and business cards. They are hunting and shooting whenever they have the time. Harry loves the steam engines, but that is only part of his fascination."

"While they are hunting game do they ever have altercations with the farmers?"

"I am sure that they do, but there's always a deal if a farmer claims ownership. They will say they are protecting the wildlife by their regular culling."

"What about Klinker's farm? Has that any game?"

"Masses," said Jenkins. "But you don't see that from the train."

"So those two could have been poaching on Klinker's farm?

"Yes."

"And would Klinker know that?"

"By all accounts he is never on the Island, so your guess is as good as mine, Inspector."

"But could there be an issue if he objected to poachers?"

"I am sure there could. They are thieves, after all."

"Well there could be a connection there that we could follow up. What about the rest of the people who work for you?"

"We have a very enthusiastic bunch at Havenstreet, mostly volunteers. Some have a story to tell, but I don't think you should class them as potential killers."

"What about you, Mr Jenkins?"

"I occasionally have a rabbit off Harry and put it into a stew," he said, not fully understanding Andy Bowen's question.

They left him to mull over their discussion. They had given him a reason to worry.

Andy had enough to speak to Harry and Ian again, but what he had learned was not unusual for Island people who had their own private tax-free side-line and probably neither could remember who asked who to ride in the cab on 8 June. However, Andy thought they should be tackled seriously if they were crawling about Klinker's estate when he wasn't there.

Poachers who snoop around might spot something or someone also doing something they shouldn't. As an absentee feudal Lord, he must have been resented by a lot of local people who might target his property if he wasn't resident on the Island.

Bruno suggested they get the poachers over to the station for a chat. It would concentrate their minds if we bring them in. Knowing what they really do in their spare time, that will put the fear of god into them and open up an avenue of investigation. Wilshire was, after all, a permanent fixture about Havenstreet.

◆

Bruno had given the task of finding Kaz Ali to PC Kevin Bell at Newport Police Station. A recent recruit to the police service, he was a local lad and set about the search enthusiastically. He was also working on a detailed background for Beale, and trying to locate Maisie Longmore.

Having lost Ali off the Portsmouth to Victoria train on the evening of the day of the murder, he returned to the details he had obtained from Marian Hislop at the school. Her records consisted of some out-of-date information from India, but nothing in the UK, neither did she have current contact information. Ali had not replied to her email invitation to the reunion, but he had telephoned and paid his dues by money order from a Paris post office in euros, so it was assumed that he had received the email with details about the school trip.

Kevin Bell set about the task by trying to reconnect with Ali's email address in Mumbai.

Bruno needed to locate him quickly so that they could complete the interviews on the '78s. Meanwhile Janet examined his notes on the school party to see if she could join up some of the dots in their relationships with each other in the hope she might uncover a lead.

She had looked at the nine school friends and from what Bruno had reported eliminated Edward Hawkins, George Lewis, Walter Mullion, Kevin Billings and Colonel Masters. That left Roger Beale, Ian Walters, Kaz Ali and James Tennant about whom there were unanswered questions and suspicions, and the hint from George Lewis that there maybe a wife of Dr Klinker. Beale's recent past, namely the five years he had been in the UK after leaving South Africa, was known about. His 25 years living in South Africa might give a clue to his behaviour, as would some background on Ian Walters before his appointment as a Professor in Oxford. She saw no obvious clues in Bruno's investigation so far, but in the absence of anything on Ali, she would concentrate on Beale and Walters, and for Andy to put some more work into Ian Harrison, the man who rode in the driver's cab with Harry Wilshire on the day of the murder, and the absence of any input from the train manager, Jenkins.

The gap that stared her in the face was how little Jenkins had been asked to contribute to the investigation. In Janet's opinion he should have been all over it, helping the police in every possible way, but had given the impression the murder was none of his business and concealed vital information.

CHAPTER 8

Saturday 16 June

Bruno had suggested noon for the meeting with Harrison and Wilshire. This left him time to take Janet to Morrisons for their weekly grocery shop and to relax over a workman's breakfast.

It had been seven months since they had bought The Lodge on Carisbrook Road, on the outskirts of Newport. It was a classic stone Victorian property in a garden setting that compelled your presence during the glorious summer that he and Janet were enjoying for the first time together. They had bought the house jointly, sharing the mortgage and expenses. The mortgage was a small percentage of the cost of the house. This enabled them both to keep their separate apartments in Newport, which they had allowed a local agent to rent out and manage. The income more than covered the total outgoings on The Lodge and provided some cash towards updating and modernisation, which they had begun. They were comfortably off.

The previous evening, they had dined at Bentley's, their local fish and chip restaurant. It served excellent fish, the licensed restaurant separated from the takeaway counter. The rapid turnover on the takeaway counter guaranteed fresh fish.

At a quiet candlelit table, Bruno ran through his week's work. It had been just over one week since he'd begun the Klinker murder case, and so far they had not discovered a meaningful clue that led anywhere. At least that is what it at first appeared. But as Janet pointed out he had drawn a distinct boundary to his investigation, and assumed the killer had to be in that net, as she identified the key moments of his week's investigation.

"Let's talk about the Class of '78," she said.

"And Jenkins and his two henchmen, Wilshire and Harrison," said Bruno, before listening to her summary.

"If Jenkins is involved in their game business, the three of them could have reason to kill Klinker. We don't know what may have gone on between Dr Klinker and the poachers."

"It wouldn't have got to murder and I don't think they would crap on their own doorstep," she said.

"First there's Beale. He's full of himself and he has a plan. Whilst Klinker was alive he was going nowhere, now he's back in the game, except what game?"

"He has never been considered a serious potential purchaser of Klinker's. He can talk the talk, but I don't think he can walk the walk. Has he mentioned his team or any partners in his project to build a theme park?" asked Janet.

"It's all talk to big himself up, according to Tennant."

"You would need an army of interested parties, and already he'd have a comprehensive plan. He has none of that and I doubt if he has the money to buy Klinker's farm. Even poor-quality farmland fetches £3,000 an acre on the Island and Klinker's farm is over 10,000 acres. That's £30 million, and nothing you've found out about Beale suggests he has, or could raise, that kind of money," she pointed out. "Klinker's murder would have shocked him the same as everyone. He's acting nervously, trying to grab some of the limelight and keep abreast of your investigation, as if he must know how close you are getting to finding the killer, so don't be surprised if he comes back to you with all kinds of imagined incidents."

She continued, "Kevin Billings has created a very successful remarkable business from a modest local family bakery. Some might say he is on his way to revolutionising the baking industry, with the equipment he is bringing into this country. He moves in a different world to Klinker and the rest of the Class of '78, and I imagine he would consider it an insult to be involved in a murder. He has also become a guru re-designing other bakeries.

"George Lewis and Walter Mullins have a personal war. If George Lewis had wanted satisfaction he'd have taken Walter on before the relationship with his wife started. He didn't because he couldn't stop her. She was bowled over by the attention from a person with charm, charisma and position. He is now happy, in another relationship and on good terms with his daughter so you can forget him.

"Mullins is an open book, a predator and a serial womaniser, but not a murderer. Even though he only performs minor surgical procedures on the Island he is a respected hospital consultant, and there are plenty of spare women on the Island who would jump at the chance of a relationship with him. A female patient will weep for her doctor and be ready to offer herself to him."

"And die for him," added Bruno, accepting that wasn't all fiction.

"Mullins has survived two divorces so he has come to terms with what he is. Klinker didn't live here, so we know little about him, and you are not going to get any clues from the people who were on the train."

"What about the poachers?"

"Don't be diverted by them, they are a blind alley. I would doubt Harry Wiltshire and Ian Harrison are connected with the killing, but as they were on the train on the day, they could have noticed something.

"The other person on the Island who can offer you nothing is Colonel Masters. For each of them it was a day out in unfamiliar circumstances and almost impossible to identify anything that happened as unusual because everything on that day was new to all of them. There is nothing in Colonel Masters' past or present that connects him to Klinker except they were at school for a few years together as young men. He is looking for a job, which he'll easily get because there are plenty of organisations on the Island looking for a retired Colonel, and from Cowes he could always travel across to the mainland. He's looking for a job, not a career.

"The three mainland-based attendees seemed unlikely suspects although Tennant said Beale did him a favour buying their bankrupt family farm, giving him an exit from having to run it. There was resentment between them. With imminent availability of a prime piece of farming land, Tennant wouldn't allow Beale a clear run at acquiring it. He has the muscle to knock Beale out at an auction, and confine him to his second-rate farm in the west of the Island.

"Edward Hawkins is an interesting man but too immersed in his art to have any reason to murder Klinker, which leaves Professor Walters, who might be helpful in discovering, any genuine suspects.

"The mystery is what happened to Kaz Ali after he boarded the train at Portsmouth Harbour. His presence at the reunion was a little odd considering where he came from, whether it was Paris or India, and his abrupt departure suggested he'd some other motive, although there was no evidence, he could benefit from Klinker's death."

Bruno had listened to Janet's analysis and arrived at the conclusion that Ali had returned to Paris.

On Monday morning they were visiting Klinker's London home and meeting Brenda Frampton. Beyond that he had nothing and was handicapped, through a lack of contact with anyone who really knew Klinker, and who had any idea of who he really was.

"Perhaps Brenda Frampton will help and once you've been to his London residence you should know more about him than any of these Island people."

◆

Wilshire and Harrison were quite relaxed when they arrived together at Newport Police Station at noon to face Inspector Peach and Detective Sergeant Bowen. Andy had prepared a list of questions based on Jenkins's statement about their other activities that were not connected to their volunteer participation in the steam railway at Havenstreet.

"Can we start by clearing up misleading statements made by you gentlemen regarding that it was Mr Harrison's suggestion that he join you in the cab on the day of the murder?"

Wilshire began by saying that there had been a misunderstanding that had arisen because neither he nor his colleague were able to state categorically whose idea it was for Harrison to accompany Wilshire on that particular day, nor did they want to voice their true reason for Harrison wanting to come on that day, so when questioned they had answered in as vague a way as they could.

"And what was the real reason?" said Andy.

Harrison spoke. "You may not know that the route taken by the track of the Havenstreet express winds through one of the finest natural habitats for wild game on the Island its very similar to a game reserve. Are you familiar with the off seasons for game shooting?"

Bruno and Andy admitted they had no knowledge at all.

"Wild rabbits and hare: you can shoot them any time from 1 January to 31 December. The roe-deer buck can be shot between 1 April and 31 October in England, and there are different dates for Scotland. Game birds have seasons in the Autumn, pheasant 1 October to 1 February, partridge 1 September to 1 February, grouse 12 August to 10 December. Duck, geese and woodcock season is during similar Autumn dates.

"Harry and I are wildlife conservationists and we also run a small business selling game, rabbits and venison to Island restaurants and private individuals who buy game from us. There are many small woods, copses and farmland where we have agreements with the owners to shoot game.

"From the bridge across the railway in Briddlesford Copse the Tuesday before the murder I saw a small group of roebuck. The Havenstreet steam railway runs through Briddlesford Copse so I called Harry in haste and asked if I could ride with him to see if we could spot the animals from the train. The demand for venison in the summer is very high so I was planning to return to that place later that day if the deer were still there."

"Were they?"

"I did see one, luckily close to the track, and returned with Harry at daylight on Saturday and we made a kill. Do you like venison, Inspector?"

"I've never tried it," said both Bruno and Andy.

It was a valid explanation of the reason why Ian Harrison had ridden in the cab on the day of the murder. However, Bruno's final question was, "Can you take us to where you conduct your game sales business?"

"Come to my premises in Ryde. I can show you now," said Harrison.

"We didn't see any evidence of the game business when we came to see you last week," said Andy.

"That's because you turned up to speak to me in the office," said Harrison. "Now I'll show you the business."

"Let's go," said Bruno.

Harrison's printing business took up about half of an industrial unit, which was split into, Ian Harrison Printing, and Game products, although Game Products was not advertised with a sign. Both businesses looked to be in a healthy state and he explained that he employed seven full-time staff. In particular positions in the printing shop were printing machines and a number of large screen computers. In a separate adjoining building was Game Products. This was where Harry and Ian employed a full-time butcher. This part of their business was scrupulously clean, the workbenches properly scrubbed down. There were two large sinks and several cold store refrigerators against the walls and one could see that these two men knew exactly what they were doing in their respective activities, and in no way was it connected with Klinker.

After politely rejecting an offer of two prize venison steaks they left the Ryde Trading estate to return to Newport Police Station. What had begun as a situation that might have a bearing on this case had taken on a different perspective. These two men's behaviour had shown that there was nothing to connect them with Klinker's murder.

"I expect their activities are unlicensed, and probably they often trespass, but that is not our concern right now. Anyway, we are too busy to pursue a relatively trivial incident. We didn't put the frighteners on them, did we?" said Andy.

"No, it's another blind alley successfully negotiated to add to the others this week," said Bruno. "See you at Ryde Pier Head for the 6.05 a.m. hovercraft to Portsmouth on Monday."

"Serious business next week, sir," said Andy with a grin as he dropped Bruno at The Lodge on the Carisbrook Road.

CHAPTER 9

Monday 18 June

Promptly at 6.05 a.m. Bruno and Andy departed for the fifteen-minute crossing to Southsea. It was a warm summer morning. The sea was calm and a smooth crossing heralded a beautiful day ahead on the Island. The sun had risen a good two hours before they met at 6.00 a.m. for the visit to Klinker's London home, where they hoped to discover more about the man, and hopefully a clue that would lead them to the murderer.

A taxi from Clarence Pier dropped them at Portsmouth Harbour station in time to pick up four bacon rolls and two coffees from the Pumpkin café on Platform 1 and catch the 6.40 train to Victoria arriving at 8.30 a.m.

The underground Circle Line took them 20 minutes to South Kensington station, five minutes' walk from 9 Adelphi Mansions in Old Brompton Road, Klinker's London home. On the journey they had planned the day starting with Brenda Frampton, Klinker's practice secretary, at his London home.

She was an attractive woman in her late forties, a well-educated private secretary who one could imagine was comfortable dealing with wealthy patients who, when unwell, went to the Harley Street surgeries for treatment. She was welcoming. Knowing they had left early and had travelled from the Island, she had warm croissants and coffee ready and insisted they relax before opening their interview with her. It was a perfect introduction to a potentially key person in Bruno's investigation.

She knew everything about Klinker's private practice and the patients he treated. By reputation he was regarded as the most skilled consultant urologist in London, and when he was not fulfilling his obligation to the NHS, to which he always gave priority time, he worked in the best-equipped private London hospitals. His patients were rich and many were from overseas.

In accordance with Kevin Bell's request, Brenda had discovered that two of Dr Klinker's patients had died following his treatments.

These patients had died in the previous two years. Guy Mendleson, a man in his mid-eighties, a retired lawyer from Reigate in Surrey, and Moran Golobieski, a Russian businessman, aged fifty-six, who lived in a mansion flat opposite Regent's Park with his wife. Guy Mendleson had been operated on at the Millennium Oaks private hospital near Caterham. He had appeared to recover from the surgery but died in hospital one week later from organ failure complications.

Moran Golobieski's operation to remove cancerous tissues in his large intestine was undertaken at the London Marlborough Hospital. In surgical terms his cancer proved to be more extensive than Klinker had anticipated from his pre-op examination. During a seven-hour operation he found large parts of the abdomen affected by cancerous polyps and removed all those affected areas. Sadly, for the first time in his professional career, Klinker lost a patient on the operating table. It affected him for many weeks, and Moran Golobieski's family could not accept that he had been a very sick man. Several times Klinker was summoned to meet people connected to him to explain, even to show with diagrams the extent of the invasive areas of his body. Oddly, at the time, he also had to explain things to men who were not members of Golobieski's family. They were Russian business associates and insurance litigators searching for an opportunity to make a claim on Klinker's professional indemnity insurance.

All questions were answered satisfactorily but not accepted by members of his family. They were shown the green forms signed by every patient before any operation, which give the surgeon the authority to undertake at his professional discretion procedures that he deems necessary in the interests of the patient. Nevertheless, some members of his family believed that Klinker might have acted with other motives and on behalf of others. The operation on Golobieski had taken place over a year ago. His family believed his problem was gallstones. He had concealed the seriousness of his illness to everyone, but gallstones would have required only minor surgery using an explosive gun, which shatters the stones in the body that are subsequently flushed out of the system.

It was obvious from her behaviour and her sadness that Brenda Frampton had been very fond of Klinker, and had not recovered from the shock of hearing that he had been murdered by a person or persons as yet unknown. She readily agreed to help the detectives in any way possible.

She did not think the Golobieski's family were the kind of people who would direct their venom towards Klinker, who had proved to them, and his rather sinister business partners, in written correspondence, the serious nature of the condition his body had been in.

After their initial investigations the men in suits went away. However, Lillian Golobieski became an intimate friend of Dr Klinker and he spent a considerable time with her.

"I think you should forget about the possible hostility towards Geoffrey from his patient's connections. Hospital consultants are a mixed bunch with a streak of arrogance, but I can't think of a situation where someone, or someone connected to someone, would go so far as to kill out of revenge or anger. And to do it on the Isle of Wight, of all places," she said. "I imagine most of his patients would never have heard of it."

"Do you think it was strange that the woman with whom he should develop a relationship was the widow of the only patient who had died in those circumstances?"

"Yes and no," she said. "The coincidence was they were both members of the same gambling club. Have you ever seen the film *Magnificent Obsession* with Rock Hudson and Jane Wyman?" she asked Bruno.

Bruno admitted that he hadn't. "What is the relevance of an old film?"

"The story is about a surgeon who causes a wealthy woman to lose her sight in a reckless driving accident, and spends years developing a cure that restores her sight. Geoffrey might have felt a little that way about the death of Moran Golobieski. Look it up on one of those online film archives. It's how I always saw Geoffrey. Is there anything in this apartment I can show you?" she said, changing the subject abruptly. "Feel free to go anywhere. Geoffrey liked spacious rooms so that he could hang up his art collection. Let me show you."

The flat in Adelphi Mansions was large with a spacious entrance hall leading to a 30- by 20-foot open plan kitchen. It had four en-suite bedrooms, a study, two lounges, a cloak-room, utility room and a patio that looked across gardens to similar luxuriously appointed properties. Its value could be estimated at well into seven figures, situated in one of the most expensive areas to live in London.

"This is a large flat, for a bachelor," Bruno remarked to Brenda Frampton.

She explained that in every room there are works of art, not by famous artists. "He visited local studios in the Royal Academy, the Slade, and Camberwell College of Art, where he bought the work of many young artists. Occasionally almost overnight a modest purchase of £40 often became worth hundreds and one artist he has supported since college days, Lillian McCain, her work sells for tens of thousands."

"What other interests did he have?"

"Many," said Brenda. "The opera, he travelled to Paris, Milan, Vienna when a soprano or tenor that he loved was

singing. He liked the cinema, the theatre, he watched football. He had a club season ticket at the Emirates Stadium to
watch Arsenal. He didn't own a car, he used taxis."

"Who were his friends, Miss Frampton?"

"Inspector, please call me Brenda. He did not have friends,
although he belonged to various clubs. The Travellers Club
in Pall Mall was his favourite."

"Is there anything you can tell us about him that might
induce somebody to murder Dr Klinker?"

She didn't answer straight away.

"I assume you knew him very well?"

"I would like to help, Inspector, but I don't know what you
are asking me. I have told you all I know about his patients.
He was a man of integrity, a gentleman. He supported any
number of charities with money and time."

"Did he ever mention his parents?"

"Often. I met them several years ago on the Isle of Wight.
After his mother died a few months ago he had to attend to
her estate, which is one of the reasons he was visiting the Isle
of Wight."

"Did he mention an old school reunion?"

"No, Inspector."

"Because it was whilst attending that, that he was killed."

"Would that be in Ryde? That's where his school was
situated."

"Yes, but not in the school, on a reunion outing. Can we
see what is in his study and the inside of any locked drawers
and cabinets?"

"Of course, Inspector, I'll check that they are all open."

Bruno regarded the intrusion into a victim's personal life
as being on the edge of immoral, except in the case of murder. Klinker's library consisted of books on the arts, litera-
ture, and sports in bookcases. A pile of recent medical journals was neatly stacked.

His address book had annotated dates alongside names

and addresses so it was possible to distinguish recent contacts with those going back several years.

Bruno had brought with him the personal effects belonging to Klinker that had been on his person when he was killed. Two credit cards had been blocked by the desk officer at Newport Police Station, as had his mobile phone account so calls could no longer be made. The technical team had produced a hard copy print out of calls made out and received in since the previous January. Whilst Bruno started to look at the contents of his desk and correspondence, Andy Bowen matched the identity of callers with the names in the address book.

Invitations to clubs, charity evenings, special event dinners and professional meetings were the bulk of current correspondence.

"Brenda, presumably you will inform those who need to know of his demise?"

"I will do that straight away," she said.

Matching the logged phone numbers against entries in the address book eliminated a percentage of them. Andy discovered only one item he considered to be of importance. During a period of four weeks immediately before his murder a lot of calls were received from one mobile phone number. Which Brenda recognised straight away.

"That is Lillian Golobieski."

"Do you know why she might have made 140 calls to his number in the three weeks before he was murdered?"

"That seems a lot!" said Brenda.

"Have you ever heard him speak about Lillian?"

"Yes, but not often," she said. "In fact, never about his personal relationships with women. He was discreet and secretive and he coveted a bachelor status."

"What was your own relationship with him?"

"It was professional. I ran his office and this place; I pay all the bills. I sign all the cheques and I look after him. We

had a love affair and lived as husband and wife for a number
of years. I liked to think we might marry, but we didn't,
because we couldn't. When I met him, he was already married. I worked as his secretary, and his marriage was not an
obstacle to me, because I fell in love with him. I know that
deep down he felt a sense of guilt of betrayal, it wasn't that
she would not agree to a divorce but neither of them would
accept the failure of the marriage."

"Was he always that way?"

"He was quite introverted, but it did not stop the most
attractive women making themselves available to him, and
he carried the status of hospital consultant in a dignified
way."

"Were you jealous?" said Bruno.

"Of course," she said unhesitatingly. "I loved him, but for
him it was not the same as when I first came to work for
him. I think he knew that. I should have left years ago, but he
wouldn't let me go."

"So, what were you hoping for?"

"Something that never happened Inspector."

"Tell us about his wife."

"Her name was Maisie Longmore. She was the hospital
administrator at the same hospital where he was a registrar,
studying to become a surgeon. It was after he became a consultant and established a private client list that we met."

"Did you meet her?"

"No," she said unconvincingly, which indicated otherwise.
"I don't know what happened to her. If you give me a little
time I'll try to find out," she said.

"Was Lillian his latest conquest?"

"Yes," she said.

Having searched his personal papers, Bruno took note
that as well as being a member of the Travellers Club he was
a member of the Oxford and Cambridge in Pall Mall and
Trotter's Casino in Carlton House Terrace. He was a patron

of The Arts Club in Leicester Square, The Tate and the Royal
Academy in Piccadilly. None of these, however, had any personal connection with him that could be followed up. They
created a picture of Klinker that was incongruous with the
Island, and explained why he seldom visited. When they had
finished their search for clues in his home, Brenda promised
to be available should they wish to return.

It was approaching noon when they left Klinker's apartment and with time to spare they indulged themselves in
Andy Bowen's favourite lunch: burgers at Five Guys, where
you can add up to eight fillings and a portion of potato skin
chips, that would feed a family of five. It was a long day and
there was no point in starving themselves.

After his visit to his home, Bruno considered what they
had discovered. Klinker was not a man to make enemies. He
accepted as a permanent feature in his life a devoted secretary, who was incapable of leaving him and making a life of
her own. He was lucky she wasn't a jealous woman or he
might have come to a bad end sooner. He trusted her fully
and allowed her total access to his business and private life.

"However nice a man he was considered to be his behaviour doesn't ring the 'nice' bell for me," said Andy. "We must
get to see Maisie Longmore."

Over lunch Andy received confirmation of the address
of Lillian Golobieski, whose mobile number had been used
to make the 140 calls to Klinker's mobile during the three
weeks before his death. When he called the number, a female
voice answered.

"Is that Mrs Golobieski?" said Andy.

"Yes, this is Lillian Golobieski," answered a lady in a
European accent.

"Madam Golobieski I am Detective Sergeant Andrew
Bowen from Newport police on the Isle of Wight, investigating the murder of Geoffrey Klinker."

"Yes," was her single word answer and then silence.

"We are aware that the deceased was known to you. Is that correct?"

"Yes."

"As we are in London this afternoon, my senior colleague Detective Inspector Peach and I would like to speak to you about him."

"I have not seen him or spoken to him for some time so I cannot help you."

"Our records suggest that you were in constant touch with Mr Klinker on this telephone number up to very shortly before his death just 10 days ago and we believe you may shed some light on his murder."

"How did you get my number?"

"Mrs Golobieski you are the subscriber to this mobile phone number."

"I cannot do that today because I am going to work shortly. You could be anybody calling out of the blue."

"We will show you proper identification Madam when we call, or we can arrange to see you at your nearest police station this evening. It is vital we speak with you today. Either it's this afternoon at your residence, or when you finish work, by which time we shall have obtained an arrest warrant."

After a protracted silence she agreed to meet them at 3.00 p.m. at her home in 16 Regent's Park Road. Bruno wanted to find out the reason for the 140 separate calls to Klinker in the three weeks prior to his murder, and felt there must be a connection.

Flat 2 at 16 Regent's Park Road was on the first floor of an elegant building in a Regency terrace facing the north side of Regent's Park. From her south-facing balcony, amongst the trees, you could see the zoo and the contours of the roof of the Snowdon aviary.

It was a large duplex apartment, the home of a millionaire, if not a billionaire, making Madam Golobieski's remark 'that she had to go to work' curious. It was Maria, the housekeeper, who opened the front door to the apartment and led them into the main lounge where the doors to the balcony facing the park were open. Almost immediately an attractive lady in her mid-forties followed them into the room, and introduced herself as Lillian Golobieski, to whom they showed their photo ID.

She appeared immaculately dressed in designer clothes ready for a grilling about her relationship with Geoffrey Klinker.

"Gentlemen, please sit down and Maria will bring us tea. I mentioned that I had to go to work so can we be brief?"

"We will try," said Bruno.

She was not hard to read with her good looks and middle-aged sex appeal. She had the demeanour of a woman of the world who believed she could deal with anyone, certainly two detectives, one aging and the other young, from a place she'd never heard of miles away.

Bruno started with, "Madame Golobieski, can you explain your relationship with Geoffrey Klinker?"

"We were friends," she said.

"Good friends?" said Bruno.

"Very good friends. He was the surgeon who operated on my husband before he died."

"That was more than one year ago. Geoffrey was a brilliant surgeon but was too late to save my husband's life, he was very ill indeed."

"And since then?"

"We were lovers, Inspector."

It was a straight answer and could explain the reason for the calls in the weeks prior to his death.

"Immediately prior to his death, over a period of three weeks, you made 140 calls to his mobile phone. Can you let us know the nature of those calls?"

"That's what people in love do," she said.

"Were you planning to marry?"

"We had discussed it and it could have happened, except Geoffrey was not the marrying kind."

"Did you find that disappointing?"

"Immensely," she said.

"You said you were going to work, what is it you do?"

"My husband was a very wealthy businessman. Have you heard of a company called Bleasnef?"

Neither Bruno nor Andy had, so she explained.

"It is a mining company. It imports precious metals, like cobalt, titanium and lithium used to make batteries for electric cars. My husband had two partners. When he died these two directors said that their agreement, which they showed to me, stated that if anyone left the company the two remaining directors had to buy out the departing director's shares for cash. Some three weeks later they came with three valuations for my husband's share of the business. The amount they offered me was £3 million, or nothing, so I took it, even though I knew the business is worth tens of millions.

Without my husband I became ill and depressed and all I could do was visit the casino. After one year I was broke. In fact my gambling debts stand at over £1 million. That is when I went to work in the casino. If I weren't broke, they'd have sued me. Then I met Geoffrey. One evening I was playing roulette and he recognised me. Nowadays I do not use my own money. I don't have any. I am a house player. When a casino opens in the afternoon someone has to start a game. That's what I do. I draw chips from the cashier and I walk around the tables and sit down and start a game. When others join me I move to another table. Geoffrey was not a regular visitor. In fact he was not a gambler. He promised to help me clear my gambling debts, if he sold his estate on the Isle of Wight. But now that is just a vanished dream, it cannot happen."

"Have you any idea who would have killed him?"

"He was not a man to have enemies, and at the casino he was anonymous. He came about once a fortnight, probably less than that, to relax after a difficult day. He used to play roulette. He had a system and he always won, but only with small stakes. When I was not working, we went to concerts, the theatre. He loved the opera. We were in love."

"Did you visit his apartment?"

"Yes, when Brenda was not there. Sometimes we went to Paris for the weekend to the opera. Puccini and Verdi were his favourites."

"Is there anything you can tell us that might help us to find the killer?"

She thought seriously before speaking.

"In gambling there are lots of shady people. None of them associated with Geoffrey, or knew anything about him."

"But you know who those shady people are?"

"I know because the casino knows who they are, as do the croupiers. Mostly they are thieves who come to the casino to play with their dishonest loot. It's a form of money laundering. They would not have come into contact with Geoffrey."

"Can you explain what was so important that you made so many calls to Dr Klinker in that time, approximately seven calls a day?"

"I already told you. He promised to help with my debts to the casino and they were putting the pressure on me to pay them."

"And what did you ask him to do?"

"I asked him what I should do, he said I should be patient, but the casino wanted me to settle."

"Did you know that he had no intention of selling his farm?"

"No."

"Did you suggest to him that he could borrow against the farm?"

"No, I did not."

"You said the casino knew you were broke and were pressing you?"

"They wanted me to sell the apartment, and they knew of my relationship with Geoffrey."

"So, what did you propose to do?"

"To get them off my back I told them that Geoffrey had promised to pay my gambling debts."

"Did they believe you when he had only promised you in a vague way to help you, and then only if he could? Did you take that to mean he would cover a big debt?"

"I hoped to persuade him," she said.

"Really?" said Bruno. "So, the casino where chasing you to chase Klinker, and that is what those phone calls were about?"

"Not entirely," she said. "I also told him I loved him," she added with a smile.

"Do you think the casino might have taken it upon themselves to try to collect from Dr Klinker?"

"They agreed to accept half in full settlement if Geoffrey paid them," she said.

"Was that agreed with Dr Klinker?"

"I don't know, perhaps they had a private meeting with Geoffrey?"

"To whom should we speak at the casino?"

"Is that necessary?"

"Yes, because if they have a note from him, they may think they can get paid from his estate."

"I do not know enough about English law, Inspector."

"Lillian, £1 million is an astronomical level of credit to advance any punter!" said Bruno.

"I was not any punter, Inspector. My husband was a billionaire until he died, then the directors of the company took his shares in return for a pittance. The casino didn't know that, did they? So, they let me run up a debt. At a certain point I knew I'd never pay it back unless I won it back, and then they keep their own money. Although I owe them, you could say that all that time I was a house player, as I am now. Without my cash buying the chips I am playing with their money. I don't know if I'd have let Geoffrey pay them anyway. He didn't have to, even if he'd signed a promissory note. So that's my story, Inspector. Yes, I did press him a lot to pay them for me, and he promised to if he sold his estate, but because they knew about him they were on to me all the time. They've stopped asking for their money, because if they take me to court where will that get them? I am a widow. I have no income, no job and no money. They will look ridiculous, Inspector. And if they win, which of course they will, the court will award them twenty pounds a week."

"I thought you said you didn't know about English law?"

"That's what I said, Inspector," she said with a smile.

Lillian demonstrated that she could get and have anything she wanted using her beauty and charm, like a twenty-first-century Zsa Zsa Gabor, and had shown no remorse at the death of her lover. Klinker was just another losing bet.

There was nothing in Lillian's story that would lead him closer to Klinker's killer. Nevertheless, Bruno thought it necessary to speak to the casino director who, according to Lillian, had somehow accepted Klinker's word, written or otherwise, that he would pay Lillian's gambling debt.

With some reluctance Lillian provided the detectives the contact details of the casino management.

"I may see you at the tables then, Inspector," was her goodbye comment.

They left Lillian, hoping they did not meet again, to visit the casino in Carlton Terrace to see what new information they might shed on Dr Klinker's relationship with Lillian Golobieski.

"I wouldn't put it past her to have set up Klinker's murder, if it meant she could get her hands on his money. She is a dangerous woman," said Andy.

"So, it's back to the Island to search for suspects," said Bruno as the taxi drove along Regent Street towards the casino located in the St James's district behind Piccadilly."

"We haven't bottomed out Brenda Frampton yet, sir."

"We will get back to her," said Bruno after we've finished with this wild goose chase.

◆

Trotter's Casino in Carlton House Terrace was the essence of luxury. The reception was elegantly appointed with a concierge desk standing to one side so as not obstruct the view of the entrance. A tall dark-suited man wearing an accommodating expression of an indeterminate age watched over the action in the foyer, principally the arrival of punters. The furnishings and decorations were luxurious to welcome and make comfortable the club's members used to these opulent surroundings.

"Inspector Peach," said the concierge, addressing the detectives as they reached his desk.

"We have an appointment with the manager."

"Yes, sir, Mr Chang is expecting you. Will you please sign our visitor's book?"

It was obvious that Lillian Golobieski had informed Mr Chang of their intended visit.

Anticipating their need for evidence of their visit, Bruno signed and Andy Bowen did likewise.

"Gentlemen, please take a seat. Mr Chang will see you shortly."

Within two minutes a smartly-dressed suit emerged and led them through the casino, past the bar and assorted gaming tables, some occupied, others waiting for the serious gambling to begin, or the arrival of Lillian Golobieski.

Mr Chang stood as the two detectives were ushered into a large comfortable office with a sitting-room area.

Once the person who had conducted them to his office departed Chang offered them still or sparkling water to drink. With them all seated comfortably, he opened the conversation.

Chang had the distinct Chinese accent of an English-speaking Hong-Kong-born man. He looked under forty and was the managing director of one of the company's flagship casinos worldwide for The International Imperial Casino group, a Chinese company that operate casinos worldwide, headquartered in New York City.

"I am sorry to hear that Dr Klinker has been murdered on the Isle of Wight," he said.

"Yes," said Bruno. "Can you help us try to find his killer?"

Chang did not answer straight away and in a moment of silence looked into Bruno's eyes.

"I will try, Inspector, and may I start this interview by stating facts that will get us quickly to the reason for your visit. Cut the crap, in other words," he said with a nervous smile.

"I was introduced to Dr Klinker by Lillian Golobieski after she had run up big debts at the casino and could not meet the call. He was a respected member of Trotter's, has been for many years. Often, he would just dine, sometimes with a lady, sometimes alone and then play roulette. He played to a system on the even chances and usually he won, but small bets. He was not on our A or even B list of gamblers."

"I understand that he promised you that he'd pay Lillian's gambling debts when he sold his farm?" said Bruno.

"Inspector, as I have said, Dr Klinker was a respected member of this club and we never engage any member in a discussion about another member's gambling debts. That never happens. If Lillian has told you that he promised to pay her casino debts that is between Dr Klinker and Lillian. We have no knowledge of anything like that. Gamblers will tell you stories but they never tell you that they ever lose. Every person out there, he gestured towards his door, will tell you they are winners.

"We had allowed her debt to spiral to a ridiculously high figure following the, unknown to us, death of her husband who was well known to the casino. He was a big punter and always covered her losses. We always treated them as a joint account. She did not tell the casino of her husband's demise until she could not meet the call. His estate was much less than everyone anticipated, and Lillian received a derisory sum for his share of his company from the other two directors. The Golobieskis ran a joint gambling account, which as a Russian billionaire oligarch, the casino let run until they asked her to settle and then discovered he had died."

"That was dishonest of her?"

"Well, she thought she would win it back. We should never have allowed it to happen."

Even Bruno knew that in a casino all gamblers are watched closely by inspectors at the tables, and by croupiers and cashiers where the chips are bought. Any unusual pattern of gambling, big wins or losses are noticed, and watched, so for her debts to have risen so quickly, unnoticed, he did not believe. They would have known from the beginning but let it go believing her Russian husband would cover her loss. So, they took a punt on her and lost.

Chang continued, "When we demanded payment, she couldn't pay. But as she is an attractive personality and immaculately turned out, we employed her as a house player. Nobody knows that. She is from Poland and has many friends here. We like to see her as she encourages our members to play. We are a gambling club, Inspector, and we don't want our members to just come here to sit about talking, drinking and eating, so Lillian brings them to the tables.

"Some while ago, she introduced me to Dr Klinker and suggested that he was going to help her pay her debts. He was a member and an occasional visitor to the club, and by coincidence the surgeon who had operated on her husband before he died. He was a shoulder to cry on, and just what she needed, a middle-aged, rich, lonely man. He fell for her and although he may have promised her that he would cover the debts, he did not do so to us. She informed the casino that he'd have a wagon load of cash when he sold his farm."

"Did you believe her? After all she is a known liar," remarked Andy.

"Any publicity to do with forcing people to pay gambling debts is bad news for casinos, so they don't do it, certainly not publicly. How would it look if a member of our club were murdered while being pressed to pay a gambling debt by us? You said he was stabbed to death in a lavatory, you think I might send a Chinese man to the Isle of Wight to kill a punter in a public lavatory?"

"I am sure there have been stranger killings," said Bruno.

"Only in Charlie Chan mysteries, Inspector. Once we are certain Lillian hasn't any assets in property or cash hidden somewhere, we will dispense with her services. A casino has always to maintain a high level of respectability and having cleaned her out she no longer represents that."

"If Klinker had sold the farm, I imagine your position would have changed as long as Dr Klinker had remained alive."

"No," said Mr Chang firmly. "His 10,000 acre farm sounds like a big business but it's a do-everything farm, cattle, sheep, fruit orchards, soft fruit, hundreds probably thousands of acres of root vegetables, including sugar beet. Dr Klinker did not do that himself. He had a very good farm manager who got well paid. Valuing that kind of business would be different to say 40,000 acres wheat on mainland UK. So, although you could be talking of twenty, thirty million, who would go to an inaccessible Island and invest that kind of money? An estate of 40,000 acres of a single crop with a woodland shoot on mainland Britain is an investment for a billionaire. There are tax and farm subsidies to be had, but Klinker's farm is for an Island person who enjoys the Island lifestyle, which I understand has a lot of natural beauty."

It was obvious from Chang's knowledge of the details of Klinker's farm that he had investigated it a lot further than he had let on.

No amount of probing by Bruno was going to get Mr Chang or the casino to admit any connection with Dr Klinker, other than they already had. They wanted to distance themselves from anything to do with a murdered club member apart from acknowledging his membership, so it was time for them to return to the Island.

Klinker had become associated with gamblers through his relationship with Lillian, and because on the occasional lonely leisure evening he'd visit Trotter's, relax, and play roulette. Gambling clubs were dangerous hangouts for such a man, full of predators of the opposite sex cleaned out of all the family wealth they could get their hands on, which usually included every cent of their husband's. Dressed in their finery, they'd sit playing gin rummy or backgammon, or as Lillian Golobieski, who was a middle-aged beauty, work as a house player encouraging punters to sit down and join her playing the tables. Lillian enjoyed the glamour of being a house player. It was the next best thing to playing with her own money.

"Have I been of help, gentlemen?" said Mr Chang, assuming their questioning had finished. At this point he stood and held out his hand and accompanied them to the reception area where a secretary phoned for a taxi.

It had been a long, complicated day. It was expected that Lillian Golobieski and Chang, the casino boss, would deny any involvement with Klinker, other than that he was a club member.

"Have a safe journey back to your Island," he said as they shook hands and he showed them into a black cab.

Bruno and Andy felt their visit to London had advanced

their search for Klinker's killer. They had eliminated any relevance in his relationship with Lillian. He had been flattered by the attention that a fading beauty looking for a rich husband, a gold digger with sharp claws, had given to him.

"Is Brenda Frampton the long-suffering martyr she claims to be? Let's put a few more pieces together before we get to her, she is going nowhere. Assume Klinker's only reason for this Island visit was to attend his old school reunion, knowledge of his attendance could only have come from or through the school secretary's office, and because he was murdered during their outing there is an Island connection. So, who apart from those who attended the reunion, and the school, knew about it? I'd assumed the farm manager's contacts with his boss were business like, and he was aware of it and if he did not have it from Klinker, who did he get it from?"

A taxi took them to Victoria station and they boarded the 18.36 train to Portsmouth Harbour station.

From their notes, and the comments from their meetings, they had learned about Klinker's life in London, and the unsensational man that he was. An ongoing relationship with Madam Golobieski could have reduced his inheritance to nothing and any allure he had seen in her would have vanished with it and he knew that. The God-given opportunity he had given her, and his sudden disappearance from her life, would have disappointed her. Dr Klinker's murderer had killed the goose that could lay her golden egg. However, as a house player in a prestigious London casino, an attractive woman would not lack attention from the wealthy gamblers, and before long she'd hook up with someone else.

"Could Brenda Frampton have killed him, and did she have a motive?"

"Only jealousy." But Bruno believed that jealousy was not a Brenda Frampton weakness or it would have manifested itself earlier, during their intimate relationship.

Their journey to London had added flesh to their

skeleton knowledge of Geoffrey Klinker, who they now saw as a real person. Especially with the introduction of Maisie Longmore, who Brenda claimed was his lawfully-wedded wife. Confirmation of that marriage would be helpful, as would finding the lady.

"Could the reason for his murder be connected with her family, who could have an ancient score to settle?" Andy wondered aloud.

"We will find out," said Bruno. "But for now, we should discount a mainland murderer."

"Even Walters?"

"No, except for Walters," said Bruno.

◆

At home, Bruno discussed the day's events with Janet. She was interested to know that Klinker was married.

"It's another dimension to him," she suggested.

Brenda Frampton knew more about Klinker than she had let on. Her residency in his apartment and knowledge of his comings and goings could be more revealing.

In their search for suspects her suggestion was to return to the Klinker farm and speak to the neighbours. Klinker's farm was a very profitable business. It had continued to be run efficiently by Klinker's farm manager. He might open the door to other Island people, who could benefit from the death of Klinker, and the sale or non-sale of the business.

The Havenstreet visitors that could not be excluded were those who only bought tickets to the museum, who did not embark on any steam train journey. They bought an entrance ticket at the ticket office, which gave them free right to roam the entire station complex. Their ticket allowed them to use the restaurant, museum, the station platform lavatories, to have a close-up look at the locomotives, and crucially to loiter around any part of the station as ostensible observers of any of the activities. The problem with that group was finding out who they were.

"It's time to open up the Island side of Klinker's business. Forget the London connection for the time being," she said.

A lingering question was why had John Jenkins not led him in the direction of the museums, and workshop visitors – instead of maintaining his focus on the train passengers and the school party. Was that intentional? It was another question to put to him. Jenkins wanted nothing to do with this murder and was not even thinking about it.

CHAPTER 10

Tuesday 19 June

The following morning Bruno returned to Clive Hall and Klinker's farm, situated on the B3399 road, three miles north of Billingham southeast of Shorwell, four miles from the southern tip of the Island. The farm lay to the south and Clive Hall, the farmhouse, was situated near the junction of the B3399 and a minor road that ran south from Billingham. In the west the farm border was Park Lane, a C road that ran due south from Shorwell to Alterfield. The farm was broadly flat across its 10,000 thousand acres, with two small lakes 200 meters off the B3399, opposite Passwood Farm, including a five-hundred-acre woodland copse with high mature trees. The land was covered in rich deep soil capable of high yield crops.

The woodland was dense around its perimeter, but once through the outer growth it was a haven for wildlife, game birds and deer, where they could breed and feed. Which makes a direct connection to Wilshire and Harrison, who would know the location of every deer on the Island. Looking at the map of the farm the woodland could be accessed from a small section of the B3399.

"They could drag a deer straight out of the trees onto a van unseen," said Andy.

This visit was to find out from Mrs Galloway how the farm was run and managed. Bruno had been especially nice to her while she behaved stoically in the light of the murder. Previously she had given off an air of subservience, quietly going about her tasks of generally efficient housekeeping. On this visit she behaved differently. She did not want any intrusion into her domain. She had allowed the police to search freely whatever parts of the manor house they had chosen, twice, and as far as she was concerned that was enough.

She did not want the reminder of the murder of Klinker continuously before her eyes. So the moment she set her eyes on them she stated that she could help them no further. This conversation took place standing outside of the entrance to the house into which she did not invite them. She did, however, answer his questions as to who managed the farm.

Dairy farming was carried on profitably, she told them, with the most up-to-date farm machinery and managed by Biff Haves, a long-serving farm manager.

"Biff Haves, the farm manager, runs the farm. He worked with Tom Klinker man and boy for forty years. He employs the labourers when they are needed mostly from early March until late October. They are all local men who, if so inclined, take on seasonal jobs in the run-up to Christmas and into the New Year, when there is little work on the farm. Biff Haves is well known on the Island and hopes to continue to manage the farm, even expand it, under new owners, because it's extremely fertile, has sheltered pastures across thousands of acres, and excellent mixed farmland and it's very profitable."

"And one other question, Mrs Galloway. Do you have much contact with Dr Klinker's half-brother, Arnold Harris? We met him when he accompanied you to identify the body of the Doctor."

"We talked about Geoffrey after that visit, and neither of us have any idea who would have done this. Arnold saw very little of him, he never knew when he was coming to the Island, and when he did come it wasn't to see Arnold," she said. "You should go and see him at the Newport Council offices. He is head of Planning."

Andy Bowen had already noted that information from an earlier meeting. Arnold Harris was a person they should visit sooner rather than later, now they had seen all of the former pupils, with the exception of Ali.

"Was it Dr Klinker's intention to sell the farm?"

"Some people think so, but I believe he had no intention of selling up and living in London. All the time his mother was alive he wouldn't, or couldn't sell, but when she died, he could. He listened to offers from farm agents, but only for curiosity."

"Do you think one of those people could have killed him?"

"Haven't a clue, odd bods turned up occasionally saying they were farm agents. No one spoke to them, apart from me, and I said I was only the housekeeper. Inspector, Geoffrey was a rich man and he didn't need the money. The tax he would have to pay on the sale would run into millions of pounds, I once asked him if he was selling, he said 'No', firmly. 'This is a stress-free haven'."

Geoffrey was born on the Island. He went to school here. He wasn't sent away to board in some fancy public school because he wanted to stay here. So they sent both boys to Ryde School."

"Does he always come back to attend the school reunions?"

"This is the first time in my time here. But he loved his school days. Find out who is behind this rumour that he was about to sell up, Inspector, then you'll find the killer."

"That's easier said than done Mrs Galloway."

"What about the neighbouring farms?" said Bruno.

"They are small and produce a mix of Island produce, some sheep and cattle. As we have no abattoir on the Island, all cattle for slaughter have to go to the mainland."

"Is that a problem?"

"It changes the mix of farming negatively," she said.

"Where can we find Biff Haves?"

"At this time of day, he will be in his office which is one of the farm cottages on the eastern edge of the farm, No 3, go back to the road, turn right, it's a mile on towards Billingham on the right."

"You are obviously busy at present; we may come back to see you later?"

"I won't be back until after lunch."

She stood in the porch and watched them drive off determined not to allow any further intrusion into her territory.

"So!" said Andy. "We'll need a warrant to get back in there," he added.

"I am not sure about that. She is only the housekeeper. But she was hostile," said Bruno. "Why do you think that was?"

"Because we came back. She thought she'd dealt with us last time."

"What does that mean?"

"She's hiding something, or she'd have told us about Biff Haves the last time we called. Remember on our first visit we got nothing from her."

They arrived at the cottages, a row of ten, all of which seemed occupied and in very good condition. No 3 had a brass plate on the door that announced KLINKER FARM HOLDINGS.

Biff Haves was waiting, and he did not seem surprised at their arrival, no doubt having been warned they were on their way by Mrs Galloway.

"I had expected you sooner, Inspector. Mrs Galloway said you had called in to see her a couple of times."

"We've been too busy since the murder speaking to the group who travelled on the school outing on that afternoon and others who were connected with the railway and based at the scene of the murder on that day. Also Mrs Galloway did not reveal your existence to us on our previous visits. I hope you are not disappointed to be so far down our list of people who knew Geoff Klinker, and are of interest to us?"

"How well did you know him?" asked Andy.

"Better than anyone on the Island."

"Then perhaps you can lead us in the right direction. What was your relationship with him?"

"I run the farm, Inspector, have done for many years. Whilst Tom Klinker was alive, he was interested in farming and we worked together on improving our farming methods. He sent me to agriculture college to learn modern methods, and we began a plan of improving our crop production, animal husbandry, calf rearing and dairy cattle, even goat farming, and four years ago we bought four alpacas; we've now got ten. We started organic vegetable production. Mushrooms became very profitable and still are. We ensured that we optimised the crop production to obtain maximum EU farm subsidies."

"What was your view of Geoff Klinker's decision to sell the farm?"

"He never said to me that was his intention," said Haves.

"Sounds like a rumour that has surfaced since his death, spread by people who'd like to buy it or cash in with him?"

"Do you know who they might be?"

"Farm agents, is my guess. Tom was good to me. He realised my worth. He gave me the second farmhouse, which would normally be the home of a son. He contributed to a good pension and I am managing director of the distribution business. We have seven lorries that deliver everything we sell to the mainland and a lot of what the other farmers produce on the Island. On return journeys we bring back food, feed and whatever an Island farmer needs. We are fully laden, out and back. The haulage business is managed by Jim Orton, a thirty-year-old Island man who worked in a similar capacity on the mainland. Haulage is a good business and we are profitable and expanding."

"So, it seems you have everything sewn up?" said Bruno.

"I have given my whole life to this farm, Inspector, and since Tom passed away, I have delivered Geoffrey a quarter of a million pounds in profit from the farm every year, so why would he sell? We are audited by Bloxham & Co., they specialise in farm audits, and they provide us valuable management information on modern farming techniques. So, *what* have I got sown up Inspector?" he said glaring at Bruno, emphasising the word *what*.

Haves had objected to Bruno's remark, because of its implications, which Bruno sensed and apologised and changed tack.

"I'm sorry I meant that in a positive way," he said.

"Inspector, the last thing I would have wanted was for Geoff Klinker to have been murdered. We are part of a family and no one as far as I know he had any grudge against the Klinkers. If the farm is sold, we will give the new owners a try and hope it continues in the way I run it. We'll see if they continue to protect the farm workers, some of whom have been here as long as I have."

"But as an employee in the end its out of your hands," said Bruno.

Biff Haves wasn't drawn on an outcome he could never imagine.

"You try telling them that, they expect me to look after them, protect their jobs. Will the new owner evict them from their homes? These are not tenants in these little cottages, they are families. It's like a small village here, over forty years they've grown like a family, married, had children, and this is their life. Geoffrey was like a feudal Lord of the Manor who has protected them."

"Are you familiar with the Island Steam Railway at Havenstreet?" said Bruno.

"I've never ridden on it, but I know of it."

"Can you guess why the murderer should choose such a location to murder Klinker?"

Biff Haves thought for a full minute before answering Bruno.

"No idea. It has to be somebody who is familiar with Havenstreet Station, doesn't it?"

Perhaps that was a logical conclusion for an unconnected person to come to, and one they'd not given enough attention to.

They bid farewell to Haves and agreed to meet again if they discovered something he could help with.

Bruno's gut feel was that neither he nor Mrs Galloway had come clean about their activities in connection with Klinker.

"Interesting to speculate how much opposition there would have been if Klinker's decision had been to sell up," said Andy.

"What is a wealthy hospital consultant living in London, who is not a business brain, going to do with millions of cash?" said Bruno.

It was an enviable position to be in, and suggested that jealousy might have been the motive of the killer. But who? The idea suggested they focus on those who stood to gain from his death. Biff Haves felt he might lose everything he had built up, so how could Klinker's demise benefit him? Unless, after Tom Klinker's death, Haves felt he had been passed over and remitting the proceeds of his labour to an undeserving master, Geoff Klinker, on a monthly basis had worn him down?

After a session of paperwork back at the station and a check through statements and alibis of those already questioned, they came up with a list of actions that needed further attention. So far, they had made little progress. Each step forward had been countered by an equal step backward. Haves had undoubtedly been warned of their pending arrival by Mrs Galloway. Why she would do that puzzled Bruno and indicated that they were concealing something so he called her to ask if he could call on her to talk about Klinker.

When they arrived at Clive Hall Mrs Galloway was enjoying tea and scones sitting on a well-mown garden lawn beneath a circular sunshade on a beautiful sunny afternoon. To Bruno's surprise, she insisted that they join her for tea. She was in a pleasant mood unlike earlier that morning. It seemed she had been expecting their return.

"Inspector, I am not the sort of person who pries into other people's personal lives, or watches the neighbours' behaviour through darkened window panes, or listens in to private telephone conversations. However, in the three weeks before his death, Geoffrey received an extremely high number of phone calls from a lady in London. From what I gathered she was desperate for money and he had promised to give, or lend, her a large sum. A figure of £1 million was mentioned in one conversation, unless I misheard," she said. "Without selling the farm I don't think Geoffrey would have that kind of money, so she was pressing him to sell. I know they were desperate calls from the way Geoffrey responded to her demands. It was as if he was trapped and she had something on him. I put two and two together and assumed that he had decided to sell the farm to accommodate this lady."

"Do you know her name?"

"It was Lillian, I don't know her surname."

"And do you know where she was calling from?"

"I assumed she was one of his London people. 'Be patient Lillian, these things take time, everything will be all right,' was the gist of his replies. At one time I thought she might be blackmailing him, but over what? He was a dedicated hospital consultant."

"I know that men can have their head turned by a beautiful lady. Perhaps they were in love? Perhaps the lady was desperate for a white knight to rescue her and suspected he had no intention of doing so. Hence the continued pressure on the phone. Perhaps he was stringing her along, and he was frightened of her?"

"What kind of woman could be desperate for such a huge sum of money?" asked Bruno.

"Not the kind he was used to, Inspector."

Bruno chose not to reveal their contact with Lillian Golobieski in the hope she might reveal something they did not know. How would she know what kind of woman Klinker was used to? thought Bruno.

"Is there anything else you can tell us about Dr Klinker?"

"I told Biff about my concerns and I know he was going to mention them to Geoffrey if he got the chance, but he never did."

"And now the problem with Lillian has gone away, Mrs Galloway."

"Yes," she said. "Unless she is mentioned in his will?"

"Do you know if there is a will?"

"That's for the solicitors, isn't it?"

"This was a lovely tea Mrs Galloway," said Andy, who whilst he had quietly listened had eaten two large plain scones, clotted cream and apricot jam, and re-filled his teacup, while Mrs Galloway had reported her suspicions to them.

"Which solicitor would that be?" said Bruno.

"He had a local solicitor whose name escapes me. Don't spend too much time searching for a will, Inspector. It might pass this estate on to someone undeserving who could have no idea what it means to a loyal band of Island families."

Bruno wanted to clarify Klinker's movements during his three-day visit to the Island to attend the reunion. What had he been doing in the days prior to the morning of 8 June?

"Mrs Galloway, do you have knowledge of where he was going and who he was seeing on those days prior to his murder, as it could open a new line of investigation?"

"No, he came and went with a polite 'Good morning' or 'Good evening'."

"When I was last with you, you mentioned that it was Dr Klinker's intention to sell that farm. Since talking with others, I did not get that impression."

"I think I said that I thought his briefcase contained papers to do with the sale of the farm. I put two and two together. I am sorry if I misled you, Inspector."

"We are just gathering facts about Klinker's activities whilst he was on the Island, Mrs Galloway, in an attempt to build a picture of his last movements and contacts and to find a motive for his death."

"Biff Haves knew everything about what Geoffrey was up to, he knew what was going on."

"In the few days before his murder?"

"Yes, I expect so. Ask him, Inspector, I am sure he'll know something."

"You have mentioned the briefcase and its contents, is it possible we can take another look at it?"

"Of course, it will still be in the study. Go ahead whilst I refresh the tea," she said, and showed Bruno to Klinker's study.

Bruno extracted a number of paper files from Klinker's briefcase. Three sets of audited company accounts, each audited by Bloxham & Co., but no correspondence concerning the sale of the farm business. The accounts were of Isle of Wight haulage companies downloaded from the internet.

The businesses were familiar to Bruno because they were Isle of Wight-based. He made notes of names and addresses of directors, and replaced them in the briefcase. The desk drawers contained Clive Hall headed writing paper, pens and pencils, but nothing else of particular interest. There were several silver photo frames with family photographs, going back many years, showing Geoff Klinker with his father, mother and half-brother, probably in their twenties. There were beach photos of two boys and dressed up in school play costumes. Bruno remained in the study, flipping through the contents of a four-drawer freestanding filing cabinet, while Mrs Galloway returned with tea. She wasted no time in confiding to him how lonely she was since Mrs Klinker had passed away.

"Madeline was a lovely lady and a good farmer's wife to Tom Klinker. She always had lots of visitors, mostly ladies from the church which she attended regularly and generously supported."

"Biff Haves said he and Geoffrey were working on something together."

"Probably, but again you'll have to speak to Haves. At the moment he's worried that someone who doesn't understand this business will take over."

His examination of Klinker's briefcase had not added much to what he already knew, but he had found two good reasons to go back to Haves, namely Klinker's interest in Island haulage businesses, which Haves had mentioned was an integral and developing part of Klinker's farm business and of which he was a director, and his whereabouts on the three days before his murder.

He did not have a particular question to put to Mrs Galloway about the contents of Dr Klinker's study, but he did ask her another question. "Mrs Galloway, during your spell as housekeeper you have witnessed the death of three of the Klinker family. In spite of these deaths in the family, will you stay on?"

Her answer was clear and obviously thought out.

"I will stay until the future of the estate is decided, Inspector, as there might be something in it for me to stay."

It was the answer he expected but it did not satisfy his curiosity to know what she might be looking for. She was, after all, getting on a bit to perform the physically tough job of housekeeper.

She reminded him that she was Madeline Klinker's sister, so Tom Klinker was her brother-in-law. She was fourteen years her junior and, when she was widowed at about the same time as Madeline, she moved into Clive Hall to look after her sister. She was the aunt of Geoff Klinker, as she is to Arnold Harris. While his mother was alive Arnold had been regular visitor, but not since, for fear of meeting Geoff.

Bruno asked if there was a particular reason for that.

She said, "No."

He detected hesitation in her answer.

Then she said, "Brothers fall out for complex reasons. They were both successful in their own fields. I think Geoff could have been more accommodating to Arnie. He was very attentive to their mother. The problem could have been resolved by Tom before he died."

"And what problem was that?"

"The estate, it all went to Geoff, whereas a little chunk to Arnie might have been fairer," she said.

"You'll never know what was in the mind of the deceased," said Andy Bowen.

This made Mrs Galloway reflective, which signalled that it was time for them to leave.

"Thank you for your time again, Mrs Galloway, we shall be on our way," said Bruno.

Although Mrs Galloway had provided some useful information, namely that he was being pressed to sell the estate by, according to her, a lady with whom he was in a relationship, it was not more than they knew already.

Biff Haves and Mrs Galloway had suggested a new line of investigation. When reporting into his Superintendent, John Barlow, at Newport Police HQ, Bruno was able to present this as progress. He was losing confidence about his ability to make further progress as he sank slowly into a muddy pool of unconnected not-quite suspects.

"Some of what I know about the Chinese is that revenge can be exacted against those who do not keep promises. Did Klinker make promises that he did not keep, like not selling the farm? Could they be suspects?"

Bruno's boss knew that the truth was, once you had interviewed every known suspect and you move onto strangers, then you've very little chance. However, he did not believe Bruno was at that stage yet. He had several persons of interest and several lines that needed clarification. He wasn't of a mind to intrude at this time because he could not add anything to Bruno's investigation except to boost the morale of both his detectives, which he duly did.

There was also PC Kevin Bell, who'd not yet got to a reportable point in his research, but he optimistically predicted that he'd soon be there.

However, Brenda Frampton surely knew more about a man whom she had been virtually married to for fifteen years than she let on.

◈

"Interesting that Mrs Galloway diverted attention from herself to Lillian Golobieski and encouraged you to go off at a tangent with the work you did with her?" said Janet over supper.

"The clue you are looking for could be in his Island home. Imagine what it was like to be him day to day. What did he do here on the Island each day? Why don't you find out what he did and where he did it?"

"We are trying," said Bruno.

By all accounts he was a lovely man entirely motivated by his professional ethics. He valued his life away from London although, as hospital consultant with a busy private patient practice, he was not too busy to enjoy the affluent life his wealth enabled and one could imagine him waking up on any day and giving it all up and returning to his roots and childhood memories. Maybe that was on his mind when he decided to attend his school reunion? What about the phone calls from Lillian that Mrs Galloway listened to?"

Bruno's notes suggested she was vague as to what Mrs Galloway had heard. Just Klinker's responses to Lillian's questions, which she had interpreted as requesting or demanding money to pay her debts. If the calls were that frequent, they probably weren't all about money. More than likely they were personal chatter, about his day-to-day activities and when are you coming back? Her life in London as a widowed woman had been turned upside down by her husband's co-directors denying her his fair share of the business he had owned.

This would have turned her into a very needy person, grasping at any man she could draw into her web. The insecurity of sensing that her relationship with Klinker had passed its peak might have inspired her to contact him constantly for reassurance. Janet, although not acquainted with every twist and turn of the Klinker case, was adept at summarising the position so far.

"Let's set aside the school chums, including Ali. He's disappeared, not unexpectedly, given he'd come from Paris for the reunion. You traced his departure away from the Island, and apart from the school he has no other connection with the Island that we know of. The Ryde School secretary should be able to tell you more about the school group, and contact with her might reveal more about them. Then there is Brenda Frampton. Did she promise to locate Maisie Longmore for you?"

"Yes, she did," said Bruno.

It remained in his mind that there was similarity in the manner of the school friends' denial of knowing anything about the murder of Geoff Klinker. It had left a suspicion that there could have been collaboration between two of the Class of '78.

CHAPTER 11

Wednesday 20 June

Biff Haves seemed happy to speak to Bruno again. He wanted to know whether he believed that Klinker was about to sell the farm; and if so, whether this may have affected the behaviour of some of the persons of interest on his now shortened list.

"The truth is Inspector, I do not know. He never made his thoughts clear to me and I saw no clues in his behaviour. A couple of years ago he talked about its value and wondered if anyone might be interested. The rest of the time we discussed plans to look for opportunities to expand. In the past two years that has been the focus of our activities."

"And that involved the freight and haulage business?"

"Yes, it did exclusively. We created a business plan based on the movement of all goods to and from the Island. There is a small premium to pay on almost everything that comes from the mainland based on the cost of transporting those goods, which adds to that cost, marginally. We obtained from Island Ferries the tonnages of freight to and from the Island for the last calendar year. From this we worked out how much freight was carried to and from by Island hauliers for the Island as a whole."

"That explains why Dr Klinker was carrying around the annual accounts of three Island haulage businesses," said Bruno.

"Correct, Inspector," said Haves. "He thought we could undercut them by increasing our freight business."

"Did Klinker talk to the companies he was researching?"

"We went to see all of them, and we talked about the opportunities for our businesses. They were polite but secretive, and definitely felt the business of freight on the Island was completely covered by them. There was no competition because we believe there is a cartel on the Island. The pricing, timetable and methodology of all the companies we looked at were identical. They do not compete with each other. They operate together, although they'll claim that supply and demand determine how they function. We calculated that with a modest investment, namely the purchase of three new transporters, we could substantially increase our turnover and more than double our profit."

"Did these other haulage companies see you as a threat?"

"Definitely. One of our targets was the live animal transport to the mainland abattoirs. We would have the capacity to handle the entire Island's volume, and that is what we are working towards."

"Would any of these haulage companies have been a threat to Klinker personally?"

"I can't answer that. I'd be surprised if one of those haulage company directors did not find his approach obnoxious, and plan to do something about him, come to think of it. "And not only a business threat," said Biff Haves. "He was a person they had met. Once they wouldn't have known who he was."

"So, what will you do now?"

"My intention is to carry on and persuade the new owners to expand the haulage side of the business. With a depot in Portsmouth we could operate along the south coast, creating tremendous potential markets for the produce we could grow."

"Who do you report to about the day-to-day running of this business?" said Bruno.

"I have only received notification of Geoff Klinker's death from the police. I have the authority, as a director, to run the business, but I would expect lawyers on behalf of the Klinker family to show up soon. To people I've had to tell, I've said he died suddenly in unexplained circumstances, but everything to do with the functioning of the business is business as usual. I am a signatory on our bank accounts, so things will not grind to a halt for lack of cash."

"Is the expansion of the haulage business on hold?"

"Temporarily, but I am ready to go full steam ahead once I have budget approval from the new owners."

"Nothing will happen until the lawyers obtain probate, which could take a while."

"One final question, prior to Dr Klinker's murder he spent three days on the Island and we have no idea of what he was doing, where he went, who he saw. Can you fill in any of those gaps for us?"

"I spent Tuesday morning with him, two or three hours, and the same on Thursday morning. Tuesday, we looked at some fencing issues, and Thursday we identified a number of oak trees in our forest that we intended to sell. That was all the time we spent together on those three days."

"Do you know which solicitors are handling the probate issues connected with Dr Klinker's estate?"

"I can tell you that his Island solicitor is Walter Brown in the High Street in Ryde, but I don't know if he is doing the probate. We have not spoken so far."

Having clarified the situation regarding the plans for the business and his ongoing commitment to running the farm, Bruno left Biff Haves to find a café for a workman's breakfast – bacon, sausage, tomatoes and mushrooms – which they knew of on Ventnor seafront across the road from the fishing port. Its shop was open every day throughout the year for fresh fish. Facing towards the promenade, meandering towards the Spyglass Inn in the distance, was a shallow paddling pond, shaped as a concrete sculpture of the Island, full of two-year-olds splashing from Cowes to Ryde. It completed the perfect setting for Bruno, notebook at the ready, to add to the mystery of Klinker's killer.

At spot on twelve stone, he could enjoy a 2,000-calorie

all-day breakfast without worrying about his weight, and since he now shared a house with Janet, Bruno had slimmed down, regularly eating the healthy food she fed him. He no longer felt or looked the ageing, overweight, grubby detective, the lonely bachelor, that his pre-Janet self had become. His newly acquired younger look he put down to her no-nonsense Yorkshire domestic disciplines, which was also responsible for her ability to surprise him with her insights into human nature.

"Perhaps he wants to buy the farm himself?" considered Bruno. "Which raises the question: has that ambition festered a long time?"

Bruno had not yet questioned him about his whereabouts on the day of the murder.

It was early in the day and plenty of time to set up a meeting with Brown. Using his mobile he located Brown's offices in the High Street in Ryde and explained, in a persuasive manner, "It has to be today."

Mr Brown agreed to see Detective Inspector Peach at 2.00 p.m.

A brief introduction that DI Peach was handling the Klinker murder enquiry had persuaded him to meet. Situated in the middle of the High Street his offices were pleasantly appointed with plenty of glass to allow daylight to brighten the reception space which had several interview rooms with glass doors and walls, in one of which he could see a tray with bottled water and drinking glasses. It was a modern legal practice.

Brochures in the reception highlighted Walter Brown's expertise in litigation, taxation, divorce, all family matters and probate.

The principal, Walter Brown, was in his mid-thirties. He had expanded from a sole practitioner recruiting expertly qualified young lawyers whose social conscience treated complex family issue areas of the law as a vocation using their knowledge and skills to help the underprivileged who found themselves on the wrong side of the law, and were consistently over-penalised when dealing with the police.

Walter Brown was not such a lawyer. He was smooth, a cultured man whose interests were artistic, mostly the theatre and music. He mentioned he had a beautiful young wife, an accomplished violinist who performed often in London.

Bruno introduced himself with identity as the detective in charge of the Klinker murder case.

"Thank you for seeing me at short notice, Mr Brown. I understand you are handling the probate application in respect of Dr Geoffrey Klinker deceased?"

"I am handling that myself and I can tell you how far we have got. It is complicated. It is a large estate and so far, we have not found a will or spoken to any relatives, so we are assuming he died intestate. Naturally we are working closely with HMRC whose levy on the estate will be high. As I am sure you are aware, probate can only be granted after the estate has settled HMRC's inheritance tax demands. The court will not grant probate until it receives a stamped receipt from the tax office showing that the levy has been paid."

"What does that mean?" said Bruno.

"If, say, HMRC ask for £2.5 million cash to grant a certificate, the beneficiary or ourselves acting, would have to raise that money and pay them before we are granted access to his inheritance. There are banks that provide this short-term facility against the estate.

"Our job is to discover and prove the beneficiaries, to value the estate, agree with HMRC the levy, then borrow the money on their behalf. Not all of it, but in Klinker's case probably most of it so we can settle HMRC, obtain the grant of probate from the court and convey the deceased's assets to the beneficiary, less our fees. They will then have to deal with the bankers as to how their loan will be repaid from the assets they have inherited which will be charged to the lenders.

"We have only just started assembling the information. I was referred to the man who runs the farm by Mrs Galloway, who was the sister of Mrs Klinker, for whom we also acted. He will come back to me with all the financial information I need to obtain a valuation, which will then be audited on site by a qualified independent valuer, probably two. As I have already said, we have a way to go."

Bruno explained, "We are trying to find Klinker's murderer. Is there anything you can tell me that might help us?"

"Obtaining probate on the Klinker estate will take many months and we have only been instructed for seven days. In that time, I have met only two people who have both been very helpful in that they would like the opportunity to buy the farm if it is to be sold. One of those is a local farmer named Beale, who farms near Freshwater, and the second is Biff Haves, the farm manager, who claims to speak for a consortium. I'd guess we are at least six months away from that."

"We are aware of those two gentlemen. They were quick off the mark," said Bruno.

"We shall make further enquiries of the Klinker family which, although it is small, could have estranged branches, and someone is working on that. That's as far as we've got at the moment, if anything strange or suspicious occurs I will call you."

"Thank you, and I'd appreciate that," said Bruno.

It had been a brief meeting that had given him confidence that whatever happened to the Klinker estate it would be dealt with professionally, and there would be no subterfuge with undisclosed interested parties. Walter Brown had confirmed Beale's determination to acquire the estate if possible. As for Biff Haves on his own, his was a pipe dream, but he did have solid Island connections that might back him and understood the realities connected with the huge money involved.

Neither Mrs Galloway, nor Biff Haves, nor Beale had disclosed their knowledge of, or that they had met with Walter Brown and registered their interest, and Mrs Galloway and Biff Haves had together instructed Walter Brown, yet neither had revealed that information to the police. No longer did she appear as just a spectator.

And how did Beale get on to Walter Brown so quickly, as Brown had only been involved for a few days? It seemed they'd hatched up something between them, and think they can keep it to themselves, but when the estate is to be sold it will be advertised across the South of England.

Bruno assumed that as Mrs Galloway is family, she hopes to gain something somewhere, as did Biff Haves.

"Beale has also been quick out of the blocks, He could only have known about the probate solicitor, and registered his interest if it had come from Galloway or Haves, and if it was from them, they must have a plan."

Bruno was tired and could not have handled another in-depth interview. He needed to switch off from Klinker for a while. He felt he was making progress and was at that point in this investigation where it was necessary to focus on detail with a fresh mind, so he adjourned to Yates Hotel, opposite Walter Brown's offices, for a drink and to catch up with Andy Bowen who'd began the day with Ryde School's secretary, Marion Hislop, to see if she could add any flesh to the bare bones she had provided in her earlier interview with the police.

"She had been very helpful, and liked having the full attention of her young local detective as it felt like I was her personal security guard," was Andy's initial response. She'd said that as a minor public school its Island location was attractive to parents from overseas, especially to families with an interest in sailing, it was safe and away from the perceived temptations of the mainland. The education standards were high and to provide scholarships it relied on rich benefactors and former pupils who were able to afford to support a scholarship awarded annually. Geoff Klinker paid for a bursary for one pupil to study a science subject. So did Edward Hawkins the artist, and Kevin Billings the baker, who also offered summertime employment to local boys and girls from the school. They were the only old boys in the year of '78 who made any financial contribution to the school.

"She said the Island was an insular community and most of the local boys who went on to universities on the mainland returned to work in Island business. Unlike other public schools, Ryde did not inspire its alumni to reach for the stars, which she stressed was her private opinion. She confirmed that her records showed that Roger Beale did win the school leavers' Latin prize in 1983.

"She could not add anything to help us. Except that she gave me another email contact for Ali, which I will pass to Kevin Bell to follow up. Although if he lives in Paris, he may not get it."

To Bruno it was progress in the right direction, as had been his visit to Walter Brown.

CHAPTER 12

Thursday 21 June

In Bruno's in-tray at the station, in a file marked CONFIDENTIAL, was new information from PC Kevin Bell about Beale. The label on its cover said: ROGER BEALE – PERSONAL FILE. This gave them a clearer picture of the kind of man he was.

Previously Bruno's suspicions against Beale were based upon his attitude and that he had something to gain from Klinker's death, as if he had planned it. But this report opened a new window onto his character, including information about his exodus from South Africa, presenting him in a different light.

He had moved to Cape Town when he was twenty-five years old after completing a Master's degree in Economics at the London School of Economics, the LSE being the leading University in its field and recognised worldwide for this subject. In South Africa he lectured on the economics of agriculture and the application of modern farming techniques appropriate to the Mediterranean climate of the Cape region, which is ideal for soft fruit, grape and wine production and all the associated trades and activities that enabled a developing export market to thrive. In twenty years, he became Professor of Agriculture and Economics at the University of Cape Town, married a South African, Helen Dettock, daughter of a prominent TV producer, James Dettock. They had two sons, Jackson and Lee, and after fifteen years they divorced. Thereafter for eight years he remained in South Africa as a University Professor and a single man, returning to the UK five years ago on the death of his father, to take over the Beale farm. Since then he has modernised the farm, changed almost everything, and turned it into a very profitable business putting into practice what he had been preaching to farmers in Cape Town for twenty-five years.

However, it was Kevin Bell's discoveries into Beale's activities that were of particular interest and are best summed up in an article in the *Cape Town Herald* of 22 December 2013, a facsimile copy of which was attached to his report:

"The South African Police office in Cape Town issued a warrant for the arrest of Roger Beale of Constantia in 2013 in connection with the killing of Sironda Ntebi, a Constantia farm employee who, with a number of others, broke into the offices of the Clock wine producers claiming an abuse of African rights by the owners who were of Afrikaans descent. The premises were occupied and the intruders were armed with guns when a fight broke out. A number of local wine harvesters were present attending a meeting organised by Roger Beale. The intruders, claiming a peaceful attendance, were accused of a violent response, which resulted in the shooting of Sironda Ntebi, who died at the scene. The killer was an unidentified person and presumably an Afrikaans farmer attending the meeting. It was a regular monthly meeting of the members of Constantia Wine Growers, who discussed viticulture methods and wine marketing and whose identities were known by all the members present. The circumstances that led to the shooting were unclear, as was the identity of the gunman.

"It was stated that the white farmers were concealing the identity of the gunman, blaming the black intruders for the shooting.

"The reason for the warrant against Beale was because following the killing he left for England, informing everyone that his father had died suddenly, and that he would be back.

"He vanished from his home in Cape Town before the

police arrived to arrest him in connection with the mur-
der. He was seen leaving dressed in black leather motor-
cycle clothing riding his Honda 1000-cc motorcycle. The
time delay between his departure and the Police notify-
ing their outstations enabled him to get clean away.

"Police throughout the Republic of South Africa have
been instructed to arrest and detain him in connection
with this murder."

◈

"So, is Roger Beale a fugitive from the South African police?" said Andy.

"This happened over five years ago and I'd imagine if he was personally responsible for the killing, he'd have been extradited to South Africa years ago," said Bruno.

"Technically he was wanted for questioning. I doubt a University professor with an unblemished reputation would get involved in a killing."

"How does the information help us find Klinker's killer? If we make him aware that we have investigated his past life, it might trap him into protecting his present situation in a manner that helps us. Let's listen to his side of the story. The South African regime is by all accounts riddled with corruption. You don't know what his life was like there, or how much he missed England. Speak to expats in South Africa, Australia or New Zealand. The glow fades quickly and all they want is to come back home, and you would be surprised how many do."

"There is no place like home," said Andy.

Bruno observed, "On his farm Beale has taken the opportunity to put into practice what he has learned, knowing from experience what works in farming and what doesn't, and for someone with his background he will know that a giant theme park on the Island is a non-starter. Kevin Bell's reports said that old Mrs Beale is still alive. She lives in a specially constructed ground-floor suite adjacent to the main farmhouse. Kevin Bell's postscript reads, 'No luck yet with contacting Ali in Mumbai, we think we have the correct contact details, but so far no response'."

"Perhaps he is living in Paris?" said Andy.

"Maybe, but that's a needle in a haystack stuff."

"Beale knows everything he needs to know about the Klinker setup and I didn't detect any hint of a South African accent."

"Now that we know that suspicious circumstances brought him back from Cape Town."

"Well it is true that his father died."

"Yes it is, but we can't be certain that he would not murder Klinker. Of course he is a person of special interest."

Bruno did not want to dilute his investigation with irrelevances and Beale's South African history did not shed light on Klinker's murder or murderer, so he decided not to draw Beale into a long explanation of the incident or the consequences.

His feeling that Beale had got one over on him he put down to his poor detective work. At least his persistence with him had caused him to offer to help them find the killer if Bruno could provide a lead. It was a gamble but it was more important at that moment to ask him about Biff Haves' activities. So, promptly at 9.30 a.m., they called him over to the Newport Police station interview room to discuss progress.

When Bruno asked to meet him at Newport to discuss developments, he was unhelpful, although after a provocative phone conversation agreed to meet at 9.30 a.m.

"I've told you all I know Inspector. You know as much as you need to know about me. You've been to my home. You know where I was when Klinker was murdered. So what is it you want from me now?"

"I want to talk about why you are determined to buy Klinker's estate. What does it mean to you?"

"I don't have to disclose my business plans to you. They are not connected to the murder of Geoff Klinker."

"Let us be the judge of that," said Bruno.

"If you tell me what blind alley you're travelling up, I might be able to shed some light," he replied.

"Do you know if Klinker left a will?" asked Bruno.

"I don't, Inspector. I spoke to the partner handling the probate application, Walter Brown, who said that he would inform me when he had obtained probate and if the beneficiary of the estate wished to sell, and it would likely take him six months. As long as I keep contact with them, I have a chance to buy Klinker's farm."

"Do you know who the beneficiary of the estate might be?"

"I never knew him well enough, but I believe he had a step-brother or half-brother, or Mrs Galloway is a family member."

"Walter Brown will find out."

"Apart from acquiring the farm, what could the killer's objectives be?"

"If it were me, Inspector, it would be because I wanted to get my hands on Klinker's estate, but as it wasn't me, Klinker's demise gives me a chance to buy something I cherished. That makes me a suspect, doesn't it?" he said. "And that's why you asked me here, Inspector, right?"

"Mr Beale, you are a person of interest only at this stage and a person I hope who will give me an inside track if anything turns up. However, you are the closest I've come to a real suspect," replied Bruno, in a light-hearted manner.

"If I can help you in any way I will, Inspector, but you are wrong to think I might know more about who committed Klinker's murder than I have told you. I knew him, for a brief time when we were at school, and I didn't particularly like him, but that was then, thirty-five years ago."

"Do you ever have any contact with Biff Haves?" he asked Beale.

"Not of choice, Inspector," was his first reply. "But I can

tell you a few things about him. Most of my Island produce, that's tomatoes, salads, vegetables, greens and roots, I sell to Tompsetts on the mainland. They are the wholesalers who sell to the big grocers. I package my stuff so it can be transported on palettes and be on the shop shelves the same day. I use Martin's, an Island haulage company, to take the produce to Tompsetts in Portsmouth who wholesale it all across the South Coast. If you lived on the mainland, you would know the Beale's brand. Everything I produce is also sold on the Island but not by Tesco, Morrisons or Asda, but go to the others and you will find Beale's products on their shelves. I am telling you this to show you that I have a profitable established business that works well for me, and I am expanding every month. I use the latest technology to produce food for the growing vegan market.

"Biff Haves is trying to take over haulage businesses on the Island and he has his sights on Tom Martin's because he knows of our relationship. I believe his plan to expand the haulage business is a good business idea but he poses a threat to my business, unless I become involved in what he is doing. He has the capacity on Klinker's farm to produce everything I grow, and from what I send to the mainland the exact size and potential for every Beale product. He could build a profitable business model and wipe me out in two years. That is what I believe they – him and Klinker – were trying to do to me by buying Tom Martin's business."

"That's another reason for killing him," said Bruno.

"Yes, Inspector, I am giving you clues all the time."

"Why don't you buy Martin's?"

"I only do what I know and I don't know the haulage business. Furthermore, no one ever becomes rich building a conglomerate."

"So, he's trying to steal your business?"

"I actually don't think he sees it that way but that would be the result," said Beale. "But by the time he gets his hands on Martin's, I will have geared up Tompsetts to come and collect."

"What else can you tell me about Haves?"

"He knows what he is doing, he is a clever guy. He runs everything at Klinker's, and has built his own little empire, and is using his position to acquire the farm. I know he has money behind him ready to make an offer once probate has been granted.

"How do you know about his plan?"

"I have friends who have told me."

"Who are they?"

"Inspector, that is confidential to me."

Bruno guessed he had a connection at Walter Brown's, but it wasn't an issue as it would not tell him something he didn't already know.

"I'll be in a position to buy from whoever owns it by the time the probate is settled."

"Can you guess who that will be?"

"I don't know his extended family, but it won't be somebody who wants to farm on the Island."

"How do you know that?"

"Because if there is someone on the Island they'd have been involved before now," Beale said in an end-of-conversation manner.

"So, it's just you and Haves and his consortium?"

"That's why I have to persuade Haves to go with me."

"And have you?"

"I am working on him."

"So far Mr Beale you have given us nothing to work on, which from a man who is all about the Island I am disappointed with," said Bruno.

"Inspector, I've given you plenty, certainly enough to exclude me. You are too experienced a detective to require my help to solve this crime. However, I think the clues lie closer to home. I'd concentrate on Haves and Mrs Galloway.

Those two are working together. I'd like you to tell me if you discover anything of interest to me," he said with a smile as he left Newport Police HQ.

◈

"No flies on Mr Beale," said Bruno, after he left the office.

"If he did it, or was part of it, he already thinks he has gotten away with it," said Andy. "And there are no clues out there that could connect him to the murder."

Andy Bowen thought Beale was a waste of time. "He thinks he is so clever."

Bruno agreed and concluded that the death of Klinker only hindered any plans he had to buy his farm.

"And he is too clever to build a theme park on the Isle of Wight. Theme parks in the UK are situated where the population has easy access for most of the year. Nobody would come to the Island in winter to visit a theme park, even a copper can tell him that. There are many types of theme park. I shouldn't imagine it is one with rides. It would have to be unique, a virtual reality theme might work, but that would cost millions to publicise and market, and Beale is not a gambler, nor is he that rich."

"We don't know what he is worth yet," said Andy.

"Not yet," said Bruno. "We can assume that Biff Haves wants to maintain the status quo. That's his business, and for all his talk about being the haulage king of the Island, I think he is a cobbler that sticks to his last."

Before acting on Beale's suggestion that the solution to this crime lay closer to home, and paying further visits to Mrs Galloway and Biff Haves, Bruno needed a line of questioning that would cause one or other to reveal something they did not already know.

Andy decided they should concentrate on what they did not know, and which of these gaps Galloway or Haves might help them to fill.

"Now we have spoken to all his available school friends, we

must keep in mind that each had the opportunity to slip into the Gents' lavatory on the station platform at the same time as Klinker and stab him to death. He was murdered and died instantly while standing at the urinal. If another passenger had entered the lavatory to use the urinal immediately after the killing, he would have slid into the cubicle at the urinal. No one did enter the lavatory whilst he killed Klinker so he was lucky and after dragging Klinker into a sitting position in the cubicle he could exit quietly and quickly immediately after, go to the window and lock the cubicle door using a stick to slide the bolt to 'Engaged'. What we do not have is a motive."

"Why don't we take up Ian Walters on his offer to discuss with him the progress we've made so far? He was one of the school party we've not yet crossed off as a possible suspect. Why would a university professor travel down to the Isle of Wight to spend the day with a group of school friends, whom he'd not seen for forty years?"

"He hasn't answered that question. Academics like Walters have big egos. There is something in their make-up, they need to be is admired. The Masters degree, the Ph.D. and the title of Professor is the focus of their life. They believe these qualifications qualify them to be admired, looked up to, when most of the time they just spout rubbish. They are not brilliant, their qualifications obtained after extended periods of study, during which time they live hand-to-mouth, stacking supermarket shelves, and they know it, but it is their way to not show it. Most of them have studied for years and years, through failure after failure, to obtain their qualifications, those small pieces of paper are all they have after sometimes twenty-five years of full-time education. After that some of them get out and go teaching, where they have to prove to somebody – anybody, students – that they are clever and therefore superior, but that doesn't satisfy their ego. They become a big fish in a small pond. We don't know enough about Walters because one size does not fit all."

"He might lead us somewhere," said Bruno. "When we last met, he offered to help and we need to get his opinion of the others who attended the reunion and why he decided to go. Before we do, let's go over our notes of our conversations with the others and see Biff Haves."

◆

Haves was available in the late afternoon, giving Bruno some thinking time before they met.

A tired and hungry Biff Haves greeted Bruno and Andy on arrival at the Klinker farm office. He had been hard at work on a distant part of the farm supervising the building of an extension to the cowsheds. It was one of those jobs he could not leave someone to supervise, he said. There was no doubt he was busy and determined to ensure the detectives understood how valuable his time was.

"Can you tell us more about your relationship with the Klinker's, as you have worked on the farm for forty years," said Bruno.

"For most of that time I worked for Tom Klinker."

"What was your relationship with him?"

"He was a perfect gentleman towards me, and treated me like a son. He promised me lots of things over the years and I believe he would have left me an interest in the farm if it had not been for Madeline Klinker. She wanted him to leave the farm to her two sons, Geoffrey and Arnold, not necessarily 50/50. Arnold, her son by her first marriage, was not interested in the farm, so he got nothing. Geoffrey recognised my value to the business so he gave me 10 per cent of the shares and a directorship in the haulage business, but nothing in the farm. Farms are family businesses; all any farmer wants is a son who's interested in the farm to carry it on through the generations, and to take on the heavy lifting as he gets old. They all know that's probably the least appealing option to any boy that's been properly educated, and has witnessed first-hand how hard and unsociable the work is. If it hadn't been for Madeline I'd be at least a part owner in the farm by now."

"Perhaps Dr Klinker would have made you a partner in the farm in time?" said Bruno.

Biff Haves didn't answer. He just smiled, screwed up his face and blew out through his mouth.

"Not in a million years."

"So where does that leave you now?"

"At present I manage and control the farm. If I owned it I would do exactly what I do now. Geoff Klinker could not have done what I do, and it will be the same with whoever takes it over. I will try to buy the farm, or become a tenant, but I will need to borrow from a bank to do that and I am fifty-eight so that might not work."

Biff Haves had given his working life to the Klinkers and it seemed that he was shortly to be denied what he believed was his right by the untimely death of Geoff Klinker and Madeline Klinker's jealous influence over Tom Klinker.

"When did you last see Geoff Klinker?"

"Early on the day he went to his school reunion. In fact, we'd planned to meet when he got back to Clive Hall. He said he'd be back at about 5.00 p.m. and suggested I drop by for a beer."

"So, you were on good terms with him?"

"Of course, I provided weekly reports on the various activities on the farm and a full set of management accounts monthly. Much of the work we do on the farm attracts European subsidies. The new cow milking plant is 80 per cent funded by the European Union Farm Commission. This farm is a very profitable business, but it has no potential for anything else but an agricultural business."

"Have you talked to Beale about the potential for this farm?"

"Not seriously."

"He has spent twenty years living in Cape Town lecturing farmers on how maximise the yield from their farms. He might give you ideas," suggested Bruno.

Andy asked, "On that afternoon you agreed to meet Dr Klinker at his home, what did you do when he didn't show up?"

"I waited about 45 minutes, took tea with Mrs Galloway, and as he'd not called on his mobile phone I assumed I had been mistaken about the meeting and planned to catch up with him the following day."

"Would it be appropriate to ask you what you were doing during the day of Friday 8 June?"

"I wondered when you were going to ask me that, Inspector, so I wrote myself a little note to remind me what I did on that Friday. I always go to the bank on Friday morning to bank cheques that we receive here and to draw cash to pay the wages, which I do before lunch for the labourers, who are all paid weekly. There are nine men on the weekly payroll. In Newport I called at Fodens who supply and maintain all the equipment on the farm. Sometimes I might do some food shopping at Morrisons while I am in the town. But I am always back by 10.30 a.m. with cash to make up the wages into the envelopes in time for 11.00 a.m. when the men go for lunch. Friday is when they take off any hours owed to them."

"And what about yourself on the Friday afternoon?"

"After that I went to the haulage yard at Wootton and worked through the journey and delivery schedules for the following week."

"Was that all afternoon?"

"No, half an hour. Our haulage yard is at Wootton Creek where I have a small yacht berthed in the water. I'd planned to go sailing during the weekend so I dropped a couple of 25-litre containers of fuel for the diesel engines."

"Did anyone see you there?"

"There are always people hanging around the yacht club. I am sure someone said hello, but I don't recall who."

"And after the yacht club?"

"I called in to Ryde Golf Club where I am a member, to play 9 holes, but it was busy and I couldn't find a playing partner so I had a sandwich and came back to the farm."

Bruno believed he understood the relationship between Biff Haves and Geoff Klinker and he struck him as an honest, hardworking, good guy. But he'd not missed the gap in his afternoon where he could have been anywhere and certainly at the Havenstreet Station mid-afternoon around 3.00 p.m. on Friday 8 June. Haves was tall and noticeable and if he'd been there someone, perhaps the ticket collector, might have remembered him, especially as he would have needed to buy a £5.00 visitor's platform ticket to enter the station compound and pass the time looking at the rolling stock laying on short track sections being restored in the museum, and visit the museum to view very early restored carriages.

CHAPTER 13

Friday 22 June

To take another look at Biff Haves they took off for Klinker's farm in the hope of also seeing Mrs Galloway, with a few probing questions. She was at home and greeted them in a pleasant, yet curious manner.

"Mrs Galloway, my colleague Andy Bowen hasn't stopped talking about your nice tea since we last called and, as there are a few more questions I'd like to ask you, we are here again at tea time."

"I was thinking it was time for tea myself, so you are just in time, make yourselves comfortable while I get it," she said. After ten minutes she returned with tea and a newly baked walnut sponge cake, which received immediate praise from Andy Bowen.

"Mrs Galloway you said you had been looking after the house for five years since Tom Klinker died," Bruno said.

"Yes, I moved in before Tom died."

"And he was your brother-in-law and Madeline Klinker was your sister?"

"That's correct, Inspector."

"So, you've known the house and family for a great part of your life?"

"Yes," she said.

"Can you tell us about Tom Klinker's relationship with Biff Haves?"

"It goes back way before my time. Tom hired Biff soon after he inherited the estate from his father and Biff has worked on the estate for forty years since he was eighteen. He, like Tom, is a natural farmer. Soon after he began working here, Tom recognised his potential sent him to agricultural college to keep up with the latest farming methods. This

farm is state-of-the-art, Inspector, and it's all thanks to Biff
Haves. Tom had promised to make him a partner years ago,
but he left everything to Geoffrey, giving Madeline a life ten-
ancy on this house."

"What did you think about that?"

"I understood why he did it. What was disgraceful was
the way Madeline forced him to do it. She wanted it divid-
ed between Geoffrey and Arnold, but he wanted to give the
lower farm, where the second farmhouse is situated, to Biff
Haves. It's about 1,000 acres and where Biff has lived for
decades, but she opposed that because he wouldn't weaken
about Arnold. Now Biff could end up with nothing, not
even a home. Geoffrey was aware that his father had promised Biff a partnership in the farm but because his interests
were elsewhere, he'd not addressed this either, even though
he derived considerable financial benefits from Biff's management of the farm. So, Biff never got his just and deserved
reward for a lifetime's work. Geoff would have honoured
his father's promise in time, but he didn't when he had the
chance."

"We understand that once probate has been obtained, he
intends to buy the farm," said Andy.

"He is too old. That is just a pipe dream," she replied
promptly. "He should retire in few years, on a good pension,
and go to Barbados. Forty years of farming wears you out."

"Who would run the farm then?" she raised her eyebrows
and didn't reply.

"Any particular reason for Barbados?"

"To escape. He enjoys the climate and, as the poet W.H.
Auden said, 'Man needs to escape as he needs food and
sleep".

"Was he the poet who wrote about trains?" said Bruno.

"Yes, he was," she said.

"Have you ever been to Barbados?"

"As a matter of fact, I have," she said.

It was a line of questioning Bruno decided to leave for another time.

"He's got a rich chap from London interested in backing him, so who knows what is going to happen? I will stay until everything is sorted as I don't have anything else to do."

"Did Biff Haves bear a grudge against the Klinker family?"

"He's not that sort of man. And the answer to your next question, Inspector, is No. I don't think Biff killed Geoff Klinker. He is not stupid, nor is he a murderer. I think he has got a very strong hand to play to get what he wants, so let's see what happens."

"We believe the murderer is a local person and nobody we have spoken to so far has told us everything they know, including you, Mrs Galloway," said Bruno. "Talking to anyone about this murder is like trying to get blood out of a stone." 'Who are you talking about?' is the normal response."

"Inspector, only a few people knew Geoff and when you speak to anyone about him, you are speaking about a stranger. He wasn't exactly a local celebrity. When he came to the Island to see his mother, they didn't go out. They stayed at home and she cooked his favourite, lobster thermidor, with some good wine. It was what she wanted to do. Biff would come to the house and they'd go through the farm business. It was very amicable, but it was during these visits that I realised that Madeline did not like Biff, she was jealous of him, and that's why Tom could not give him a partnership in the business. Nobody crossed Madeline. It was her way or the highway. Geoff would have done as soon as the dust had settled after her death, but she's only been gone three months so he didn't have time. Have you spoken to Arnold?"

"Only when he came to the mortuary. Nobody liked him here, and he never visited his mother when anyone else was about, or expected. Tom didn't like him, and Geoff couldn't stand him. When they were boys, neither had anything to do with the farm. So, there was very little in common between them."

"There must be people who like him," said Andy, buttering a scone and applying liberal dollops of jam and clotted cream, in an almost artistic manner, having already polished off a slice of walnut cake.

"Do you have any contact with Roger Beale?" said Bruno.

"The man who has a farm near Freshwater?" asked Mrs Galloway.

"Yes, he was one of the reunion party, a classmate of Geoff's."

"It's funny you should mention him. He came here yesterday, introduced himself as a friend of Geoff's, said he was thinking about buying the farm once probate had been completed."

"That's interesting," said Bruno.

"Yes, it was a complete surprise to me," she said.

"What surprised you? Was it him, or that he knew that probate was proceeding?"

"Both," she said.

"It was you that instructed Walter Brown, isn't that correct?"

She hesitated before admitting that she had visited Walter Brown, but wasn't sure that she had instructed him to apply for probate. "Biff came with me so perhaps he could confirm that."

"How did Beale know about probate?"

"He snoops around the Island."

"He said he wanted to walk around the yard and outbuildings." 'I'm trying to work a few things out,' he said. After half an hour I made him a cup of tea, and we had a pleasant chat, and he expressed his condolences about the murder. He implied that he knew Geoff well, which I know he did not. No one knew Geoff well. Said he wanted to continue running the farm as Geoff would have liked, in his memory. Those were his words. That made me laugh."

"Had you met him before?"

"No, he is a friend of Biff's. Biff brought him to the farm a couple of times recently. I don't know what they discussed but it was farming business, that's why I was happy for him to walk about the yard."

"Do you think he will buy the farm?"

"It will depend on the price. You can't say that farmland fetches much per acre on the Island. It is likely to be a low price, not a mainland price, so I've no idea, Inspector."

"Has anyone else been nosing about?"

"I've not seen anyone but if anyone shows up, I will let you know. Now you tell me, Inspector, how many suspects do you have?"

"Not many," said Bruno. "Or I wouldn't be here talking to you."

"Am I a suspect?"

"You are of interest, Mrs Galloway. It's a complicated investigation. I am not yet sure what the motive was for killing Klinker. You've helped me a little, Mrs Galloway, so now we are going to be getting back to our base to see if anything has come in for us."

Once Andy had finished his beloved afternoon tea, he left Bruno commanding her attention whilst he took another look at the silver photo frames displaying old family photographs on the oak table in the entrance. One that caught his interest was of Mrs Galloway and Biff Haves together on what appeared to be a holiday location. To study it further he took a copy on his mobile phone as evidence of a relationship between them, something they had not considered. Bruno realised how much in command of events surrounding Klinker's killing she was. When he considered his alternative theory that this could be a two-person murder, it prompted a rethink of his impression of Mrs Galloway, even to the extent that she could be the architect of Geoff Klinker's death.

At whatever age she was, she was not the grubby house-keeper she presented, beneath it she was far from being a frumpy old woman and less than a handful of years older than Biff Haves. That they might conceivably be a couple, working together, fitted with Bruno's idea that this murder could have been committed by two people.

The conversation between Andy Bowen and Mrs Galloway demonstrated that she was fully capable of acting a part and becoming a different person. Discovering the new Mrs Galloway was his new challenge, and he needed a closer look at the relationship between Haves and Galloway, to pursue his notion that they were responsible for a murder.

Bruno and Andy agreed about this.

"Biff Haves would know all about Beale, including his South African past, and had expressed a willingness to part-ner him taking over the estate," said Andy. "Hence Mrs Galloway's comment about seeing him about the estate. She said Biff Haves had brought him to the farm a couple of times recently, so when he showed up alone, she allowed him to wander around for as long as he wished and then gave him tea and a chat. Yet to us Beale was disparaging about Haves. Maybe that's just a front? When I asked him if they'd made contact, he replied 'Not of choice,' yet her report is quite different. I want to know his exact movements on the after-noon of 8 June because we've not discounted the possibility of two persons committing this murder. Beale would have been at Havenstreet with the school party while Biff Haves says he was putting fuel into his boat at Wootton Creek, and was back at the farm having tea with Mrs Galloway late afternoon."

CHAPTER 14

Monday 25 June

Bruno decided to accept Professor Walters' offer to visit the crime scene on the Island for two reasons. Firstly, he wanted Walters to analyse the murder by providing all the information they had gathered so far. The second was to see if he revealed anything that only the murderer would have known.

When he called to arrange his visit, he was very pleased to accept Bruno's invitation to visit the Island and analyse the case so far.

Although he lived the furthest away from the crime scene, they had not eliminated him from their list of suspects. Crime was after all his bread and butter, and history was full of crimes committed by people who dealt out their own form of justice. Amongst those were doctors, lawyers, policemen, judges and probably criminologists.

He was excited to be invited to Newport Police Station to meet the senior staff and to help find Dr Klinker's murderer. Bruno had prepared a copy of their daily worksheet since 8 June to bring him up to date with the events that had taken place since and where the police had got to in their investigation.

"Did you immediately think it was one of the school group, Inspector?" was the first question Ian Walters asked Bruno.

"No, it was a convenient place to start and where I felt a clue might lay or be obvious."

"And did you find one?"

"I'm not sure, it's true to say I have ideas, but so far not a reliable clue."

"This summarises where we have got to," he said, and offered Walters their notes. "They are a record of each interview with each individual in the school party," said Andy, passing over a slim file of about 20 sheets of A4 paper.

Walters didn't skim through the sheets, he read each page at the speed of a slow reader, and then reread some paragraphs before taking hold of a police mug of tea and slurping down several gulps.

"Not much in those that connects them with Klinker," he said. "Although we were all there with an opportunity to commit murder. Apart from us, the relationship between Beale, Haves and Mrs Galloway requires further work, as does finding Ali, but the rest have no connection with Klinker and the farm. Mullion the hospital consultant, Lewis the pharmacist, Hawkins the painter, Masters the retired Colonel and Klinker complete the list of professionals."

"I agree," said Walters. "The first four have no link to Klinker, so let's put them aside. James Tennant has established himself and came to the reunion to tell everybody who might have knowledge of his business failure on the Island, how successful he had become with his garden centre ventures. He would definitely have found an opportunity to tell Roger Beale, but that is miles away from a connection to Klinker, so that accounts for six. Kevin Billings is too successful and unconnected to have an axe to grind with Klinker, they live in different worlds, so that eliminates seven which leaves Ali, Beale, and myself.

"What about other suspects?"

"You mean Biff Haves and Mrs Galloway? Mrs Galloway features in your report as an elderly member of the Klinker family, a potentially harmless old lady, if one exists."

"I have come to the conclusion after two brief meetings that she is not what she seems. I don't believe she could have committed the crime, but she cannot be ruled out as an accessory. If we consider that Biff Haves is involved," said Bruno. "So far, we have not succeeded in contacting Ali, but we have to live with that, which leaves Beale."

"Nothing we have points to him as a murderer, let's say we are watching him, as we are Biff Haves. And finally, there is me," said Walters. "But I would not be here trying to help find the murderer if it had been me."

His rider suggested the opposite to Bruno.

"As Beale and Haves seem to be on track to acquire the business once probate has been obtained, I assume the funding for its purchase will be in place in time, and even if there is another bidder their pole position should guarantee they win. Walter Brown of Ryde will know if Klinker left a will and who the beneficiaries are. Did he have any living relations, apart from his aunt, Mrs Galloway, and a half-brother, Arnold Harris?" asked Walters.

Bruno replied, "We believe Dr Klinker has a wife, or an ex-wife. They parted twenty-five years ago and we are searching for her. We don't think there are any other relatives. Our investigations have concentrated on unconnected parties living locally who we know were there or thereabouts, like the station staff, who we've interviewed."

"Let's assume that Harris inherits the farm. Check out his whereabouts on the day of the murder. He will know if he is in line to inherit the estate and will be waiting for confirmation from the lawyers. A half-brother would rank behind children who share both mother and father, in this case Geoff Klinker. However, a properly written and witnessed will changes everything, and that is something the lawyers will not disclose until after probate is proven as I see it," said Walters. "Four people need to be eliminated from your enquiries. Beale and Biff Haves, Arnold Harris and Ali – if he can be located."

"And Mrs Galloway?"

"Yes, and Mrs Galloway," added Walters.

"Let's go across to the murder scene at Havenstreet Station and have a chat to whoever is working today," he suggested.

The small outside lavatory with mid-twentieth-century

fittings and open to the elements was a grim site for a murder. The killer had stepped into the lavatory off the platform pavement with killer blade at the ready while the victim stood, back to the killer, in full flow, peeing in the urinal. He did not turn to see the killer enter behind him, and was dead within seconds of receiving two lethal stab wounds. The two stab wounds would have been delivered with considerable force and accuracy; the killer would have known precisely where on the torso to stab the victim. He was dragged into the adjoining cubical and placed on the pedestal before the blood seeped through his clothing. From outside the small window the killer had slid the door lock to show engaged and fled, returning undetected to join the throng of people who'd left the train or were gathering on Platform A for the next departure to Wootton, or to re-join his Ryde School chums finishing afternoon tea in the café.

Walters examined the lavatory for 15 minutes re-creating the scene in his mind, and concluded that the murderer was either one of the school group or a person, or persons, who had travelled on the train, waiting for his arrival on the platform. It was busy so the killer would have had to have been physically near the victim to follow him into the lavatory prepared to kill him within seconds of Klinker unzipping his flies to urinate.

However, in the very short time it took to kill Klinker the murderer was running the risk of detection, if another person entered the lavatory. At this point Walters directed the detective's attention to the brass screw fixed at waist height protruding no more than 1 centimetre on the outside of the lavatory entrance door.

"What do you think that's for?" he said pointing to a small dirty hinged metal plate with a hole that fits over a staple and is secured by a pin or padlock. This hasp was fixed to the upright on the inside of the exterior lavatory door. "It was crucial for the killer not to be interrupted. If there were two people involved in the killing it was simple, but one person needed some protection, and I guess he would have fixed the bolt and hasp so he could slide the bolt across whilst killing Klinker, and not be caught in the act. So, the murder was well planned with at least one reconnaissance visit before the event, and because the killer had detailed knowledge of the layout of the Havenstreet Station it seems to eliminate non-Island residents and everything points to a single killer familiar with the layout of this station. Inspector, I would like to see the body before I make any further observations."

Police did not need a warrant to inspect a corpse, so they called the mortuary late afternoon and arranged for Walters to get a close up.

Bruno hung back as they entered the body storage section, as did Andy Bowen who had already witnessed the corpse.

From a distance they watched him study the body of Klinker lying face up and then ask the attendant to turn the body on to its side so that he could examine the two knife insertions. The first had cut an artery and penetrated the heart, the second other organs and the liver. They had been administered with maximum force; a lunge so fierce it would have rendered Klinker lifeless in just a few seconds.

"Do you think Walters was pleased to return to the Island?" Andy asked Bruno while they waited for him to examine the corpse.

"Very pleased," said Bruno. "The twenty-first-century Sherlock Holmes. Sitting in his rooms in Oxford, until some distressed person calls with a horror story that prizes him from out of his armchair to go and investigate. If we think Walters is a suspect it's because we see him as capable of committing the crime and he was present on the day, which is not the same as donning the cloak of the famous detective," said Bruno.

"What's the difference?" said Andy.

"With Walters we are watching for him to show us

something only the murderer would know, whereas Holmes was showing us something the murderer did not know."

"That is your role, sir," said Andy,

Bruno was flattered at being compared to the master of all detectives, and felt obliged to make his young assistant a similar gesture.

"And you would be Doctor Watson, I suppose?"

"If you say so, sir."

"I am not clever enough to solve crimes like Holmes," said Bruno.

"Isn't it Doctor Watson who solves the crime?"

"He digs up clues which isn't quite the same," said Bruno. "And I have Doctor Janet Gibson for that role."

"Is your lady a real doctor, sir?"

"Yes and no," said Bruno. "She has a Ph.D. in one of those subjects to do with child psychology, but she would never style herself as a doctor.

"Did you know that Conan Doyle wrote those stories when he worked as a General Practitioner in Portsmouth?"

"He was a local boy, then?" said Andy.

"Yes, he was, in one way. I don't think he came from Portsmouth but he lived in Southsea from where he practiced medicine as a GP. This inspired him to write the Sherlock Holmes mysteries. In the 1890s he played as goalkeeper for Portsmouth Football club."

Ian Walters finished his examination of the body and returned to where Bruno and Andy stood inside the exit.

"I was curious about the type of wound and the angle of the knife blade as it entered the body. I believe the killer was tall, 6 foot at least, with powerful arms, capable of a swift horizontal thrust with the knife, with his right arm. Then, winding his left arm completely around the victim's neck and shoulders to support his body and prevent it from sliding to the floor, he eased it backwards placing it in a position on the pedestal in the small cubicle, before closing the door and exiting, and from the ventilation window sliding the engaged bolt across with the aid of a stick securing the door to the cubicle."

Bruno listened to Walters repeat the killer's act of murder a second time. His description being identical, word for word an exact repeat of his report after exiting the lavatory. There was something in his repetition of the murder that he didn't quite get.

To eliminate Walters, he needed more from him. His findings so far were helpful, and as the afternoon was drawing to a close, he called Janet to persuade her to give the Professor a bed for the night in their partly renovated home. Unsurprisingly she jumped at the idea. It was an opportunity to let him talk and to pick his brains, and to get Janet's view on whether he was capable of murder. She could think of nothing better than spending an evening with an Oxford Professor of Criminal Jurisprudence trying to eliminate blind alleys.

Walters accepted Bruno's invitation. It had been his intention to stay over and visit places he remembered from his school days on the Island. He came from a naval family. His father had risen to the rank of Admiral and had returned to live in Portsmouth in retirement. During his adolescence he had been a border at Ryde School.

After Ryde School he had read Law at the internationally respected School of Law at King's College, London, now known as the Dickson Poon School of Law.

"He seems to be have been a lonely driven, student, which fitted with his career in academia," she said.

After graduating with a first-class law degree he remained at King's College funded by the college to complete a masters degree and then with further funding from the university undertook research for his Ph.D., which included time visiting prison inmates, analysing and categorising motives and why murderers commit the ultimate crime.

After King's, he became a university lecturer and during the course of the next fifteen years taught at two universities in the south if England, Exeter and Portsmouth. Continuing his research into criminology as a prison visitor, he wrote papers and books on aspects of the criminal mind, eventually winning an appointment as a lecturer, and then as Professor of Criminal Jurisprudence at St John's College, Oxford.

As a prison visitor Walters learned why people commit crimes. Some people who were unsuccessful in their lives killed in the knowledge they would be found out, and others committed murders wanting to be found out.

Over dinner in the midsummer sunshine he repeated his observations about the site of the Klinker murder, and the manner of the killing. How the killer had inserted the fatal stab wounds and he had exited the public lavatory, leaving the entrance to the cubicle showing ENGAGED.

"Do you think an Island person committed this murder?" Janet asked him.

"Without doubt," he said. "The site was known to the killer, and he could have prepared more than one site. If he couldn't get him at Havenstreet, he'd try somewhere else."

Walters, having lived on the Island until he was eighteen, would know it very well, and he was keen to show that he had come to the conclusion that it was an Island person, directing any suspicion away from himself.

"Roger Beale, who attended the reunion, is trying to buy the farm after probate."

"I remember Beale," said Walters. "Affable, a teacher, lived in South Africa, came back to the Island when his father died."

"Previously Professor of Agriculture at Cape Town University."

"You mentioned that since Klinker's father died Biff Haves had sole control over the farm, the bank accounts and the new haulage business."

"Yes."

"Could Beale buy Klinker's?"

"Maybe, with bank help. He is a farmer with a demonstrably excellent record that any farm mortgage finance company would back."

"I would get an independent accountant to do an audit of the Klinker farm accounts to see that everything adds up, likewise the haulage business," suggested Walters. "Confirm that Haves is running an honest business."

"That can be done as part of the valuation for probate. Biff Haves could covertly have become rich by stealing from the businesses in ways that anyone with total control can, and do. Klinker's increased presence could have threatened him leading to the discovery of a discrepancy. It is a line worth examination. It's a known fact that directors control businesses, not shareholders, or in this case one shareholder."

Walters confirmed Bruno's assessment of Biff Haves and in accordance with his instructions, Andy would discover his exact whereabouts on the afternoon of 8 June, then they could take another look at him.

During the evening Walters described examples of the criminal mind and how they usually failed through shoddy execution. He illuminated the probability that many more crimes than people imagined went unsolved and on top of these was the crime of murder. How frequently is the true cause of death unknown?

That Walters was unmarried, suggested he was totally absorbed with his professional work.

After he departed the following morning, Janet said he should not be excluded as a suspect because of his job or where he lived, but because he had shown no sadness or condolence at the murder of a school friend. His analysis was cold and impersonal.

"By what standards do criminologists judge themselves?"

was her question that Walters did not answer. "Do you search for the perfect crime, the unsolvable crime?"

"But not necessarily to commit it. No one is suggesting that Klinker's murder is unsolvable," said Bruno. "Klinker's killer had certainly worn gloves while he was engaged in the murder, so there were no prints or DNA to use as evidence. Evidence in this case is so far lacking."

Taking the advice from Walters, Bruno put in place an examination of Klinker's farm and the associated haulage business accounts, which Kevin Bell extracted from Companies House.

The filed accounts for the businesses as limited companies for the previous three years' trading, up to 31 December, were accessed on the station computer and showed exactly what had been stated, that Geoff Klinker was paid about £250,000 per annum in dividends.

They showed that the company was doing extremely well. The balance sheet indicated that a substantial sum of money had been reinvested in the business during this time, all coming from profits earned by the businesses. This money had been used to acquire and establish the haulage businesses and buy the latest transport vehicles where each truck could cost in excess of £100,000. The profit and loss account showed that profits had increased substantially each year of trading, and turnover to more than £4 million in the year ended 31 December 2018.

The haulage company profit and loss account reported a healthy position and increasing in value, and the notes to the accounts showed an interesting state of affairs as regards the ownership of the business.

Biff Haves had been allotted 25 per cent of the company shares with Geoffrey Klinker shown as the owner of 75 per cent. Biff Haves was shown as a director on a salary of £25,000 per annum. Geoff Klinker was the other director. However, a note in the accounts stated the shares contained a pre-emption clause that in the event of either shareholder wishing to sell his shares for whatever reason they had to be offered to the other shareholder at par. It's a standard clause in a private company's articles to protect minority shareholders.

"What does that mean in this case?" said Andy.

Jack Roswell, the local chartered accountant, was the man Newport Police called on for financial advice whenever the station officers requested an explanation or clarification. Biff Haves would have been fully aware of the benefits to him of Klinker's demise, and acquiring the 75 per cent Klinker holding at par for just a few thousand pounds automatically made him a rich man, and with a following wind his collateral in the haulage business might have made him capable of offering to buy the Klinker farm when it came up for sale. o's explanation of the accounts gave Bruno a clear motive for the murder. Jack Roswell confirmed that the accounts were in order, with no irregularities in the accounting system. In his two previous interviews Biff Haves had not shown any inconsistences, although as any investigator knows consistency does not imply truth.

He had claimed that on the morning of 8 June, he'd worked on the farm from 7.00 a.m. to 11.00 a.m., but had not said what he was doing. In four hours, he would have accomplished a memorable amount of work. A clarification of his precise activity on that day was vital to Bruno. The time to commit this murder could be measured in minutes, and the time that the murder was committed could be accurately set against the arrival of the Isle of Wight Steam Train back at Havenstreet station at 3.00 p.m.

Bruno needed to understand Haves' movements throughout 8 June in short time slots measured in minutes in order to eliminate him, or to raise him from being a person of interest, to being a murder suspect. He let Andy visit Haves for a third time alone. It might lower his guard if he saw he was being interviewed by the number-two detective.

CHAPTER 15

Tuesday 26 June

Haves was busy in his office at 9.00 a.m. the following morning, when Detective Andy Bowen arrived to "rough him up".

"Detective Bowen, surely you do not think I am involved with Klinker's murder?" was his initial response to Andy Bowen's sudden appearance. "I assume you've exhausted all your other suspects?"

"In our work we have to dot every *i* and cross every *t*, and that is why I am here, I have still got some *i*'s to dot and *t*'s to cross. Can you tell me again your whereabouts throughout Friday 8 June, particularly on the afternoon of that day?"

Andy Bowen had checked his notes of the previous interview with Biff Haves in which he had explained what he did on 8 June in general terms; now, Bruno seemed to want it minute by minute.

"We're preparing the combines for harvesting in 4 weeks' time. It's easy with our new machines, because the manufacturers tell us what state the machine is, and they come along and service, or repair if it needs it. I checked crop growth in the north-east quarter. Spoke to the livestock manager, and I had egg and bacon for breakfast with Mrs Galloway on my way to the bank.

"I got back at 11.00 a.m. after collecting cash from the bank in Ryde. It's a little antiquated paying cash in brown envelopes, but my men don't all have bank accounts and there isn't an ATM anywhere near the farm.

"I was here until 11.30 a.m. having started at 7.00 a.m., everything was in order so I went to Wootton where our haulage business is located. I always do on Fridays."

"How long were you there? Half an hour?"

"There is a week's work to examine and always an incident or two to discuss. Then I filled two 25-litre fuel carriers with diesel from the yard bowser, and took them down to my boat in Wootton Creek. With this weather I planned to go sailing over the weekend.

Wootton is a short drive to Ryde golf club, where I am a member and decided to have lunch and play nine holes with anyone who fancied a round of golf. It was a beautiful afternoon but it was also Friday, and the course was fully booked so I had lunch, sat on the terrace and read the newspaper."

"What time did you arrive at the club?"

"One o'clock, thereabouts."

"What time did you leave club?"

"It could have been 2.00 p.m., not much after," he said. "Then I returned here in time to relieve Lesley, my office lady, and make a few phone calls. I left the office about 4.00 p.m. after checking with Phil who lives next door. You can see his house there," he said, pointing through an office window at a detached well-kept farm cottage. After that I called in for tea with Mrs Galloway, and to wait for Geoff to show up for the beer we had agreed."

"Could anyone remember your visit to the golf club on that afternoon?"

"They might do, Inspector. I spoke to one or two of the members, but as I said it was busy with members and an influx of visitors. This is a holiday island, and golf societies come on three-day visits and play all the courses in the summer."

"Can we talk about your relationship with Roger Beale?"

"We don't have a relationship," said Haves.

"But you meet regularly?"

"Not regularly, we meet occasionally to discuss farming matters."

"Is it true that you have given him confidential information about your business here, in advance of probate being obtained, and you have together planned to purchase the Klinker estate?"

Biff Haves was visibly uncomfortable with how this interview with a police officer was progressing, and was unsure how he should respond. He considered what he and Beale had discussed was confidential. It was sensitive business information that could materially affect the value of any purchase.

"I've given him nothing that is not in the public domain and at Companies House."

A partnership with Beale was his big opportunity to achieve his lifelong ambition of at least part-owning the Klinker estate. Hence, he felt his deal with Beale should not to be divulged to third parties, especially the police.

"How is your investigation progressing, Inspector?"

Andy wasn't prepared to give any information to Haves about to whom they were speaking, so his answer was, "Slowly." That was all he said.

Andy had decided he had taken his meeting with Haves as far as he could so with a serious tone and for a reason he could not explain, he bid Haves good morning, and left to report his meeting to his boss.

For him, Haves was now a person of interest. His close connection with Beale posed the question whether this murder might have been carried out by these two. Klinker's death could have given them the opportunity to realise their ambitions. Bruno listened attentively to Andy's report as it was of critical importance to their investigation.

"Let's consider the possibility that for Haves obtaining the business is a two-stage exercise. Klinker's murder is not going to gift him his beloved farm. Then he has to buy it, which alone he cannot do. That's where Beale comes into it. What about the men who work for Haves?"

"They are not men with whom Haves might have a personal relationship. They are working men, the opposite to what Haves aspires to be," Andy continued. "So where does that leave us?"

"Mrs Galloway has given us the impression that Haves and Beale were buddies," noted Bruno.

"I believe her," said Andy. "Any suggestion that Haves could raise cash on the Island or with banks anywhere on the mainland to buy Klinker's would not be correct. He might run a good business but how would he operate on his own if he had to meet the payroll every week? That's been Klinker's responsibility since his father died, whether he was regarded as an absentee landlord or not.

"His father has been dead five years, during which time he has expanded the business by buying up haulage companies, knocking some out I bet, and improving every operational activity on the farm. Even if Biff Haves claims credit for this, he has accomplished this with Klinker looking over his shoulder and signing the cheques. I think the partnership he was denied by the old man is significant. It suggests that Biff Haves isn't quite what he seems. Who is to say that he doesn't bear the grudge that Mrs Galloway denied when you asked her? Let us do as Walters suggested, check the money in the company bank accounts, Haves' alibi, and anything else we can find out about Beale's movements on 8 June."

Meanwhile Bruno updated his commander on progress. No one was more conscious of elapsed time than he was. When you have spent every waking hour trying to solve a problem for several weeks, and you have made so little progress, you plant doubts in your own mind and in the minds of those who you report to. Fortunately, Superintendent John Barlow, Bruno's boss, was sufficiently experienced in trying to crack unsolved murders. He did not need to interrogate Bruno, he trusted his work ethic, and was sure results would come.

He had worked with Bruno for nearly two years and he had no doubts in his ability as a detective, and was confident he'd crack this case given time.

Andy had taken the opportunity of driving from Ryde Golf Club to Havenstreet. It had taken him less than 30 minutes. If Haves had left the club on the 8 June, as he had said, at a little after 2.00 p.m., that would have given him time to prepare and position himself ready to kill. Furthermore, his movements and time management throughout the day guaranteed that he was in the right place at the required moment. Earlier at the golf club Andy was the epitome of discretion learning from the club secretary how busy they had been on the afternoon of Friday 8 June.

"It can be mayhem on Friday's," he said. "Mornings we have weekenders getting in an early round, the Retired Old Boys meet later in the morning, they play Stableford and stay for lunch."

He remembered Biff Haves calling in at about 1.00 p.m. on that day. He could not remember if he was in the club to play, he didn't think so he may have had lunch, because tee-off times were available and he did not play.

Andy remembered that Haves had said the course was fully booked.

"Perhaps he didn't have a playing partner," said Andy.

"There is always someone to play in this club. If a member calls in for lunch, it's usually a short stay, a quick lunch, a sandwich or a burger and a drink."

"Do you have CCTV anywhere in the club?"

"We have a CCTV camera over the entrance to the Pro's shop which is in the left-hand side of the car park."

"Does it record the visitors to the club?"

"No, it's there to record break-ins and deter thieves at night, but Alistair, our golf pro, should be able to help you if the camera was on and if he archives the recordings."

In the Golf Pro's shop Alistair explained that the camera served several purposes, apart from security at night, although he could not understand why thieves would break into a golf shop.

"There is no cash left in the shop, and what would a thief do with golf equipment? No golfer would buy off the back of a lorry. I don't keep an archive, but the camera recycles every 21 days. So, the day in which you are interested, 8 June, should still be on the disc. I can return to 8 June and you can browse through the day if you have time?"

Andy did have time, so he sat as a desk at the back of the shop whilst Alistair set up his laptop for Andy Bowen to read his disc, fast forwarding to 1.00 p.m. on 8 June.

From 1.00 p.m. the shop was busy and if Biff Haves had come in Alistair could have been forgiven for not remembering him. It was a small shop loaded with golf stock with just enough room to move about. Andy was lucky because the camera recorded a visit by Biff Haves at 1.53 p.m., leaving six minutes later without making a purchase. The camera confirmed his presence at the club. His departure from the shop also signalled his departure from the club, it had to be assumed. Then it allowed him ample time to drive and park at Havenstreet Station in time to meet the arrival of the 3.00 p.m. train from Smallbrook with the school party, murder Klinker, return to the farm and join Mrs Galloway for tea at 4.30 p.m.

Although Andy's investigation confirmed that Biff Haves had time to commit the murder, why would he have chosen the steam railway station, which could only be entered through the ticket barrier, and leave him trapped should a complication arise. If he had wanted to kill Klinker, he could have done so at a multitude of opportunities around the farm. Chewing him up in a combine could have been an accident. He reported to Bruno that although Haves had the time to visit Havenstreet and kill Klinker, it was not a plan he would have thought up, in preference to easier, certain and safe alternatives.

Bruno agreed that he should remain just a person of interest.

The death of Klinker posed a greater threat to his ambition of a share in the ownership of the Klinker estate. Whilst the farm remained in the ownership of Klinker he was secure and Klinker knew he couldn't run the farm without him. Likewise, Beale had not displayed any signs that indicated he was a killer. In spite of a perceived arrogance he had acquired from his two decades living in South Africa, under the various different political regimes, he had survived in a senior academic role.

His professional background and his attention to his business were a million miles from the murky business of murder. It was surely beneath a man of his intelligence to believe that the only way he could achieve an objective was through murder.

Beale's life in Cape Town had highlighted to him the importance of his English heritage and his ambition was to bring his two sons to England to finish their education at British universities. His care for his mother at the farm, and the improvements on the farming methods he had introduced had created an enviable Island business, and that did not show the character trait or the mind of a murderer. In Bruno's mind Beale and Haves shared an ambition regarding the Klinker estate and were patiently waiting the outcome of probate before pouncing either individually or together to acquire that business.

Bruno recalled the conversation he'd had with George Lewis, the pharmacist, who had stubbornly insisted that the murderer was not an Islander, because he was so sure of that if an Island resident had murdered Klinker he would not have been capable of continuing to live on the Island because of the constant reminder of his evil act and being found out. He probably thought that would absolve him of any suspicion.

Janet was disappointed that on his visit to see Mrs Galloway, he had not elicited some gossip about how life was lived at Clive Hall, and what kind of relationship she had with everyone there.

She suggested that he or Andy Bowen should return one afternoon with a bunch of flowers. She believed that if a woman had secrets she might share them with someone who understood the loneliness she must be experiencing at Clive Hall.

Meanwhile Bruno's thoughts turned to Brenda Frampton.

CHAPTER 16

Wednesday 27 June

Bruno arrived at Newport Police Station to meet Andy in a creative frame of mind. He had a number of angles to explore, and liked the opportunity to throw out off-the-wall, unlikely scenarios, so he invited PC Kevin Bell who was developing his analytical skills to sit in on the brainstorming session.

"Haves and Beale," began Bruno, "their relationship is of pure convenience. Beale can buy the Klinker estate but he cannot ignore Haves, who currently controls the entire Klinker business and could steal up on the blind side, unless he keeps him in his sights. Haves and Galloway are devious but not necessarily complex. They have erected a wall of silence which we've not penetrated yet."

"Are they lovers?" said Andy.

"Let's say they know each other very well."

"We know she is a chancer," said Bruno, not quite understanding himself what he meant.

Professor Walters is on the radar but so far just a keen observer. If he was the murderer, they'd not yet discovered a motive and Bruno suspected there was nothing as solid as evidence to support a loose gut feel. Kevin was still hopeful of finding Ali. He had collected information about platform cameras and received some film from two of the stations between Portsmouth Harbour and Victoria. He also confirmed about the stations en-route that had no cameras.

"What about Brenda Frampton?" said Andy.

"She gave us very little, considering she was effectively married to him for years and years."

"Is that all we've got Brenda Frampton? I thought we had done with London. It means another trip to Klinker's London home. Didn't she say she'd locate Maisie Longmore for us?"

"Yes, she said she'd try, and finding her is becoming more important."

"Set up a visit to Kensington tomorrow. Perhaps there is more to her than we've cottoned on to so far."

Bruno needed to explore her relationship with Klinker, while she had lived with his obsession with Lillian Golobieski. She had admitted she was in love with him and accepted his infidelities, but to what extent did she have to suffer them, and how long before that love turned to hate, at which point she might decide to kill him? It was one scenario for the imagination but not an avenue Bruno wanted to pursue now.

Now that the man she had loved for two decades was dead, she had admitted that for many years they had lived happily together as man and wife, but their love had become stale, although they continued to live together occupying separate bedrooms in the apartment.

Often, she did not see him, except in the consulting rooms, where she continued her work as his secretary. But when he was home, she cooked his meals and they dined together, continuing as they had when their relationship started.

"We remained good friends," she had insisted.

CHAPTER 17

Thursday 28 June

The next day, their journey was familiar and straightforward. Brenda Frampton was welcoming, helpful and ready to answer any questions.

"Brenda, we need to explore his relationships with people in his circle in London. Is there anyone who might want to harm him?"

"I did not meet his friends or acquaintances in recent years. When we were younger, we had lots of mutual friends, but as he became busier and more in demand, he had less time, almost no time for socialising. Sometimes he would eat in his club and come home late, so days could go by when I didn't see him. I felt his presence and he needed to know I was here. Eventually when I said I thought I should leave, he was horrified. He said this was my home and wouldn't agree with my leaving. At first I was uplifted by that, until I realised that he dreaded the thought of living alone. I didn't think he could live alone, and I became afraid to leave for fear of what might happen to him."

"He never mentioned the Isle of Wight to you?"

"Yes, enough for me to think there was something he didn't like about the Island. He thought it was hostile. Since his father left his estate solely to him, he said he could feel the resentment towards him everywhere, and because of the lack of affection, he did not think he could move there permanently."

"Did you ever visit the Island?"

"Fifteen years ago, I went with him to see his parents. They were nice, his father was a working farmer but he had other interests and his mother was well known on the Island. She dined with the Island MP and all that. The first time, we went to celebrate their thirty-seventh wedding anniversary. The second visit was soon after, when he kept his promise to show me the Island – very enjoyable. Those were the only two occasions Inspector, nothing more," she added.

"When he said they were an unfriendly lot, whom was he referring to?"

"He was not specific. Everyone, I think. He felt their attitude to a stranger. It's a small Island inhabited by three types of people. The workers who do the jobs and make up half of the population; the elderly retirees, reasonably well-off from the mainland, who make up almost the other half; then there is a small group, less than 1 per cent who come and go and own most of the Island, with big houses, farms and family estates that have been handed down since the sixteenth century. Geoffrey became one of those when his father died. Since then, for the past five years, his mother has been trying to get him to move there. The farm is a well-run business by the manager who worked for his father for thirty-five years, and Geoffrey would only have been in the way.

"Being a hospital consultant is a vocation, it's not a job or a profession. Medicine is a calling on an elevated level. You get better at it the longer you do it, so the longer you want to do it. He had no enemies that I could put a name to in London. Most of his associates would not know where the Isle of Wight is and certainly not that he had an estate there. He wouldn't have told anyone."

"He told Lillian Golobieski," Bruno pointed out.

"Yes, that was unwise," she said.

Her eyes focused on Bruno for a split second, but long enough for him to know he'd given something away in his reply.

"You've met her, haven't you, Inspector?"

"Yes," said Bruno.

"And what did you think?"

He knew he had to give the right answer to her question.

"I am middle aged and unmarried, although I have a partner. I am a provincial detective and I live on the Isle of Wight, which you've indicated most Londoners have never heard of. I can be read like a page of an open book. Yes, she flattered me as if I was a superior being, like I imagine she did with Dr Klinker. However, I saw her for the gold-digger she is. A fading beauty, interested in one person – herself – and money. There are successful, professional men who only see what is on show. Because of the pressure their work puts them under, Lillian is the perfect release, but the serious relationships these ladies crave are seldom there. Did he invite you to the Island when his mother died?"

"Yes, he did, we travelled together and I looked after him."

"What will you do now?"

"I will stay here. One thing he did for me in anticipation that one day he might die was to put the lease – and it is a long lease, 130 years – in joint names, and as we never married with a specific instruction transferring any Klinker interest to me, so if either of us suddenly passed away the leasehold would be owned entirely by the survivor."

"Will you attend his funeral?"

"Of course," she said.

"If I haven't found his killer by then, will you be my eyes and ears and tell me if you notice anything strange?"

"Of course I will, Inspector."

"And how about Maisie Longmore?"

"I think I know where she is working and I am waiting for my friend to provide me with contact details."

"Can you make it urgent, please, Brenda?"

"Yes, Inspector."

Their departure at 11.00 a.m. gave them time to catch the train from Marylebone to Oxford to see Ian Walters for his further thoughts after his visit to the Island earlier in the week.

At 12.04 p.m. he was waiting on the platform at Oxford City rail station to meet the two detectives, as Bruno had suggested, for an update on progress. Although the University summer term had ended Oxford was teeming with visitors and students from overseas attending short two-week intensive courses introducing them to the subjects they planned for their future careers. The Professor had reserved a table for lunch at the Randolph Hotel in the centre of the city. What puzzled Bruno was that although Walters was at the reunion, he had not conveyed to them one original thought on the day, about the other attendees, the journey through the Island beauty spots, or his own impressions of the suspects, so that Bruno was unable to place Walters at the reunion. He'd attended in the same capacity as his other school friends, but so far, not as one of them, and he'd not given him a lead to follow.

Because he was running out of places to look and people to investigate, Bruno had returned to Walters who remained something of a hollow man. It had been at the Professor's instigation that he'd pursued his investigation of Biff Haves, so while a substantial lunch was ordered, in what Walters described as an historic Oxford hotel that had witnessed some amazing occasions, Bruno detailed their interview with Haves.

"We confirmed that his prompt 2.00 p.m. departure from Ryde Golf Club gave him an opportunity to drive to Havenstreet and murder Klinker." Andy did not accept that he could have undertaken the variety of different tasks he did on a busy working day prior to a murder, which required exact timing and precision. If he were planning to commit a murder, he would have dedicated time solely to that crime.

Walters suggested that his busy day could have represented his alibi. His journey time from the club to the station could have been planned. He might have accessed the station on a £5.00 ticket unnoticed by changing his appearance and clothing in plenty of time for Klinker to arrive on the journey from Smallbrook. All he had to do was position himself and wait. The professor's opinion convinced Andy that in the case of a murder one had to anticipate the unexpected.

He was interested in Brenda Frampton's inheriting the Kensington apartment. It was compensation for not marrying her, and a sign of his insecurity wanting to keep her close to him. Although she benefited from his death, it was not a motive for her to engage in any skulduggery to get her hands on something that was already owned by her and Klinker.

During lunch, Walters wanted to know what their thoughts were, their gut feelings, if any, about where they were going. Bruno explained all their meetings so far, which Walters picked over, asking questions and exploring avenues they had already thought about.

As the professor had nothing concrete to contribute, lunch became an opportunity for Walters to deliver a lecture on criminology, highlighting murders resulting from jealousy and envy, when a person is given or is credited with something that another has forever longed for.

"Was there anyone amongst those they had interviewed that fitted those personality traits?" said Walters.

"Perhaps," said Andy. "But not as so far revealed to us."

"What about Lillian Golobieski?"

"That requires more personal information than we've had time to gather so far, and jealously doesn't seem an appropriate motive in this case," said Andy, wondering if Walters might start on a psychological study of their suspects to determine their character weaknesses.

Andy was educated to Ian Walters level in the working of the criminal mind and was therefore able to understand his approach completely. He and Bruno had increasingly felt that Ian Walters was a person of interest on the fringe of their investigation, a person with an as yet unknown motive. This was only a hunch stimulated on the occasions they had met, particularly as they had accepted his offer to help them based on his expert knowledge of the criminal mind. Now this lunch meeting seemed pointless because his interest was not to discuss their list of suspects and their possible motives, but to find out what they were thinking, while revealing nothing about his own theories.

After settling the lunch bill, which included two bottles of Saint Emilion, they declined Ian's offer to drive them to the railway station on the basis that a half-mile walk would clear their heads and give them the chance to stroll between the historic college buildings of the finest academic institution in the world, and also that he was over the limit to drive.

Having drunk more than half of the wine he had become less lucid than at the start of lunch, more apt to reveal himself which, if they had stayed a little longer, might have given them something else to work on. Lunch had persuaded Andy to take another look at the professor's CV, to which end on their return train journey he called Kevin Bell at Newport Police Station HQ and asked him to look at the establishments he had claimed to teach at, and see if the local newspapers during his time at each establishment had reported any unsolved murders. Bruno listened to his call, which set him thinking about Professor Walters as a suspect. He had noticed as lunch had progressed how Walters had become more overtly superior in his attitude towards them. It was only Bruno's decision to pay the bill that had enabled him to reject the wine waiter's offer to bring a third bottle of Saint Emilion.

After their long heavy lunch and a journey from Oxford via Paddington, the tube, Victoria to Portsmouth and on to the Island, he was in a relaxed mood for supper with Janet, with whom he'd kept in mobile phone touch with on the journey. She was ready to report on her visit to Mrs Galloway that afternoon after school had finished. Bruno had thought for some time that Mrs Galloway had a story to tell that two male detectives had not been able to get out of her. So he had asked Janet to act in the guise of a police counsellor and visit Mrs Galloway, who Detective Inspector Bruno Peach thought might want some help living alone in a large house after its master had been murdered.

◈

Janet had taken Bruno's suggestion that she might learn something of value from a one-to-one with Mrs Galloway, who was surprised to see her and accepted her gift of a large bouquet of summer flowers enthusiastically, finding a vase and arranging them whilst Janet introduced herself.

"Mrs Galloway, did you have much contact with the doctor before he left for the school reunion?"

"Some of the time he was here, he played the piano. It was very warm so he enjoyed the garden, and walked around the farm, saw Biff Haves, but he stayed on the farm most of the time. When I asked if he was looking forward to the reunion, he said he was not sure, but he did not elaborate on that remark. I don't think listening to the life stories of a bunch of strangers was quite his cup of tea," she added.

To learn anything, Janet had to get Mrs Galloway to talk about the Klinkers, and her sister and nephew Arnold Harris, who could, in the absence of a will, inherit the Klinker estate. Given that Harris had looked after his mother for five years since the death of his step-father, Mrs Galloway would have known him very well, although she had not mentioned him in her previous meetings with the detectives. Was she deliberately keeping him out of it, knowing that he might inherit the estate, or was it something else? Perhaps she and her nephew were in it together, concealing something important?

Janet's next question gave her the answer she was searching for. It was her off-the-beaten track way of thinking that was Bruno's reason for asking her to pay a visit to Mrs Galloway.

"How long have you known Biff Haves?"

"Over twenty years. He has been such a loyal servant to the Klinkers."

"He is not married, is he?" said Janet.

"No," she replied, without adding one word.

"Perhaps he never met the right person?"

"Maybe," she said, and walked out of the room to get the tea.

In Clive Hall's main lounge were a dozen, shiny, clean silver photo frames with old and recent family photos. They had been polished and stood out as a feature. Janet believed that pictures on public view in a house were to be looked at by visitors as well as the occupiers of the house. Some were old photos, but others were more recent.

In one early photo, which must have been thirty years old, both boys were dressed in stage clothes. When Mrs Galloway, returning with a tea tray, spotted Janet looking at the photo collection. She was keen to tell her about and the persons featured in the photo display.

"They were always in school plays and loved dressing up. Arnold went on to acting with the Ryde Stagers Amateur Dramatic Society. He still runs it."

One photo showed Madeline Klinker in a family group, and the second, placed in a prominent position, was of Mrs Galloway and Biff Haves standing together on a pier somewhere, which was definitely not Ryde Pier. It had a seated rain-protective shelter behind where they stood, which seemed to run the length of the pier, which Janet thought she had seen before, but couldn't remember where.

It indicated that they knew each other on a social level, and the placing of the photo of them so prominently in the house, manifested something else.

"As boys and young men they appeared in many Gilbert and Sullivan operettas, and when they were in sixth form they both appeared in *A Passage to India*. They were only one year apart in age, Arnold was in the upper sixth when

Geoffrey was one year behind. They loved drama. Madeline was very proud of her two boys.

Arnold looked after her until she passed away, he stayed here when she recovered for some of the time, but he was sensitive enough not to be in residence when Geoffrey came home. This was Geoffrey's kingdom and he was king of the castle."

"Did Geoffrey recognise Arnold's contribution towards looking after his mother?"

"No, he believed it was Biff Haves who really looked after her, with my help of course."

"Why was that?"

"In truth he knew quite well it was Arnold, but he wouldn't acknowledge him or his contribution."

"What was Arnold's reaction to Geoffrey's murder?"

"Fear. He was frightened. If someone could kill his half-brother for no known reason, a person who had hardly any connection with the Island, he feared they might target him for the same reason. In his professional life Arnold makes a lot of enemies. He is responsible for recommending or rejecting planning applications before they go before the council committee. It's a powerful position, and he gets plenty of abuse, letters and phone calls. He hasn't been here for some time, although he phones me often."

"But he hasn't been to see you since his mother died?"

"Not since the funeral. He cleared a few personal items of hers, but nothing else. He's welcome, but there's nothing for him here now, so he doesn't come over. He has an important job and he is the director of an Amateur Theatrical Company in Ryde. They put on plays during the year, Shakespeare and Noël Coward. They are very versatile and Arnold usually has a leading part. They travel all over the Island and in October they have a festival at Shanklin Theatre. He is a good actor and if he had gone to an acting school when he left school, he could have been a professional. That's what he really wanted to do."

"Is there an incident in the past, however far back, that might have caused anyone in the Klinker family concern, given what has happened?"

"Not in the time I was close to them. Geoff would never harm a fly."

"Mrs Galloway, can I call you by your first name?"

"Of course, it's Sheila."

"And you call me Janet. Sheila, you said your husband passed away before Tom Klinker?"

"Correct, so I came to look after my sister. Two widows. She was eighteen years older than me. I was a mistake, my mother said. She insisted she call me her housekeeper, even to her friends – especially to her friends. She never called me by my first name, I was always Mrs Galloway."

"You've no children?"

"No."

"What do you do here, now you don't have your sister to look after?"

"I am busy straightening things out for the new owners."

"Any ideas?"

"It will be an Islander for sure. I love this location, the Island."

"Like Biff Haves?"

"Exactly," she said with a broad smile.

"How do you manage your house in Ryde?"

"It's let. The agents manage the property and call me when the washing machine breaks down."

"Where is it, the town centre?"

"It's on the esplanade facing the Solent."

"Will you move back when this is sold?"

"I am hoping the new owner will retain my services."

Janet had been there about 30 minutes and was about to enjoy a second cup of tea, when in walked Biff Haves. He did not knock, just strode in. Surprised to see Janet there, he said good afternoon, quite casually.

Mrs Galloway said, "Hello Biff, so you've come for tea as well?"

"That would be nice," he said and sat down.

"Mr Haves, as I was about to leave, I will say goodbye and let you enjoy your tea." Janet grabbed her backpack, said goodbye to Sheila Galloway and went home.

⁂

"On my way home I thought about the photo of Sheila Galloway and Biff Haves on the pier. There was something very familiar about the deck of the pier. It was the rows of seats that ran through the centre. As a Yorkshire girl, where did we go on holiday?"

Bruno could not even guess.

"I'd swear the photo was taken in Scarborough. It would have been on holiday. If they went there together, then there is something between them. We are searching for a murderer who may have had an accomplice, and these two could be who we are looking for."

Bruno was interested in her suggestion. She had established a relationship between Mrs Galloway and Biff Haves that had changed his perception Biff Haves. She had not concealed her support for him although she had played his chances down of succeeding in acquiring the Klinker farm, by referring to his age and lack of collateral.

"It doesn't change much," said Bruno. "I still see them as innocent bystanders in this murder. I need to know more about them. Where does Haves live, and what does he do in his spare time?"

Janet's next observation concerned Arnold Harris. "Would Harris have left Mrs Galloway on her own at Clive Hall after his mother died?"

"I don't think that would be normal," said Bruno.

"Only if he knew she had a fall-back in case of emergency?"

"You mean Biff Haves?"

"Yes."

"The only way we'll find out is from the horse's mouth," he said. "If Haves had not shown up, did she have anything else?" said Bruno.

"No, we had talked enough, but it has given me the personal contact if I need to speak to her again."

Bruno was pleased with Janet. She had learned useful information about the Klinker household. All that was left was to plan her next assignment.

CHAPTER 18

Friday 29 June

Fortunately, Arnold Harris was available to meet them, before he went into a Planning meeting.

"Mr Harris, on the morning of 8 June, Geoff Klinker left Clive Hall at about 9.30 a.m. after a meeting with his farm manager. He was going to a school reunion, promising to return to Clive Hall to have a beer. At that time he was quite involved with the farm, although he left the day-to-day running to Biff Haves, and from what we can find out he had no intention of selling the farm. Is that your understanding?"

"I have no idea what happened at Clive Hall on 8 June, or if Geoff had any plans to sell the farm, so I really can't help you. My mother did not give me the impression that Geoff would sell once she passed away, but that was a while ago."

"Did Mrs Galloway have any idea of what he might do with the farm?"

Harris turned the question back on him. "What has she told you?"

"She said she thought he would sell." Bruno gave that less than honest reply to get a reaction.

"Really, I wouldn't know, Inspector, and if she had known of that decision I am the last person she would tell."

"Since your mother passed away you don't go to Clive Hall?"

"No, it holds unpleasant memories for me, personal things."

"What is your impression of Mrs Galloway?"

"Aunt Sheila, or Mrs Galloway, as mother insisted on calling her, because she showed her off as her housekeeper. When Tom was alive mother was the housekeeper, but when Tom died, she wanted help, and as her sister had fallen on hard times, she took her on, on strict conditions. I didn't think it would work but it did, although she disliked it when I came to see Madeline. Mrs Galloway is very manipulative and she'd give anything to stay in Clive Hall."

"What about the house she owns in Ryde?" said Bruno.

"Did she tell you that? Inspector, she is flat broke. The house on the Esplanade belongs to Biff Haves. If she has to leave Clive Hall she'll have nowhere, unless Biff Haves takes her in."

"Is it possible you could inherit Clive Hall?"

"It is possible, but unlikely. Tom and Geoff would have prevented that possibility, with some legal angle. Geoff will exclude me in every possible way. Tom left everything to Geoff on the condition that he executed a will that specifically excluded myself. So, Inspector, if I did, by some stroke of fortune, end up with Clive Hall, Mrs Galloway would be out the door on day one. And to tell you the truth, I would be over the moon."

"Wouldn't you soften your approach towards your aunt?"

"Never. She didn't exactly make my mother's last few years a bed of roses. They didn't like each other, and 'Mrs Galloway'," Harris smiled at the use of the housekeeper's name, "almost prevented me from visiting her in the end."

"I've always found her to be very pleasant," said Andy.

"She knows how to handle men. She had a terrible reputation as a young woman, according to my mother. If she offers you scones and jam, be careful."

"You mean they might be poisoned?" said Andy.

"They might be," said Harris.

It was a warning Andy Bowen accepted open mouthed.

"I am not a farmer, so would I keep the farm? Yes, I would. I like my job here protecting the Island from greedy property developers, but I'd do a deal with Biff Haves."

"You'd have lost all your money then," said Andy.

"I'd have gambled everything I own that if either of us were to get murdered, it would be me. Some of these property developers would like to kill me. Maybe one day someone will. Finding my killer will be easy. You'll find their name on some 'turned down' planning application. Is there anything else, Inspector?"

"Yes," said Bruno.

"Where were you on the afternoon of 8 June, the day Geoff Klinker was murdered?"

"I was in Southampton on that day at a local authority conference. Second Friday in June every year. That was the day of the closing dinner, where I hosted a table."

Bruno was satisfied with his interview with Harris. He was a man who was satisfied with his lot, and any officious traits he might have, he could employ in his dealings with property sharks. Andy Bowen made a note of the Local Authority conference venue that he'd get checked out. Inheriting the Klinkers' farm seemed the last thing on his mind.

The next question was Mrs Galloway's real situation.

If her tenure of Clive Hall was based upon a few lies, it did not require a great deal of a policeman's imagination to see that with Biff Haves' help she could become the mistress of Clive Hall. Whether the two of them could have contrived Geoff Klinker's murder was a very unlikely long shot, but having already investigated the potential involvement of Biff Haves, it was not necessary to retrace their steps.

◈

At Newport Police Station PC Kevin Bell, their university-educated computer guru, was proving that he was no PC Plod. With a number of actions in the Klinker case pending he had concentrated on Professor Ian Walters.

Walters' first degree at the London Law School took four years from 1985 to '89. Further research, a Master's degree, and then a Ph.D. in Criminal Psychology took him through until the mid-1990s when he finally finished in the summer of

1995. By which time he was twenty-nine years of age and, for the first time in his life, looking for a job. In the fifteen years until he obtained his first lectureship at Oxford University, he held three positions.

His first job was a teaching post at Portsmouth University on a newly-created course titled Criminology. During four years in this position he lived at his parents' home. Living with a retired Admiral had its advantages, although his mother, an institutionalised bridge player, thought he was a sponge. He took everything on offer and gave nothing back, even though he was well able on a University salary to contribute to the daily running costs of a well-appointed apartment in a fully serviced block of modern luxury dwellings. She thought he'd learned a way of life from the criminals he studied, and would inevitably one day become one of them. She saw him assume their identity and sympathise with them as a victim, a form of Stockholm Syndrome. She thought criminals should be punished, generally more severely than they were.

PC Bell had taken a few hours to visit the Walters' apartment and to speak to Jim, the concierge of the building in which Admiral and Mrs Walters occupied the penthouse apartment. Jim, an ex-sailor, knew the Walters well. Both the Admiral and his wife in their eighties were still living there. After presenting his police identity, Jim was very forthcoming with information and gossip.

"What did you think of Ian Walters?" PC Bell asked him.

"He was an angry man craving attention, which no one gave him. After four years of living here, he changed jobs and took up a position at the University in Exeter, but the reason he left Portsmouth was because of an incident at the prison. He used to visit an inmate serving a life sentence for murder. He was his counsellor, and the man was due for release in months. The prisoner was found murdered soon after his visitor Ian Walters had ended his counselling meeting and

had left the prison. The killer was never found and no details
of his murder were made public. The police came here three
times. First they wanted a statement, then they wanted his
notes of his visits. Then they wanted to know about his job
as a Criminal Psychologist and any theories he might have
as to why this person he knew well might have been stabbed
to death. I got the feeling that the police who came here
thought he knew something he wasn't prepared to tell them.
He was not a very sociable man. I never had a conversation
with him about anything. That third visit persuaded him to
move away from Portsmouth."

"How did you get this information, Jim?"

"I know Admiral Walters. He was an admiral and I was
a Petty Officer. We're both Naval pensioners, but we are
still shipmates. He sits down here in the hall and talks to
me about all kinds, including his family. I occasionally see
his son when he visits his parents. Sometimes he stays over.
At Exeter University he replaced a retiree as the lecturer in
Criminal Jurisprudence, and continued to visit long-term
prisoners, principally murderers. There he wrote papers that
were circulated within his profession. As a criminal lawyer he
occasionally found himself confronted with a convict whom
he was convinced was innocent. Then he would arrange the
appeal process on their behalf, with Legal Aid lawyers, and
so on.

"In the West Country the Police and Prosecution Service
responsible for obtaining the conviction were not happy to
reopen a case and especially when a university lecturer was
meddling and trying to prove a point. The first time he tried
this with a prisoner the conviction was upheld, and he was
banned from continuing as a Prison visitor. He gained a bad
reputation with the Devon Constabulary and after a few
years he moved on."

"So he was no friend of the police?" said Bruno.

"Those incidents showed a concern for men who were

driven to kill. Murder was his special subject," said Jim. "I get most of my stuff on Ian from his parents, who are a lonely pair. I don't think he gives a toss about them really," he said. "No doubt he'll inherit their flat when they pass away."

After Devon Walters returned to London working as a criminal analyst for the Ministry of Justice and the Home Office producing data on which government ministers make decisions on prison, policing, sentencing and law changes.

Jim said he didn't recognise a compassionate need in Walters to help his fellow man and he hadn't worked out whose side he was on, or any purpose in what he does.

◆

Bruno was impressed with Kevin Bell's information source. He'd obtained more useful information from Jim the concierge at the apartment block about Walters than they had in each of their meetings. Jim's observations proved that they were dealing with the right person.

What Bruno did not have was anything about his personal life. Even when they called to see him at home, there was no suggestion of any other person in his life.

"So, what drives him?" said Andy.

"Ambition, insecurities, and after thirty years trying to be one step ahead of the criminal mind through his direct contact with them, he considers himself the expert. He's at the top of his profession and when you reach that level you try to prove or disprove accepted theories by experimenting."

Bruno believed that they knew with whom they were dealing, but he had not helped yet. Therefore he remained a person of interest and a person on the other side.

"Could this have been an opportunity for Walters to settle an old score with Klinker and at the same time use all of his experience to commit the unsolvable murder?" said Andy.

"He doesn't need an old score to settle," said Bruno. "And would he choose this place and this time?"

"His ego demands that, although a spectator, he is

involved. It takes place on an occasion where he is a participant, like the school trip. He has to be questioned as one of nine suspects."

"What is our next move with Walters?"

"We indulge him, tell him how we are getting on. He sees we are nowhere near ever making him a suspect, so he leads us in wrong directions whenever we give him the chance, whilst we try to walk in the killer's footsteps and recognise something unusual. There is always a pattern to serial murders. Just enough instrumental violence to kill."

"Why don't we tell him the truth about Haves and Mrs Galloway, the silver photo frame and let's see what he comes up with?"

"Good idea."

In an email to Walters, Andy told him what they found out from Arnold Harris about the Clive Hall setup whilst Madeline Klinker was alive.

Walters' prompt email reply was a simple instruction: "Find out what Mrs Galloway was up to on 8 June. You know that she had tea with Biff Haves at Clive Hall at 4.00 p.m., while he waited for Geoff Klinker to return for a beer to discuss farm business. You don't know her other movements on the 8th. They could have met at Havenstreet station at around 3.00 p.m. and murdered Klinker. You should let her know that you know she's been telling lies, and although the lies are not significant, they are character-defining. She's been living in a bubble you should burst. The photograph of them on holiday proves or suggests that Haves knows all about her, and both have a close tie to Clive Hall and the Klinker farm. It would be interesting to hear if Beale has a view on Haves and Galloway. I could not see Mrs Galloway accepting him as Haves' business partner."

◆

As the focus of Bruno's investigation switched, he still had to find Maisie Longmore, Klinker's wife or ex-wife. It was a peripheral enquiry but a victim's ex-wife might light up a dark corner in Bruno's investigation.

A call to Brenda Frampton, who'd promised to try and locate her, produced a negative response, but the call had awakened her promise to him, and he sensed a positive response from her soon. She had inside knowledge of the hospital management structures throughout the Health Service, so if Maisie Longmore was still working, that is where Bruno believed she would be found.

He felt Mrs Galloway's exposure had been the direct result of Janet's impromptu visit. She had clocked their picture on Scarborough Pier, and been present when he arrived for tea. "As if he owned the place," was her comment. Now, as Walters had suggested, was the time to burst her bubble and find out whether there was something in her activities on the afternoon of Friday 8 June that linked her to the location of the crime.

◆

By coincidence it was 3.30 p.m., time for tea, when Bruno and Andy called at Clive Hall. They had phoned in advance with a couple of questions and asked if it was convenient to call.

"Yes," she said, sounding not at all nervous at the detectives paying her another visit.

When they arrived, she had dressed for tea, looking years younger. In her mind there was no need to continue the pretence of the dowdy, downtrodden, hardworking housekeeper. Bruno recalled that on earlier visits she had been irritated at their sudden appearance, which they now took to be because she hadn't been warned of their arrival in enough time to spruce herself up.

It was not their intention to refer to the matters that had been brought to their attention by Janet or Arnold Harris. Andy opened the conversation by inferring that they had only come for her delicious tea, as if what they wanted to enquire of her had been thought up by him, to justify a visit for tea.

Bruno let Andy talk, and between mouthfuls of scone, jam and cream, he busily asked her to complete his record of their last visit by telling him what she did after Geoff Klinker left the house to go on his fatal school outing.

"After Geoff left at about 9.00 a.m. I watered the garden, swept the patio and made scones. I had prepared a light supper, poached salmon fillets for Geoff on his return. At around lunchtime I drove to Ryde, and parked in the High Street. It's one-hour free parking. I went to buy some toiletries and some cleaning materials. I went to Hurst's for a padlock, had soup and a roll in Greggs for lunch. I drove down to the Esplanade for an ice-cream and watched the hovercraft come in with day-trippers, sat in the sun watching the families paddling in the sea for about an hour, and then I came home. I often do more or less the same thing."

Knowing the geography of the Island well, Andy commented that Ryde was some distance from Clive Hall.

"That's quite a long drive to do some shopping?"

"Yes, Inspector, but Ryde is my home town, and the Esplanade is like my front garden. It's further than Newport, but it's more of an outing. I got back at 3.30 p.m. At about 4.00 p.m. Biff Haves arrived. He was here for about an hour. When Geoff didn't show, he went home."

"Okay, Mrs Galloway, I don't think we shall be troubling you again, except for one more question. Do you have any records of your purchases in Ryde?"

"I doubt it, it's three weeks ago," she said.

"But just for the record, you paid cash, then?"

"Of course," she said.

Bruno's opinion after her explanation of what she did in Ryde was that she could have easily have been at the Havenstreet station for the crucial part of the afternoon, namely between 2.45 and 3.30 p.m., and even have assisted Biff Haves in the murder of Geoff Klinker. But to link them both to this murder, they needed something else.

He believed that they were ploughing a legitimate furrow with Biff Haves' plan to purchase the farm by legal means.

"Smart, isn't she?" said Andy, as he drove his boss back to Newport Police Station.

"I am not sure," said Bruno. "She was relaxed and gave nothing away. We can think the same of her now as before we went. She told a story in which she could have been anywhere between 1.00 and 3.30 p.m. She likes you, though."

"That's because I like her scones."

"I noticed," said Bruno.

What he couldn't see was whether she had to be a suspect, so she and Haves remained persons of interest. Janet thought the latter and Walters was all for awarding them with the title of suspects, even principal suspects. Their position seemed to muddy the waters, and was not Bruno's intention. Clarity and evidence were what he was looking for, and he couldn't see that with Mrs Galloway.

⁂

Although he had not discovered a single piece of concrete evidence that would trap Klinker's murderer, after three weeks of hard work Bruno thought they were nearer to closing in on the killer by what they had eliminated. The tub full of lucky dip prizes was not empty, but nothing so far had given them that crucial piece of information. But there were still parcels to retrieve from the bottom of the tub that needed just a little more effort to pick out, one of which held the clue that had so far eluded them.

On top of his desk at the station was a message: "Please call Brenda Frampton", with a London telephone number.

She had acted immediately on Bruno's reminder of the previous day. To his delight, she had discovered that Maisie Longmore now held a senior management position in the most convenient location possible: Queen Alexandra's Hospital in Portsmouth.

He had thought she might have retired, as people who

work in the health service do at about fifty-five, which is about the age he guessed she would be. Having located her, he had to decide what he could gain by contacting her. It must have been years since she had been in touch with Geoff Klinker and as a bringer of bad news, he could only cause distress. Therefore he needed to be clear as to how she might help his investigation. He imagined that Brenda had not at first wanted to involve Klinker's estranged wife in his murder by disclosing her whereabouts.

With Maisie Longmore's contact details, she became a person of interest they needed to speak to, but not on a Friday afternoon.

On the list of outstanding actions was more detective work to be done on Kaz Ali. Andy Bowen reminded him of this, but he might not have done so it if he had realised that it would cause Bruno to drag him off to Portsmouth on a Friday evening.

"He disappeared from the 17.11 p.m. Portsmouth to Victoria train on Friday evening, somewhere between Portsmouth and Victoria. We have to make the journey at the same time and see what happens at each stop," said Bruno.

"As long as we make the journey at some time, would that do?"

"No, Friday is the end of the week and people travel differently on that day. Some are going away for the weekend. It is busier at different times. People take half-days or leave work earlier. We need to see it as it was."

"If he was flying back to Paris, why would he alight at any of the intermediary points?"

"We don't know, but he did not leave this train at Victoria."

"Assume he wasn't going back to Paris, at least not that evening. I think we need to look at the stops, the cameras – where there are cameras – and where he could have left the train unseen. We know the time of the train he caught, and we know which stops the 17.11 p.m. train from Portsmouth makes on Friday evening. We'll go and look at the station layouts."

To examine the mystery of his train journey, and as it was late Friday afternoon, they sped across to Ryde hovercraft terminal and caught the 16.20 p.m. to Southsea in time to take a taxi to Portsmouth Harbour, and catch the 17.11 p.m. to Victoria, alight at Havant and consider the possibility that Ali had also done so.

At Portsmouth Harbour station, the CCTV cameras showed all persons departing on the 17.11 p.m. train to Victoria on the evening of Friday 8 June, and at Havant station all passengers who left the train at Havant at 17.20 p.m.

The 17.11 p.m. was a commuter train, bringing back people who work in Portsmouth. It was also taking people to London and stations in between for the weekend. A surprising large number of passengers alighted the train at Havant Platform 1, which was covered by cameras along the entire platform, and showed everybody who exited the station through the ticket barrier. In an examination of passengers boarding the 4.00 p.m. hovercraft to Southsea on Friday 8 June, a clear image was visible of Kaz Ali, an Indian gentleman in dark sunglasses. No person leaving the train at Havant bore that image. It was a sunny day and a number of passengers were dressed in T-shirts and shorts and wore sunglasses, but no passengers leaving the train bore any resemblance to the Kaz Ali who boarded the hovercraft at Ryde. Footage from the camera showing the passengers leaving the station confirmed the footage on the platform, so they assumed he had remained on the train and he had continued his journey to Victoria and on to Heathrow en route to Paris.

Bruno wasn't able to extend his investigation to Mumbai to chase down Kaz Ali, or send his willing assistant Andy Bowen. So, for now, he assumed that the bona fide Kaz Ali had attended the reunion and, as cameras were not infallible, that he'd returned to Paris or some other pre-designated destination via Victoria.

Andy Bowen had a different take, which was based on the speed of his departure from the Island, and then from Portsmouth to somewhere. If an airport was not his destination it was somewhere in the south of England where the sudden appearance on the TV or internet of a murder on the Isle of Wight could not cause those around him to associate him with it. That implied that he was a temporary visitor to this area who had slipped back into his normal surroundings and social environment, which could be anywhere, but more likely to be local.

Although his departure from the Island had been swift, it was no more so than the others who all cleared off pretty quickly once they'd had their afternoon tea and said their goodbyes. Ali's departure itself was not a cause for suspicion. The hovercraft and train timetables dictated the rest of his journey.

Bruno had suggested that Andy Bowen ask Marion Hislop to send an email to Kaz Ali's Mumbai address. This, they hoped, would confirm his email address in Mumbai, as Kevin Bell had received it.

✦

There was one more item on Bruno's list of actions marked urgent, which was to call Maisie Longmore at Queen Alexandra's Hospital in Portsmouth. She was fortunately at work and reception put Bruno through to her direct line.

After introducing himself, she said that she was expecting his call because Brenda Frampton had told her that Detective Inspector Bruno Peach, of the Isle of Wight Police, would be calling. She had communicated the dreadful news about Dr Klinker to her.

"Brenda was concerned the she'd given my details to the police."

"Did she say why I want to see you?"

"She said you would explain. But that my husband Geoffrey had died tragically."

"That's right, Miss Longmore, but the details can wait until I see you face-to-face. Can we meet on Monday?"

"Of course, you know where I am."

"I will arrive at 11.00 a.m. on Monday at your office and I shall have my colleague Detective Sergeant Andy Bowen with me."

Bruno had thought that Brenda Frampton had Maisie Longmore's contact details, as they were old friends. They were two more people with an intimate knowledge of Dr Klinker.

"Before we go," said Bruno, "I want some photographs of the school party on the day, that means asking the group to copy us in on any pictures taken by members of the group of each other, particularly a picture of Kaz Ali."

This would mean a busy Saturday morning for Andy and Kevin Bell.

CHAPTER 19

Monday 2 July

Surprise, surprise, early on Monday there was a reply, which Marion sent across to Andy Bowen. It read as follows:

My dear Miss Hislop,

When my father, Kaz Ali, who is ninety years of age, replied to your earlier letter, he did confirm visiting Ryde School between 1978 and 1984. It was to take my brother Kaz aged thirteen to join the school as a pupil, and I know that regularly when he was returning to England on business, he would travel down to see Kaz there. Our business is importing machinery from Europe. You refer to an invitation to attend a reunion at the school which my father does not remember as it was probably intended for Kaz, who currently lives in Paris at 13 Rue de Petit Pont, 75005 Paris 5. Please try his Paris address and if you fail to find him come back to me.

Yours sincerely,

Hari Ali.

"So, Paris it is," said Andy Bowen to Bruno. "There and back in one day on Eurostar." But today, they first had to cross the Solent.

◈

Bruno had previously visited the Queen Alexandra Hospital in Portsmouth on police business, so he knew it was a 20-minute taxi journey from Clarence Pier hovercraft terminal. At 11.00 a.m. Maisie Longmore had cleared her desk and was waiting for the arrival of the two detectives.

Her position at the hospital was Chief Executive – in other words, the boss – with over thirty years' experience, running NHS hospitals, and it showed through the behaviour of the staff towards her. Her office was typical of the senior executive manner she projected. They sat across from her in a comfortable meeting area to the side of her desk, with tea and coffee available from flasks.

"Inspector, please tell me all you can about my dear Geoffrey."

"Can I begin by asking your relationship with him?"

"He was my husband. We were married just thirty years ago. Although we have not lived together for twenty years, neither of us wanted to divorce. I am Roman Catholic and we were married in the Catholic Church. Geoffrey never asked me for a divorce out of respect for the vows we took together. He knew that for me it would be hard to break them. Had I asked him for a divorce, I know he'd have granted my wish."

"The sad news, Miss Longmore, is that he was murdered on the afternoon of 8 June on the Isle of Wight."

"Oh dear," she said. "Poor man." And before she shed a tear, she said, "Please excuse me," and got up and left the office, to a room out of sight. She was gone for twenty minutes, and when she returned she was watery eyed but fully composed.

"I am sorry to have left you so long, but Father Jerry came straight over. He was in a ward nearby and we prayed together for his soul in peace.

"I have not seen Geoff for some time, so I don't think I can help you at all in your search for the murderer. I don't know any of his colleagues or his family. I only know he is well through Brenda, who I speak to every three or four weeks, we are old friends. I knew her when we worked together many, many years ago. That is when he met her.

"Is it possible for me to arrange for a priest to visit the place he is lying in rest? I am assuming he has not been buried? I want a priest to say a prayer with him. It is important to me, Inspector."

"I can arrange that, Miss Longmore, if you tell me a day and time."

"Can you tell me where he is?"

"He is in the mortuary at St Mary's Hospital in Newport on the Island."

"Would tomorrow morning at 10.00 a.m. be all right?"

"I will arrange to be there myself, just to make sure," said Bruno. "Is there anything else you would like to know from me?"

"Inspector, I will have to think this through, and now I know the circumstances of his death, talk to Brenda. The news that someone has killed my husband is so devastating, I do not want to know anything more at this time."

"Miss Longmore, at the moment we have a number of suspects. We've come to see you in case there was something you can recall about someone, even if it was a long time ago, that could help us. Was there a colleague, or a person he might have fallen out with?"

She sat and thought for a brief time, on the edge of an emotional moment. Containing her emotions, she stood up and led them out of her office, saying goodbye with a wave, leaving her secretary to phone for a taxi to take them back to the hovercraft.

◆

Back at the station Andy Bowen confirmed an appointment for Mrs Geoffrey Klinker, accompanied by a priest to visit the body of Geoff Klinker at the St Mary's Hospital mortuary the following morning at 10.00 a.m.

Seeing Kaz Ali now became Bruno's priority since he'd learned of his residency in Paris. It had confirmed his existence and the story he had told his school friends about living in Paris. That he had disappeared off the radar during his return journey from the Island did not seem important. Nevertheless, he was still wanted urgently for questioning in connection with the Havenstreet murder. Confirmation of his existence had not absolved him of his part in the police investigation and the need for him to be seen. However, for two detectives to travel to France to interview a potential murder suspect, who was not a European national, required permission from a higher authority than Bruno's. To do it on the quiet, by travelling to France on Eurostar, could create difficulties if they were to decide that Kaz Ali should be brought to the UK for questioning under caution.

After listening to Bruno's pitch, Johnny Barlow realised that their investigation was slowing down and they were desperate for a breakthrough, so he could not reject their request to go through official channels, which involved the International Police Division requesting the French police to visit Ali at the address provided, and arrange an interview with Ali for the UK police officers in Paris. This process was started once Bruno passed Ali's details to his Superintendent, who said they would set up a meeting with Ali in Paris as soon as possible.

◈

The only interest of Jenkins, the manager of the Havenstreet railway, had been to silence all discussion and behave as if it never happened, which had stopped employees on the spot on the day from coming forward with even the slightest comment or observation. Jenkins made fear-inducing comments like "Do you really want to become involved in a murder enquiry?" to a member of the restaurant staff who had seen two of the school party visit the Gents' lavatory at the same time.

However, Bruno decided it was time to revisit the murder site with Andy Bowen and re-create the scene of the murder. After three weeks, somebody might have remembered a small incident they had not previously thought relevant or mentioned.

From a number of phone calls on Sunday to members of the school party, Andy had obtained photographs of the reunion that had been delivered to the station on Monday morning. These were mostly of the rolling stock, and the countryside, and although Ali appeared in three of the photos, they were side-on or showing his back. It gave some indication he was there, but was not a full frontal.

They arrived at the busy Havenstreet Station just after 2.00 p.m. and in spite of Jenkins's hostility, informed him that they were going to re-create the murder for the benefit of the staff who were broadly the same as on the afternoon of 8 June. They would ask them to come forward with anything that happened, not just an unusual incident, but anything they recalled at that particular time. There were seven members of staff that Andy Bowen briefed about the incident. Between 3.00 and 3.30 p.m. they assisted Bruno and Andy to re-create the murder scene, as it was on the day, which they stated would be at precisely 3.10 p.m., the estimated time of the murder. Anything at all that they remembered leading up to 3.10 p.m. and afterwards, until 3.30 p.m., would be of interest.

Andy arranged for the platform guard to place the usual toilet out-of-order signs either side of the Gents' lavatory for the designated 30 minutes and retired to the cafeteria with Andy at 3.00 p.m., occupying a part of the café that the school party had occupied. Five staff were involved in witnessing the reconstruction, the same five who were on duty on 8 June. Three in the restaurant, the ice-cream sales lady who had a clear view of the Gents' lavatory door from the sun covered ice-cream kiosk, and the platform guard who had been keeping the waiting passengers clear of the platform edge.

Andy, acting as "the victim", sat facing Bruno as he could exit the café unseen by Bruno, who sat facing the exit door. At exactly 3.09 p.m. he stood up and made his way to the exit door. Five seconds later, and perhaps fifteen paces behind Andy, Bruno stood up and followed him at the same pace along the platform and into the Gents' lavatory. Ninety seconds after following Andy into the Gents', Bruno emerged and stepped behind the small brick building and out of sight at the back of the lavatory. Through the open window he simulated securing the bolt that prevented anyone from entering the lavatory. Bruno returned alone to the café and sat quietly until at 3.30 p.m. when Andy returned. The detectives agreed to return at 6.00 p.m. when the café closed to discuss the re-creation of the incident which they assume led up to the killing.

They spoke to Jenkins about any thoughts he might have about the murder since they'd last met. He had nothing constructive to contribute and he transmitted the feeling to both detectives that the last thing he wanted was for the police to find the killer who would go on trial and attract a mass of negative publicity to the Isle of Wight Steam Railway.

At café closing time, the five staff who'd witnessed the simulation and John Jenkins assembled in the café where Andy Bowen provided them with drinks before turning to the main event of the afternoon. They had all thought very carefully about the staging they had witnessed.

Mary Samuel, one of the volunteers, was the first to speak.

"I remember when they all got off the train, some of the men went to the Gents', but three or four did not. They collected tea from me and a slice of cake. The two men that you were replicating sat at different tables whilst everyone had returned and were taking tea and cake. After 10 minutes the first gentlemen stood up and spoke to one of the others in the party, and said something like, 'I will be right back.' As he left another gentlemen followed him out. I don't remember either coming back, I presume one of them did, but I didn't see them come back."

"Can you remember the appearance of the two gentlemen who left one after the other soon after they had all taken tea?"

"Well the first gentleman was tall and one of the most

elegant, a real gentleman, they were all gentlemen really. The second man wore a smart suit too."

"Could you identify him?"

"I think so, Inspector."

"Thank you very much, Mary, that helps a great deal."

The other two ladies in the restaurant had been serving the tea and cake to the school party and others who had come in for tea and were mingling about and did not see either man leave the restaurant. Jackie on the ice-creams, situated on the entrance to the café, also recalled two men leaving the café one after another and going into the Gents' 20 metres away. She didn't remember seeing either of them come back.

"There is just one more thing that I would ask Mary and Jackie to consider. We have a few photographs that were taken by the school party, and I would like you to look at them and see if the two gentlemen you saw go to the Gents' lavatory are in the pictures," said Andy as he laid out the photographs he'd been given. He let the ladies study them for a short time. Both Mary and Jackie identified Geoff Klinker as the leading man, and also, they were both fairly sure that the gentleman in the dark blue suit was the man who followed Klinker into the lavatory.

"Ladies you have been most helpful. Thank you for staying behind and recalling the afternoon for us. We are having some difficulty getting to the bottom of this tragic event, but your input has been invaluable. Finally, grateful thanks to Mr Jenkins for setting aside the time to be present whilst we re-created the crime scene."

◆

On the way back to the station Bruno was elated. Both ladies had told them what they needed to know.

"Now we must see what Kaz Ali can add to our investigation."

"What about Jenkins?"

"He is just worried about the negative image a murder might have on his business."

"It could be a positive image like Agatha Christie's *Murder on The Orient Express*," said Andy. "Everyone wants to travel on it."

"That was fiction," said Bruno.

"Don't you think more people will come her when this story gets out?"

"Murder in the Havenstreet Steam Railway Gents' lavatory? I don't know."

CHAPTER 20

Tuesday 3 July

While Andy reported in to the station to get them to chase the French police about interviewing Ali in Paris, Bruno arrived at St Mary's Hospital in Newport to meet Maisie Longmore and Father James, a Catholic priest from her local Catholic church, St Mary's in Ryde. While he said prayers in the private ceremony in the presence of Maisie and the body of Geoff Klinker, Bruno stood away from the couple and out of earshot of the whispered prayers from Father James.

Their blessings took fifteen minutes and afterwards in the hospital reception Bruno spoke to Maisie Longmore, who asked only when it would be possible for her to bury Geoff Klinker, informing Bruno that it was her duty as his wife to arrange that.

Bruno then asked her to contact Walter Brown, the Ryde solicitor, with proof of her position as Geoffrey's wife, so their probate investigation could proceed in the correct manner. If she had an independent solicitor, she should also instruct him to act for her, on the basis that Walter Brown were proving the value of the estate for the Revenue. She promised to do that.

Bruno replied that he did not know when the Coroner would release the body but would find out and tell her. With that she left with Father James to return to where she had come from. He would have welcomed a conversation with her but it was not the occasion and not with a priest and it could wait. He didn't know if Geoff Klinker was Catholic, but her visit with a priest comforted her and satisfied her wish to honour the man who had deserted her. Having been married to a man who by general consent was the last person on earth anyone might want to murder, it must have come as a great shock to her. With a little time, she might find something that could help his investigation. Her appearance at this stage of the investigation and her beneficial claim over the Klinker estate, if any, would put the cat amongst the pigeons.

◆

Back at the station Andy had been successful with the French police who had spoken to Kaz Ali at the address he had given them, and they could arrange an interview in Paris at short notice. For Bruno and Andy that meant the next day. The Gendarmerie in Paris set up a meeting at their headquarters for 12.00 noon and Andy got his wish, a journey, on the 7.20 a.m. Eurostar from St Pancras non-stop to the Gare du Nord in the centre of Paris.

CHAPTER 21

Wednesday 4 July

From the Gare du Nord it was two stops on the RER to Cité, the headquarters of the French Police unit and location of the meeting.

Kaz Ali's willingness to meet British police on French soil surprised them. If he were suspected of killing Klinker, Bruno would have to provide irrefutable evidence to convince a French court to extradite Ali back to the UK to be formally charged, which they did not yet have. An inconclusive sideways shot from a cheap camera, showing that he was present at the school party outing, was not enough. They were relying on a contradiction in his story and his recollection of the events on the day to trap him.

The gendarmes wore smart uniforms and two remained standing in the room during the interview. Two other French officials were introduced to Bruno and Andy before Kaz Ali entered the room. Monsieur Astor was a French lawyer experienced in French extradition procedure, he spoke good English. They restated the position of Kaz Ali, inspected the English arrest warrant, which Bruno had obtained should justification unfold, and very pleasantly said, "Gentlemen we are ready when you are, we are just observers to ensure that any outcome is consistent with French law."

"Detective Inspector Peach, there is another matter of which I am sure you are aware. That is, Monsieur Kaz Ali is an Indian citizen. His country would oppose any application by a foreign jurisdiction to drag one of their citizens back to stand trial for murder in the UK, however solid the evidence you may have."

When Kaz Ali entered he was not what the British detectives expected. He could not have behaved less like a murderer. He was expensively, smartly dressed, wearing a jacket and tie, polished shoes and smiled warmly.

"Good afternoon gentlemen," he said. "You have come from the Isle of Wight. I went to school on the Island, and I have fond memories of my time there. I understand that you wish to speak to me about the murder of one of my good friends, Dr Geoffrey Klinker. How can I help you?"

They all sat before Bruno started.

"We'd like you to tell us of your movements on the day he was murdered, namely Friday 8 June."

Ali was well-spoken in a good English public school manner.

"To put your minds at rest gentlemen, or," he said with a smile on his face, "to blow a hole in your suspicion that I might be involved or even committed the murder of Geoffrey, I was in Paris throughout the entire day. I left my apartment in Rue Petit Pont at 8.00 a.m. and walked across the Pont Neuf to my office in the Rue de Rivoli. I do it every day and it takes 20 minutes. I arrive around 9 o'clock with a coffee. I carry it up from Starbucks in the arcade at street level, with a warm croissant, a French habit I acquired many years ago. I was not alone in my office. I have a personal assistant, an engineer, and two computer operators. My office is the purchasing department for Ali & Co. We import machinery from several European companies and export to India. With our location in Paris and the euro as our currency, these give us advantages we need, as most of our equipment comes from Germany. I won't go further about our business. That is not what you want to know.

"I was invited to a reunion two or three months ago, but we are busy in our office in the summer. Travelling is so much easier now so members of my family come to Europe in June and July. As a result, a visit to my old school to see people I have not seen or spoken to, in some cases since I left Ryde, was a trip I could not justify.

"I am truly sorry about Geoff because I did keep in touch with him and whenever I was in London. I'd give him a call, and we would dine together and catch up. He was a marvellous surgeon, so I hear, I am so sad to think that somebody thought so badly of him."

Bruno began by describing the time and place of the murder, and the gruesome violence suffered by the victim. Ali was silent and visibly shocked.

"Mr Ali, a person purporting or claiming to be you attended the school reunion, who we believe could be responsible for killing Dr Klinker. Can you provide evidence that you were in Paris on the 8 June between the hours of noon and late afternoon? Is that possible?"

"There are several things in my office that recorded my activities during that time."

"Perhaps we can see those before we leave?"

"Yes, that can be arranged, Inspector."

"Is there anyone you know who might want to put the blame for this murder on to you?"

"I can't think of anyone, Inspector. If I travel through the archive of my mind, I would never come up with someone who would try to frame me for a murder on the Isle of Wight. It is unbelievable."

At this point Bruno produced the two photographs showing a partial picture in profile of the man who pretended to be Kaz Ali on the day.

"Can you recognise this man?" he said pointing to the man in the suit that the ladies identified as following Klinker into the Gents' lavatory.

Ali studied the two pictures.

"We might be the same height, but I am at least twenty pounds heavier. He's about the same age, he dyes his hair and, in that light, he looks like an Indian gentleman. What is his reason for impersonating me?"

"Is he an Indian gentleman?"

"He looks like he could be," said Ali. "But not someone I know."

"But he is someone who knows you?" said Bruno. "And he knew you were not going to the school reunion."

"So, who could that be?"

"The payment for your attendance at the reunion was made in Paris, and if it was not you, it was someone who was sure of your whereabouts on that day. If they do not live in Paris, they came to Paris to make the payment, phoned the school secretary, although a phone call could have come from anywhere confirming that he would be attending the reunion. That suggests somebody in Paris is trying to frame you for Klinker's murder."

"It does, Inspector, if you believe my impersonator is your killer."

"Would he impersonate you for a different reason?"

"It's a mystery to me, Inspector, and somewhat far-fetched."

"Tell us about your occasional visits to London when you used to meet Klinker socially. You are the only one of his schoolmates who had any contact with him. When was the last time you met?"

"November last year. If I stay one night we dine at the Oxford and Cambridge Club, where I stay. If I stay two nights, the second night we dine at the Travellers Club nearby. I visit England because we buy equipment from two companies in the midlands."

"How do you travel to London?"

"I fly from Paris Charles-de-Gaulle to Heathrow and then by train to Paddington. What we had in common was the opera and the theatre, so sometimes we went to the Royal Opera House."

Bruno's interrogation of Kaz Ali was becoming a chat about an old friend. To get it back on track he asked him if there was anyone in his circle of Paris friends who would want to set him up.

His answer was, "Definitely not! It would be absurd. My French friends are totally unconnected with the UK or aware of my schooling in the UK. Inspector, the impersonator is a person who knew I wasn't going on the reunion and pretended to be me, not through any connection. He was also a person who knew the location like the back of his hand, so to speak, that seems obvious to me. But did he commit the murder? You've not convinced me about that, Inspector.

"If you have finished the interview, I will take you on a short walk to my office, and you can see my diary for 8 June."

Having run out of avenues to explore with Ali, and embarrassed by the suggestion that the mystery impersonator need not necessarily have murdered Klinker, Bruno was pleased with the offer of an honourable escape, but not before signing forms of a satisfactory outcome where no charges were made or were pending against Kaz Ali.

It was a short walk to the offices of Ali & Co. It was not the modest place Ali had described. It was a reception, comfortably furnished, which led into a similarly comfortable open plan layout. There were five people working at desks, three ladies and two young men. The men were Indian in appearance. It was to one of them that Ali addressed his question.

"Can you print from my diary my activities for 8 June this year?"

To Bruno he explained, "I haven't the faintest idea how it works, but everything I do is recorded in my diary page on the computer. Ayam can give you a copy. So, are you going back to London now?"

"Not straight away," said Andy. "I don't know Paris, so with my boss's permission I'd like to see at least one famous site, like the Eiffel Tower," said Andy.

"If you look out of this window you can see it, on the other side of the river, three kilometres away."

Ayam appeared with a computer printout of Ali's diary on 8 June, which he gave to Ali, who studied it for a minute then passed it to Bruno. Until noon he had received three calls, wrote three emails to named customers and left for lunch with Herr Block, a German sales representative from Siemens in Hamburg. At 3.00 p.m. he had sent an email to Herr Block, thanking him for a splendid lunch at the Tuileries Garden restaurant, and confirming an order dated 8 June for a Digiset 350, to be despatched to Chennai on the 8 September. Some pricing data was given, with shipping information and finally as further proof of his presence in Paris on the afternoon of 8 June he authorised a transfer of €100,000 to Siemens in Hamburg as a deposit on machinery ordered. The bank transfer was timed at 16.27.

Bruno was happy that his presence in Paris had been confirmed by an unconnected party. He passed the printout back to Ali, who didn't take it. Instead he said, 'Keep it for your records, Inspector.'

It was approaching 1.00 p.m. and he said, "I am sorry I cannot offer you lunch, gentlemen, but I have a meeting shortly. I hope I have been of help today. I have certainly tried. On a sad note if I could attend Geoff's funeral, whenever it is, I would like to."

"I'll make a note," said Bruno. "And thank you for seeing us so promptly."

They shook hands and he showed them to the exit. At the cab rank outside Bruno hailed a Mercedes taxi.

In the cab he spoke in perfect French to the driver: "*La Tour Eiffel, s'il vous plaît,*" then said to Andy, "I've never been up the Eiffel Tower either. I've worked out as long as we're on the 7.20 p.m. from Gare du Nord we'll be in time for the last train to Pompey and the ferry. We gain an hour going back."

The line of visitors waiting to ascend to the first stage was just a 10-minute wait. Ascending to the first stage provided a sensational view of the city from four sides. On this clear day was all the way to the horizon, about eight miles in each direction. At 1.25 p.m. lunch was still be being served and that was what interested Bruno. Over a table in the window, facing The Tuileries gardens, the Champs Elysées and the Arc de Triomphe, they enjoyed the full menu and a bottle of French château-bottled red wine.

"Andy, this lunch is on me and then we have all afternoon to enjoy Paris. We'll visit Notre Dame, the Latin Quarter, the Île St Louis and, if we have time, a river trip. The metro takes 20 minutes to the Gare du Nord."

"You've obviously done this before, sir?"

"Yes, I brought a lady to Paris once, some time ago. Today I regard as a win, we've eliminated Kaz Ali, and we are searching for an Islander, who has full knowledge of Ryde School and has the bottle and skill to impersonate an Indian gentleman, with a reason to kill Klinker. Ali said the impersonator need not necessarily be the killer. It would be weird if he wasn't," said Bruno.

"It comes back to the school party?" said Andy.

"It is something to think about, but not now," said Bruno. "Let's enjoy lunch. The French will, and I will show you something of Paris on the way home."

Andy was truly impressed with his boss and his knowledge of Paris. After lunch Bruno took Andy on a whistle-stop tour of the Left Bank, starting with the Panthéon, in which revered French authors were buried, the last one in recent times was Alexander Dumas. Then they went to Notre Dame cathedral and saw the cathedral treasures, and at the Petit Pont caught the river launch to see Paris from the river Seine.

It was then just after 18.00 and time for a taxi back to the Gare du Nord for the 19.20 to St Pancras.

Bruno had satisfied his young assistant's curiosity about the world's most beautiful city, and whetted his appetite for a return visit.

They had also eliminated Ali from their list of persons of interest and set about the task of finding his impersonator.

Everything went as clockwork on their return journey, and they arrived in Ryde at 11.59 p.m. and shared a taxi to Newport arranging to meet mid-morning.

Between a shower, cup of tea and bed, Bruno gave Janet her daily update, setting her the task of finding a solution.

He had reached one of those, "Where do we go from here?" moments. He did not feel that he was far away from finding the killer, but since 8 June, after all the questioning and interviews, nothing had been said by anyone that opened up the case.

Although Bruno was tired and it had been a very long day, he was never of a mind to shut Janet up when she was raring to go.

She had waited all day for this debrief. "Let me look at those photos of the group showing the man posing as Ali," she said.

He took them out of his bag and gave them to her.

After she had studied them for a few minutes, she said, "We know this man is not Ali, but he must have met him and known something about him, enough to get by in a quick chat with a group who'd been at school with him forty years ago. None of those who attended the reunion have said they did not think it was him. If someone had suspected it was not the genuine person, during the day and after lunch and a generous wine consumption, they might have mentioned it amongst themselves or certainly to you during your investigation.

"If they had spoken to him, blown his cover, he could have laughed it off, called off his murder and gone home. But nobody did, so he is a good actor and must have been very pleased with his performance. It would have swelled his ego. All he had to do then was kill Klinker in the pre-arranged place and vanish. So, we are looking for a tallish man, immaculately dressed, an Indian or someone disguised as an Indian gentleman, familiar with the Island, who wanted Klinker dead. And these photographs prove that none of the others were involved, and that includes Haves and Mrs Galloway. It was an outrageous stunt that was executed by somebody who fled back to the mainland. So we know who we are looking for, Bruno," she said, having summarised the situation so precisely.

This left him with the $64,000 question: who *was* he looking for? He would think about that tomorrow.

CHAPTER 22

Thursday 5 July

Nevertheless, when he met Andy in the morning their first act was an examination of what everyone had said, of whom one of the principal contributors had been Janet, who had lain awake listening to his report of his meeting with Kaz Ali. He'd agreed with Andy that another attempt at tracing the movements of his impersonator from the time he boarded the 17.11 Portsmouth to Victoria train on 8 June, was a starting point and more might be gained from a second visit.

Andy was certain that the moment he had escaped the Island in the hovercraft he would use the first opportunity to shed his Indian persona and resume his natural identity so as not to leave a trail. Once aboard the train at Portsmouth he would cease to be Kaz Ali. His next move would be to get off the train as soon as possible breaking the physical connection with Kaz Ali. If Andy's analysis was correct, this meant that he was one of the passengers who got off the train at Havant, less his disguise.

"So that's were we start, by looking at the people who left the train at Havant. If we can identify a lookalike, then we can trace his movements from there."

◈

At Havant station the manager was ready and had set up a screen for a frame-by-frame look at everyone who got off the 17.11 from Portsmouth.

Ignoring the children and females, they looked at every man who passed through the exit gate. If their journey ended there, the machine retained their ticket.

They studied each male one by one and no one resembled the physique of the man in their photograph. It took five minutes in elapsed time for all the passengers to pass by and somewhat longer to examine them without spotting the physique they were looking for.

"Let's carry on until the next batch of passengers pass through. Remember our suspect is disassociating himself with the 17.11. He might delay his exit and mingle with the passengers leaving the next train."

Amongst those who disembarked from the 17.23 from Portsmouth was a passenger that resembled the physique they were looking for, except that he was not dressed as Kaz Ali had been when boarding the 17.11. He carried a Sainsbury's plastic shopping bag. He wore a white floppy hat, appropriate for the weather, and sunglasses. He was either dark skinned or wearing make-up, and his shirt sleeves were rolled up. He was not recognisable as a person they knew.

"That's him!" said Andy. "That is our Kaz Ali."

He passed thorough the ticket barrier, nose to tail, with the other passengers off the 17.23 train.

"If he is Kaz Ali, then the person with the plastic bag did not board the train at Portsmouth."

"We have to be sure of that," said Bruno.

"He went to the lavatory," said Andy. "To set himself right and to break the 17.11 connection."

"So, we've spotted somebody who looks physically like our suspect. But where did he go from the concourse at Havant?"

They downloaded images of the passengers showing their suspected murderer, then Bruno and Andy left the platform.

"Let's walk around," said Andy. "And see where you can go to from here. My guess is he'd want to get away from here as quickly as possible leaving no connection or trace."

"To go where?" said Bruno. "Back to the Island?"

"Possibly," said Andy.

So far, he had done remarkably well, his assumptions proving correct. There were four options at Havant, a bus, a taxi, a car or to walk.

A bus, but to where? A taxi, likewise and traceable. So it had to be a car.

"So, he'd have parked some place early and joined the commuters to Portsmouth, caught the ferry to Ryde, and then a taxi to Havenstreet."

"Except that we think he's an Islander?" said Andy.

"Do we?" said Bruno. "If the murderer is an Islander this Havant jaunt does not make sense. Perhaps the bogus Kaz Ali had no intention of returning to the Island that evening? Having vanished into thin air on the Portsmouth to Victoria train it was mission accomplished, and he could assume his proper identity and return to the Island anytime."

"We'll have to come back to that. Let's look at all the places he could have parked a car."

It did not take long. The car park had an hourly charge with increasing rates up to a 24-hour charge. Outside the station yellow and double yellow lines stretched as far as one could see. The side streets, undoubtedly the place to park, would have filled up early.

"He would have chosen to park in the car park, because he would not risk his car being stolen or removed for parking in a restricted area."

"So how can we make a check on car registrations?"

"There might be a camera recording cars in and out. Let's find out from Universal Car Parks, who run the parking. But first, let's have some coffee at the station and check the Gents' lavatory," said Bruno.

He felt that Andy was on to this suspect so he'd go along with him, as so far he'd proved right.

While he ordered the coffee and two bacon rolls, Andy got through to Universal Car Parks, where mention of his name and rank escalated his call to a manager who could answer his question and who explained this car park offers 30 minutes free to all customers. That meant you could see persons off and on trains, without paying for parking. You got a ticket by punching in your car registration number, then inserting cash or credit card up to 24 hours. Your registration was printed on your ticket, you put it on your dash, and that's it.

"Okay," said Andy. "So, the machine prints the reg number on the parking ticket. Does it retain a record if these registration numbers?"

"It has a memory for up to one month."

"If we provide you with a registration number, could you confirm if that car was parked in that car park on a certain date?"

"Up to one month, Inspector."

"How many tickets does the machine issue in one day?"

"Some days over one hundred others it might be twenty," the UCP manager said.

"Thank you," said Andy. "I will come back to you."

He noted his name and direct line and he believed, with some work, they could link one of the cars to the bogus Ali.

"If the machine recorded all the plates on 8 June, then we look for an Island plate."

"Say our man hired a car?" said Bruno.

"Then we trace him through the hire, sir. If we identify the bogus Kaz Ali, we have our man," said Andy.

"As long as the man doesn't have a cast-iron alibi?" said Bruno.

"We shall see, but not a watertight one."

"Universal said they would let us have the records for 8 June once they have an official police request. I'll do that from the station, sir," said Andy.

Bruno's weekly activity report was positive that he had cleared up the Kaz Ali disappearance conundrum, and released him from suspicion during their visit to France. Bruno had, however, not yet ruled out the possibility that the man they'd not yet identified scurrying away from Havant Railway station might be innocent of murder.

It had been a busy afternoon in the café on the 8 June, and although two ladies witnessed two gentlemen from the school party follow Klinker towards the Gents' lavatory, a different incident could have occurred.

◈

"Klinker could have been followed into the Gents' by any-one, and Ali's impersonator could have walked on by. If you exclude him and Walters you are back to square one, but not quite," said Janet, whilst she listened to his day's findings over supper.

"I can't see the point of Havant unless you're going to a mainland location, and Havant to Guildford, or Southamp-ton, seems more logical. The combination of two taxi rides, a hovercraft and a mainland rail journey, a parking issue, as well as the game of impersonating an Indian businessman is not what an Island murderer would do. Don't you think this could be a set-up to make it look like it is a mainlander?"

"I don't know," said Bruno.

"Tomorrow is Friday and I am taking my parents to Shanklin Theatre to see a play performed by Ryde Amateur Theatrical Company. It's called *Separate Tables* by Terence Rattigan. Have you seen it?"

"No," said Bruno.

"Well I've seen it at the Playhouse Theatre in Leeds with my parents ten years ago. I think you'll like it. Get your mind off Klinker for a few hours."

Bruno enjoyed Janet's attempts to broaden his mind. One of the hazards of his profession was that it absorbed every waking hour, shutting out intellectually challenging pastimes.

CHAPTER 23

Friday 6 July

Andy was already working on the registration number list that had been received at the station from Universal Car Parks first thing.

There were 437 parking tickets issued on 8 June from two ticket machines. Season ticket holders had a windscreen badge and were not included. Andy had excluded tickets timed after 9.00 a.m. for less than eight hours, on the basis that our suspect could not have got to the reunion in Havenstreet in time. It left 27 tickets for vehicles that had parked by 9.00 a.m. for periods beyond 6.30 p.m., for which he'd requested ownership details from the DVLA.

When Bruno called Brenda Frampton to inform her of his meeting with Maisie Longmore, she said, "Maisie was coming to stay on Saturday to commiserate with me as we were both close to Geoffrey. She will want me to help with the funeral arrangements."

The existence of Maisie Longmore, or Mrs Geoffrey Klinker, changed the game for many of the participants in this murder enquiry, and it would be interesting to see the effect on members of the family.

❖

Before their visit to Shanklin Theatre, Bruno entertained Janet's parents, Jack and Lorna Windsor, to a pre-theatre dinner at Pavarotti's Italian restaurant in Shanklin. Lily, the Sardinian owner, had often served him an enjoyable meal whenever he visited his mother in Shanklin. It was an authentic Italian restaurant where the entire family, her chef husband and three sons, were involved in the business. Janet's father was a former Yorkshire bank employee with a generous index-linked pension. He was dull with a banker's brain and with Island bus passes. They lived well in a modern bungalow, a mile's walk from Janet's new home in Newport. They were happy that their daughter had met someone, although for no reason Bruno could determine, Jack always gave the impression that he had to be cautious in the company of a police inspector, where the opposite was true. It was Bruno who tended to be cautious in the presence of this Yorkshireman, with his eyes that could see right through you. Janet did not disclose her ulterior motive in bringing Bruno to the theatre on a Friday evening, which they normally reserved for themselves and where they dined at their favourite seafood restaurant. This she kept to herself, anticipating it would prove her instinct correct and reveal itself to Bruno during the play.

Separate Tables had been a stage hit in London in the mid-1950s, and as a film starring Rita Hayworth, Burt Lancaster, Deborah Kerr and David Niven. It takes place in a small hotel in Bournemouth. She remembered the play by Terence Rattigan, an English playwright popular in the period after the war, who died in the late 1970s, as an interesting play about relationships.

Janet had bought the best seats in the third row of the front stalls. The Shanklin Theatre had been saved from demolition ten years ago by Island Theatre lovers who volunteered to work without pay in all the required positions to keep it open. In ten years, it had prospered, ran productions throughout the year and made money, which was used to preserve the fabric of this 100-year-old theatre, and market the productions throughout the Island.

Janet Gibson had followed Bruno's progress on the Havenstreet murder case as long as he had been in charge of the investigation. She thought that Brenda Frampton, Maisie Longmore and Klinker's half-brother Arnold Harris, could have plausible motives. Singly or together, they could have had a reason to kill him, but Bruno had set them aside.

The time had come in her mind seriously to consider the others, beginning with Arnold Harris. He could have an accomplice who murdered Klinker, while he was away from the Island in Southampton as he claimed to have been. Until the appearance of Maisie Longmore it seemed likely, unless a will existed leaving the Klinker estate to someone else, that he would inherit it.

Mrs Galloway had told Janet that Arnold Harris was the director of the Ryde Amateur Dramatic Society, and it took up all of his spare time. So, seeing him acting the part of Major Pollack in a play in which she knew the storyline was an opportunity to watch him play a character who had something very personal to hide. The theatre was packed and Arnold Harris's performance might reveal something new to Bruno about Harris.

If the Kaz Ali who had been present at the Ryde '78 school reunion had been an imposter, then the imposter had put on a brilliant acting performance, because none of his school friends had noticed anything unusual about him. He was one of them. If that man was an Islander – and of that there could be no certainty – then he might at the very least be a member of the Island's only Amateur Dramatic Society.

This was her reason for bringing Bruno to see this play.

This performance by the Ryde Amateur Dramatic Society was superb, and as the curtain fell on this polished amateur production, the audience rose to their feet and applauded the cast to many curtain calls. After the curtain finally went down the audience spilled onto the pavement, having thoroughly enjoyed this spectacular revival of a successful West End play. Bruno had enjoyed the production as had Janet and her parents, and they discussed it at length in the car back to Newport.

After bidding goodnight to Janet's parents, they sat at their kitchen table, and over a nightcap discussed the play.

Bruno let Janet chat through the performance, highlighting her sympathies, until she got to Major Pollock.

There was something familiar about his performance he said at which she pulled a copy of the programme from her handbag.

"Major Pollock was played by Arnold Harris," she said.

"Yes, he is the director of Ryde Amateur Dramatic Society. Mrs Galloway said so. He was very good," said Bruno thoughtfully.

"Take a look at those photos taken by the school party on the reunion," said Janet, who'd retrieved them from his briefcase.

They showed the side and back view of the man in the reunion party posing as Kaz Ali. They studied both the pictures and came to the same conclusion: that the actor Arnold Harris, acting the part of Major Pollock, was wearing an identical suit as that worn by the bogus Kaz Ali at the school reunion.

"It looks like the same suit!"

"If it was the same suit, then we've got our man."

"Not yet," said Bruno. "But it does point the finger at Harris."

"Is there any feature of the suit in the photographs that one could say with certainty is the one being worn by Harris in the play?"

Like Bruno, Janet didn't believe in coincidence, and she admired his sense of connectivity, which had served him extremely well in his career.

"It's on tomorrow evening, so let's go again and study Arnold Harris' performance as Major Angus Pollock and, if we can, get a picture of him in the suit."

She had decided how she could pose as a photographer from the County Press newspaper and get him to pose for her.

Fortunately, Major Pollock was dressed identically to the

previous evening, but the opportunities to take a photograph were limited, until the final curtain, when Janet took a picture of the cast taking their final curtain call. The movements and stance of Major Pollock, with his occasional back to the audience sequences, gave them the opportunity to compare the suited actor with the strangers moving around.

Having watched two performances of a play, in which Arnold Harris acted a brilliant Major Pollock, Bruno saw the suit as important. It highlighted Klinker's half-brother, as a person of interest, and demanded re-examination of the recent interview with him, in which he had stated that on 8 June he had been in Southampton attending a Local Authority annual conference.

The photographs taken by the reunion attendees depicted Ali standing in a certain position creating a distinctive body shape. It was Major Pollock's similar stance in some scenes during the performance that convinced Bruno that he was on to something.

CHAPTER 24

Monday 9 July

Andy Bowen's first job on Monday was to confirm Harris's whereabouts on 8 July. He'd claimed to be at a conference in Southampton throughout the whole of that day, having stayed in the hotel on 7 and 8 June. Bruno needed to piece together his reported movements of the 7th and 8th until he departed the hotel on the 9th, after the conference closing session on the morning of 9 June.

The "Local Authority Annual Conference for Senior Local Authority Employees" was held in different venues every year in different parts of the country. Andy Bowen started with the organisers who had promoted the LGAC, as the Local Government Authority Conference was called. They were a London-based private company named European Exhibitions International Ltd, and were helpful. Their general manager, Alan Browne, emailed Andy Bowen a list of delegates which showed where they had come from, a copy of of the events which showed the name of the speaker and the time of his presentation. Arnold Harris was listed as being the chair of the question and answer session, which started at 5.00 p.m. on the opening day, 7 June.

Friday 8 June was a busy day, there were seminars on a range of local authority services subjects, and in an adjoining hall exhibition stands manned by companies that supplied products and services to local authorities nationally.

The conference organiser said it was a successful conference. Delegates and exhibitors were slightly down on last year, but that was blamed on the venue. Harrogate or Scarborough would have attracted more delegates with wives, whereas Southampton didn't have the same appeal.

Throughout the day of 8 June there were seminars and a

talk on Local Authority issues and at 8.00 p.m. a 45-minute
talk was given by Arnold Harris, Chief Planning Officer for
the Isle of Wight County Council, about planning applications and dealing with property developers.

◈

Mid-morning, Andy Bowen visited the Southampton hotel
conference venue, where the banqueting manager ran
through the three days of the conference.

"It's always busy, with people buzzing everywhere. They
are 45-minute slots for each seminar, and in between the
exhibitors grab you to show you systems and equipment
which they've spent one or two days setting up," Alan
Browne told him.

◈

Andy returned mid-afternoon with an idea of how Harris
might have spent his time at the conference. He confirmed he had occupied room 343 on the third floor of
the hotel for the nights of the 7 and 8 June and that he
chaired a welcoming opening session of the conference at
5.00 p.m. on the 7th, and in advance had booked to attend
two seminars on the 8th during the morning and afternoon sessions at 11.00 a.m. and 3.00 p.m. In the evening at
8.00 p.m. he had given a talk about handling the difficult
questions he received from property developers when their
planning applications are rejected by the planning committee. He returned to the Island sometime on Saturday
the 9th.

Andy's report on his visit to Southampton supported the
statement Harris gave them when they saw him a couple of
weeks earlier, principally that he was away from the Island
on the day of the murder. Andy confirmed with Alan Browne
that Harris had played a full part in the conference. So how
could the man in the suit on the train have been Arnold
Harris? Or the man who followed Klinker into the Gents'
at Havenstreet? It did not reconcile with his presence at the

two seminars in the morning and afternoon of the 8 June at the conference.

"In addition to booking a place on these two seminars, did the attendees sign in? If Harris signed in, and confirmed his presence at either or both, then we are barking up the wrong tree. What about the person off the train at Havant?" said Andy.

"I think he is our man, but is he Arnold Harris? European Exhibitions International, who organised this conference, is a marketing company. Names, addresses, contacts and attendees are their bread and butter, so they would have a record of who attended every session, and the subject matter in order to plan next year's conference, so we must look at what they have. Their business is to attract as many delegates, exhibitors and presenters that the delegates want to hear from. So, they will research the industry. Let's talk to them about the seminars that Arnold Harris signed up for and can they confirm his attendance."

"In London?" said Andy.

"Yes," said Bruno. "Tomorrow first thing, set it up today if you can. Harris is all we have, and if we confirm that he is not the man in the suit, we are back at square one."

"Up the creek," said Andy. "Shouldn't we visit him again?"

"No," said Bruno.

"We are not sure about this man in the suit. Could he have been Walters, or somebody else?"

"That's a different puzzle," said Bruno. "Let's complete the Harris puzzle first."

CHAPTER 25

Tuesday 10 July

European Exhibitions International, as the name suggested, put on exhibitions in major European capital cities. Their business was run from offices on the top floor of the old Simpsons department store in Piccadilly, now Waterstones' flagship bookshop. Bruno and Andy arrived just after 9.00 a.m. and were greeted by Tom Laird, the marketing director.

"Gentlemen, you want to discuss our recent Local Authority conference and exhibition in Southampton?"

"Yes, we want to talk about the seminars that you presented. Particularly we need to see the list of attendees for the 11.00 a.m. and 3.00 p.m. seminars on Friday 8 June, to confirm that Mr Arnold Harris attended these two seminars."

"Arnold Harris is very well known amongst Local Authority Conferencing. He often opens and closes the day's activities. He did that for us in Southampton. These two seminars were, 'Pedestrianisation and Route Planning' at 11.00 a.m. in the morning and 'Maintenance of Public Lavatories' at 3.00 p.m. He signed up for both, and paid the attendance fee when he reserved his place in February. Both presentations took place in the Queen Victoria suite. As you turn up, we ask you to sign in and show your pre-paid ticket, or pay to enter. I will find the records of these two seminars and organise some coffee for you."

Whilst this was being served by a pleasant lady, Laird returned with a navy blue pocket folder with a white sticky label showing QUEEN VICTORIA SUITE, 8 JUNE, and a list of four seminars: at 9.00 a.m., 11.00 a.m., 3.00 p.m. and 5.00 p.m. Inside the folder were four thin plastic envelopes, one for each.

"So, we are looking at 11.00 a.m. and 3.00 p.m."

Each folder had several sheets. The name of each paid delegate was listed in alphabetical order on the left-hand side of the page, with a space for a signature to the right-hand side.

Laird watched the two detectives as each selected one of the clear plastic envelopes, extracted the lists, and searched for the names of Arnold Harris. His name was listed for each presentation, but he did not sign in alongside his name in either seminar to confirm his attendance; neither, it was noted, did half the names on the list.

Tom Laird suggested that Arnold might not have signed in. "Although he would have been in attendance, because he is well known and has an official status, so I wouldn't regard his not signing as an indication he did not attend," he said. "At the bottom of the page there are some handwritten names, from whom our receptionist would have taken payment by card."

In view of Laird's comment, a lack of a signature could not be conclusive evidence that Harris did not attend, although he could have been elsewhere during the day, including taking a day trip to the Island.

◆

On their return journey with what could prove to be this crucial tide-turning evidence, Bruno and Andy got to work analysing all the information about Harris.

Bruno wanted to fill in the blanks before interviewing him again. Being in possession of Kaz Ali's invitation to the school reunion implied that Marion Hislop was involved. And what was the significance of the mysterious journey to Havant after his departure from Havenstreet shortly after 3.30 p.m. on 8 June?

Andy Bowen felt they had cracked the case against Harris and that he was their man. Bruno, however, wasn't convinced he had enough pieces of the jigsaw yet.

"Let's get off at Havant," he said to Andy during the last

part of the return journey to Portsmouth. "Let's walk around, re-enact if you like, and try to figure out why Ali would stitch together such a complicated manoeuvre. If we could place him at Havant, early or late, he could not have attended the Local Authority seminars. What about the details of the owners of vehicles that were parked that day?"

"Should be waiting for us at the station, sir."

◈

At Havant they alighted from the train and followed a small group through the ticket barrier. Outside the station these passengers quickly dispersed in several directions. Beyond the concourse at roadside, the detectives walked left, and left again in search of non-restricted parking. It took them 15 minutes before they reached a section without parking restrictions, and a similar distance in the other direction.

"Our suspect would have parked in the station car park," was Bruno's conclusion. "He would not have driven around in his frame of mind, searching for a place to park. So, let's look at the cars that parked throughout the day at the station car park."

Back at Havant station the twenty-seven registration numbers were waiting for them, but none was recognisable as an Island plate.

"It is possible he doesn't have a car with an Island plate. People who come from the mainland sell their cars here, that's a question we can ask him," said Andy. "I don't see the killer wanting to worry about where to park."

"He could have taken a taxi to bring him and arranged for a different car firm to pick him up off the 17.23 p.m. arriving at Havant," said Andy. "Havant to Southampton in the rush hour would take an hour by car. By not attending the seminars Harris had time to catch the Havant to Portsmouth train, cross to the Island as Kaz Ali, spend the day with a bunch of men who wouldn't remember him, kill Klinker, return to Havant, drive or take a pre-booked car ride back to the Southampton hotel in good time to chair the function in the evening," noted Bruno.

"Have we solved this murder?" said Andy.

"Only in our minds. I feel we are quite desperate to latch onto the only person outside the school group who had a connection with Klinker, and are motivated in that conclusion by the fact that he had an obvious motive: he believed he was his only living relative, and therefore would inherit the Klinker estate. If we could prove that Harris was pretending to be Kaz Ali on that day, we could charge him."

Bruno wanted time to sleep on it. Everything seemed to point to Harris, but would a murderer concoct such a complicated runaround if he were set on homicide?

Andy was convinced that Harris was their man. "He's the closest we have to a suspect. He obviously believes he will inherit the estate which he has always considered it partly his right."

"The facts mark Harris out, but do not add up to make him a killer," said Bruno. For him it was a personality issue, he did not recognise Harris as a murderer.

"Let's talk to him and get the low-down on this intricate plot, and let's tell Walters about this scenario. I'd be interested in his response."

"Are we still looking at Walters' employment history?"

"We are, and Kevin will update us at the station."

◆

Kevin Bell had worked hard gathering information about Professor Walters and his employment record since finishing his doctorate at the King's College Law School in London. Kevin Bell's report covered fifteen years, and three principal periods of employment at Portsmouth University, Exeter University and at the Home Office in London, looking at some local press and talking to the local police. At each, several murders, so far unsolved, had taken place, all of middle-aged men, mostly with professional status, such as accountants and solicitors.

Kevin believed if he had undertaken a nationwide survey of unsolved murders he'd have found some consistency. What was it about middle-aged men that made people want to finish them off?

"Can he complete the who, where and why list for us?" said Bruno to Andy, the recipient of the report.

"Let's go through it with him and he might do just that."

"Kevin, open up the Professor and from your research tell us what he is really like," said Andy.

Kevin recounted Walters' biography from the beginning. "He was born in Portsmouth in 1966, an only child, the son of a high ranking serving naval officer, he attended various preparatory schools until he was thirteen, and success in the common entrance got him into Ryde School where he was in the top set for almost everything. He was regarded as a clever boy.

"He went onto London University's prestigious Law School in 1984. He took a four-year course to graduate, and won a research fellowship to complete his master's degree and then a Ph.D. in Criminal Psychology. He was awarded his Ph.D. in the summer of 1995 when he was twenty-nine and left London in search of a university teaching position. By chance he secured a lecturing post at Portsmouth University and moved to Portsmouth to lecture in Criminology. Socially he did not make friends or enjoy a pleasant reputation. Portsmouth was an unusual place for a newly-qualified high-flying academic to return to. Portsmouth University was not a 'high seat' of learning for his lectures. Many of the students on the criminology course were destined for careers in the police or the probation service. So why, at a time in his life when his contemporaries were progressing their careers, did he return to Portsmouth? Surely more interesting and academically challenging positions near to major criminal courts in London were options? After eleven years living away from home studying in London, we traced no friends or interests in the Portsmouth area, so it was not a pleasant surprise to his parents when he informed them that he was staying with them, albeit only at first until he could find a flat of his own."

His four years in Portsmouth were uneventful and all Kevin could obtain was a confirmation email that gave his dates of employment at Portsmouth University. After Portsmouth he accepted the position of senior lecturer in Criminal Jurisprudence at Exeter University, where the University had close liaison with the West of England Police constabulary who called on the Exeter University criminology department when in difficulties with unsolved crimes.

Kevin continued, "Walters responded promptly and was not found wanting in his willingness to help. He re-established himself as a prison visitor until a convicted murderer he was counselling got murdered in the prison lavatory. The killer was never found, but it was assumed an inmate with a grudge was responsible.

"As Walters was visiting the prison on the day the prisoner was murdered and because of the freedom he enjoyed in the prison to move around unescorted, the police were interested in his movements in the prison at the time of the murder, but he was of little help to them.

"His other mission at Exeter prison was to listen to convicts' grievances, and if any inmate could convince him of their innocence, he would take up their cause, and persuade the authorities to conduct a legally aided appeal. This gained him an unwanted reputation with the Devon Constabulary, so bad that after five years he was virtually run out of town."

"He moved back to London working as a research analyst for the Home Office. His return to London coincided with the world financial crisis, austerity, and the hostility of the prison service to poor pay, overcrowded prisons and an increase in violence towards prison staff. At the Home Office the Home Secretary intent on prison reform provided Professor Walters with a platform to introduce new ideas for prison management based on his experience in Portsmouth and Exeter, where he gained a reputation as a protector of the oppressed, making his CV look impressive," said Andy. "Which probably won him his Oxford University professorship.

"What we don't know is the opinion of him at Oxford University. He may or may not be known to the local police. I would be surprised, from his previous pattern of behaviour, if he were not known to them in some capacity. He has been at the University for eight years so let's find out about him from them. We can't go unannounced to his place of work, so let's start with the Oxford City Police."

CHAPTER 26

Wednesday 11 July

Superintendent Nigel Woodruff at Oxford City Police Department agreed to meet the two Island detectives the following day. Woodruff was an experienced policeman, having served the same Oxford Constabulary for thirteen years, long before Ian Walters joined the University.

Bruno took some time to explain to the Superintendent the background to their investigation, where they had got to, their interest in Walters, and what they had discovered from his previous employment. He explained the gruesome nature of the murder – its location, the type of weapon and the place on the body of the victim where the blade was inserted – and the fact that there had been no trace of a weapon at or in the vicinity of the murder.

"What we have not so far examined is how he has conducted himself in his present job, and before we go probing about, can you help with our enquiries?"

"Do you have any information on him that could be of use to us?"

Woodruff replied, "Inspector Peach, he is known to us and has been for several years. In the beginning he presented himself as a criminologist who could help us with suspects or convicted criminals who may have been responsible for other unsolved crimes. He implied that he could tell from their demeanour whether they were guilty of related crimes.

"I think he is very experienced in analysing the criminal mind and he has written his findings up in books and police journals, but he was not helpful to us. In truth to some detectives he was a bloody nuisance, interfering with their suspects and not sharing what had been disclosed to him in confidence. After we rejected him, he presented himself

to the prison authorities and persuaded the prison governor to use him as a prison visitor and advisor, where he was
allowed to test a programme he had developed to prevent
reoffending. It's the biggest problem prisons face. How do
we stop 80 per cent of the prison population from returning
to prison within twelve months of being released? Professor
Walters' idea was to make the treatment of returnees so hard
that it would deter first offenders. Returning to prison for
a second time would automatically incur a longer sentence
and the conditions would be hard labour."

"That could work," said Bruno.

"It would be impossible to persuade the judiciary who
think that the punishment should fit the crime."

"Sir, could we see police records of unsolved murders
in the area of Oxford since Professor Walters joined the
University eight years ago?" said Andy.

"At a guess there are very few of those. Maybe just a handful, even less," said Superintendent Woodruff.

"We'd like to see if any of them are in any way however indirectly connected to the Professor. For example, the
Klinker killing took place on a school reunion at which
Walters was present. It is too early to suggest that he was
connected with the killing, or even that he was an observer,
but there are certain coincidences in his past that if they had
been repeated anywhere else would cause us to look deeper
into his connection."

"We can do that but not until my backroom staff have
time to look back over the period," said Woodruff. "If his
name appears in connection with any unsolved murder, I
will call you. That is the best I can do."

"How long will that be, sir?"

"I will get it done as soon as I can. But I will try to get it
to you in one week," he added in a very positive note as they
departed.

"Great news," said Andy Bowen, who was now convinced

that Arnold Harris was the killer. "We can wrap the Klinker killing up in a week. Do you think the Oxford Constabulary will come up with anything, sir?"

"Yes, I do. But we'll carry on with the work we still have to do in the mean time, like nailing Arnold Harris, or anyone else we have in our sights," added Bruno.

◆

"Yes, Inspector, you've come back so I expect you want to tell me how you are getting on," said Harris as they arrived as the Newport County Council offices unannounced. He did not appear surprised by their reappearance at his office.

"No," said Bruno. "A number of your actions have revealed themselves during our investigation, which concerns us, namely your movements on the day of Dr Klinker's murder. However, at this moment we shall not exercise our right to caution you. Are you worried about anything connected with the murder of your half-brother?"

"That is a strange question to put to me, Inspector!"

"What you have said so far doesn't agree with what we have discovered during our investigations. I will lay my cards on the table and then ask you to comment," said Bruno.

"You claimed to be at the Solent Hotel on the night of 7 and 8 June?"

"Correct, Inspector, and I take it you have checked that?"

"We have and we have also checked the two seminars at which you reserved places."

"At two specific times during the day. The mid-morning and mid-afternoon seminars, and then the early evening seminar. And that is all in order, I take it?" he said.

"Not exactly, Mr Harris. There is no evidence that you attended the morning or afternoon seminar. If you did not attend either of these seminars you would have had time to go to the Island and be in a position at Havenstreet station to murder your brother."

"Ridiculous, Inspector, you almost make me laugh. If I

had any intentions of killing my brother, I wouldn't have chosen a week when I was on the mainland and he was meeting a group of his old school mates on the Island. Do you think I am daft? Inspector, I believe that I am potentially the big gainer as a result of his murder, and everybody who has any connection with the Klinkers knows that. I would have guessed I was the prime suspect from day one.

"My brother and I didn't hit it off on all sorts of things, but I would never hurt him, certainly not to get my hands on his estate."

"Can you explain why you did not sign in for the two seminars you claim to have attended?"

"Inspector, I have a different role to play at the annual Local Authority Conference than just as a delegate. I always open the conference chairing a question-and-answer panel. That gives the conference organisers an idea of what the delegates want to get from the conference, and we can amend that if necessary. I don't, as a rule, sign up to attend the seminars I want to attend. I pay early when I book to attend and that gives me the option to wander in and out if I don't like the content or the speaker."

"So, you attended these two seminars on that day?"

"Inspector, I didn't keep a diary of everything I did over the two days. Perhaps Tom Laird can help you. He is the manager of the event. I know him well as I've worked with him over many years and what I do for Tom Laird's company is voluntary."

Bruno hesitated at this point in his interview. His dilemma was that if he suggested that Harris had played the part of Ali on the school outing, he could have been laughed out of the building, and then to claim Arnold Harris, impersonating Ali, was the murderer seemed an even remoter possibility. So as he did not yet have a cast-iron argument that would make his case. He resisted accusing him of impersonating Kaz Ali on 8 June, and therefore of murdering his half-brother.

◆

After they left Harris, Andy Bowen was confused by Bruno's reluctance to introduce this matter, because he felt this might break Harris down and lead to the possibility of a murder charge.

"Harris isn't going anywhere. He's confident and secure as things are, and I believe he wanted to bring up the subject of Ali which would provide him a stage to act upon, but I did not give him that opportunity," said Bruno. "Not until I am 100 per cent convinced one way or another."

CHAPTER 27

Thursday 12 July

"She was not unhappy that we were going to visit her again," said Andy to Bruno, who felt he had an inside track with Marion Hislop. If there was anything she knew, his charm would get it out of her, although if she *were* involved, his conviction that Arnold Harris was the murderer would produce nothing. How could such a delightful lady become involved with a murderer?

As Bruno and Andy travelled to see her at Ryde School, on the dashboard of Bruno's car was a copy of the theatre programme of the play Janet had taken Bruno to twice, *Separate Tables* by Terence Rattigan. It listed on the centre pages the details of the production by the Ryde Dramatic Society, and the cast of actors in the play. Andy Bowen casually picked it up and read whilst Bruno drove. Alongside the cast list was a passport-size photograph of the principle players. It was a small cast, of which Arnold Harris was shown as Major Pollock, above a photo of Marion Hislop playing the part of Sybil.

The sight of her name against her photograph alarmed Andy Bowen. She was the Ryde School secretary who had organised the '78 school reunion and outing to the Havenstreet Steam railway.

Bruno hadn't mentioned her to him because he had not read the theatre programme. Neither had Janet linked the actress on stage as the Ryde School secretary. However, it did shed more light onto their search for a connection between Kaz Ali and Arnold Harris. Marian Hislop and Arnold Harris had something in common, and it was she who had dealt with Ali when he'd decided not to attend. Had she buggered up the emails to India?

Bruno was surprised he'd not spotted the link or recognised her in the cast. In truth he was only paying attention to Harris on the night.

He had still not changed his mind about Harris. He did not understand the impersonation of Ali, or anyone who would do that, but her involvement added something that needed investigation.

At Ryde School she was an outstanding secretary. She was effectively the school manager and what happened on a day-to-day basis she handled. Acting with Arnold Harris regularly indicated they knew each other well, and if he did impersonate Kaz Ali on the school reunion, surely she would have known about it, or even been a partner in the plan. If she was involved in some kind of deception, then could she have played a part in Klinker's murder?

"Interesting," said Andy, who wasn't sure if his discovery increased his belief that Harris killed Klinker. Having spent more time with Marion Hislop than had Bruno, he could not accept that she would be involved with a murder. She had a very pleasant personality and he had liked her, and as he remembered she had reacted very helpfully when providing information about the school reunion.

Bruno decided to present Marion Hislop with the facts about Kaz Ali as far as they had discovered them, and try to get her to offer an explanation.

She had already told the police she had received Ali's fee via a money exchange from Paris. Whoever had represented Ali at the reunion must have done that. She should be able to cast a light on the payment details, which she should be able to confirm by providing sight of correspondence and the payment vouchers from France.

"Miss Hislop, we are having a problem with locating the Kaz Ali who attended the school reunion on 8 June. We traced the real Kaz Ali to his Paris home, via his family in Mumbai, and visited him there. We have proved that he did *not* attend the reunion. So who did? You informed us that you received payment by money order from France, and a person representing himself as Kaz Ali attended the reunion."

"That is correct Inspector," she replied. I did receive a international money order, which I cashed as the Post Office."

"Do you have a counterfoil or receipt?"

"No, a money order is like a postal order, they stamp it and give you the cash."

"Was it in euros or sterling?"

"Pounds sterling, of course, Inspector. I can show you the entry in my ledger if you wish?"

"Didn't pounds sterling in a French money order seem strange to you?"

Bruno did not ask to see the book entry as he was certain it would be in order.

He then played a bold card based on Andy Bowen's recognition of her in the previous weekend's playbill at the Shanklin Theatre.

"Can I congratulate you Miss Hislop on your performance in *Separate Tables* on Saturday evening."

"Well thank you, Inspector. It was a great success! Did you enjoy it?"

"My lady and I loved it, and we also liked Arnold Harris."

"I was lucky to be allowed to play Sybil, the landlady, Arnold chose me for the part."

"You were brilliant."

"Arnold played Major Pollock, he is a very good actor you know."

"You are aware that he is Dr Klinker's half-brother?"

"Yes, I do, and I feel very sorry for Arnold."

"Did he have much to do with his brother?"

"I have no idea, Inspector; you should ask him. I think it will have affected him considerably, and the play will have taken his mind off it, such an awful thing to have happened."

"Is there anything else you can tell us about Arnold Harris?"

"Like what, Inspector?"

"We have spoken to him several times about the murder, and for a man who has suffered many setbacks in the past few months – the death of his mother, and the end of his obligations towards her, then the murder of Dr Klinker for no apparent reason – he is remarkably upbeat."

"That's because, deep down, nothing worries him. He desperately wants to know why someone would want to kill Geoff, in case the same reason might apply to him."

"And what might that be?"

"Clive Hall and the farm. He knows that he probably stands to inherit the estate and that places him in an unenviable position. It's the last thing he wants. He could not take the responsibility."

"Well maybe that will never happen," said Bruno. "And even if it does there are plenty of buyers. He could sell it on, and walk away from it."

Bruno felt that beneath the small talk they were engaged in, was an intriguing relationship between her and Arnold Harris, which she was not revealing to him.

"How long have you been a member of the drama society?"

"Over twenty years. We put on two main productions every year, one in the summer, and the other at Christmas. We like to do Charles Dickens in the winter, and a period drama in the summer. However, this autumn we were planning a change, a new play called *An Indian Summer*. We shall start our rehearsals in September with a cast read-through."

"What is it about?"

"India in 1947 just before independence when all the Brits had to give up their privileged existence and leave India. The play is about a senior diplomat who has a mistress and a child, both of whom he has to leave behind, or does leave behind."

"I am sure there were many of those at that time," said Andy.

Marion Hislop wasn't what she appeared to be, and Bruno was struggling to think how he could get her to open up. Like Harris, she was an attractive middle-aged person, and he did not believe that either of them lived simple lives. Something they did, either as individuals or as a couple, lit up their lives, and all he could see was the Ryde Amateur Dramatic Society. It reminded him of a Church of England parish church in Newport in which a scandal surfaced several years ago. The organist was caught *in flagrante delicto* with the lady choir soloist behind the altar by the vicar. As an understanding clergyman he cast a blind eye, so they carried on their relationship, regularly. Since then, attending a different church with Janet, he'd convinced himself that the organist and a leading lady chorister were also up to it, and that it was a feature of their activities. Now his focus lay with Marion Hislop and Harris. If Harris had impersonated Kaz Ali in order to murder Klinker, she would have been involved. The only way he was going to find out was to accuse her of assisting Harris. She was not going to open that door.

Bruno decided to back off for the time being. He needed some more evidence to accuse them of the crime of murder. In view of their involvement with the Ryde Amateur Dramatic Society, and its plan to produce a play about India, although it might be a wild idea for a leading member of the cast to impersonate a living individual, the events surrounding the actions of the impersonator on the day suggested otherwise.

Their investigation of the car park at Havant Station had produced no reliable follow-up to link Harris's sojourn in Southampton with a journey back to the Island to attend the school reunion. However, his actions suggested that something could have been going on. Could he simply have been attending the school outing just to practice his acting skills, or to impress Marion Hislop? Or could it simply be to satisfy an inflated ego?

With grateful thanks to Marion Hislop both detectives took their leave of her and returned to Newport station.

◆

Andy Bowen remained unconvinced of Bruno's cautious approach, but admired the web his boss was weaving. Like Bruno, he was now less certain that Harris was a murderer.

Bruno had decided that the only persons of interest capable of Dr Klinker's murder were Beale, Ali's impersonator, Walters and Biff Haves, perhaps with the aid of Mrs Galloway. With Walters they were waiting on the results of Superintendent Woodruff's examination of the Oxford City Police Constabulary records for knowledge of any murder with which Walters had any connection. Often, after five weeks, Bruno's boss would call a halt to a murder investigation, and it was shelved until time could be made available to continue.

On this case Bruno was failing and soon his boss would give him something else that would edge the Klinker murder to the bottom of the list. Andy's opinion was that Harris had killed his half-brother to get his hands on the Klinker estate. Bruno could not see why he'd risk everything he had in life – a well-paid secure job, status and a lifestyle he enjoyed. Why would he exchange these for a millstone round his neck? So he resisted Andy's suggestion of taking a more aggressive approach by arresting Harris and Marion Hislop on suspicion.

"Make Marion Hislop believe that Harris is guilty," said Andy. "Accuse him of murdering Klinker in the lavatory and then he might explain himself. We know that Ali did not attend the reunion and somebody else did, using his name, for some extraordinary reason, and we think that man is Harris. If it wasn't to murder his half-brother, what was he up to, and why?"

"We have no evidence to charge Harris," said Bruno. "But we can visit him and probe his relationship with Marion Hislop, and frighten him. Her confessed juggling of the money order is suspicious, and the reason to visit him is because he knows her well. Suggest to him that she might be involved, because she admitted contact with somebody who claimed to be Ali who coughed up the 75 quid to go on the trip, an amount she paid into the school funds after cashing an international money order, for which there is no paper trail. If he thinks we suspect her and he is close to her, he will come up with something which may open the door and confirm your suspicions that he is a killer."

Bruno accepted his young assistant's hypothesis. To avoid seeming heavy-handed, he agreed that Andy should return, alone, and gently try a different approach.

While Andy Bowen set off on his mission that he believed would prove that Arnold Harris had killed Klinker, Bruno sifted through the peripheral information he'd gathered in the course of the investigation. Beale, with or without Biff Haves, thought he was a shoe-in to buy the estate. However, he hadn't reckoned on James Tennant's interest, or the existence of a Mrs Geoffrey Klinker who, if she proved her marriage, unless Geoff Klinker's will stated otherwise, would inherit the farm. With family business connections on the Island, which was once her home, she might be overjoyed to become involved in the management of the farm. If she could run a large NHS hospital, she could certainly run a farm business. So, there would be no sale to anyone.

Obtaining probate on the estate of a person who has been murdered can take forever, and is never less than six months. Either Beale or Biff Haves, as far as Bruno could work out, had the cash to buy the Klinker farm. However, Tennant could also be a potential buyer. His business suggested he had collateral and his mainland banking connections would support him, which put him in pole position. It would exact revenge, and satisfy any family resentment against the Beales, if he could be reduced to the under-bidder at an auction sale of the Klinker estate.

◆

At lunchtime Andy Bowen returned from his meeting with Arnold Harris and reported the outcome.

Andy had started with Harris's explanation of the receipt of Ali's contribution to the school outing. He expressed the police doubts about its plausibility, which suggested to them that she might have some knowledge or even be connected with Klinker's killer. Harris was concerned, so to explain her behaviour he had to explain his part in the act of deception and their reasons.

"I have been a friend of Marion's for more than twenty years, and I can assure you that she had no connection with my brother's killer. Our friendship started when she joined the Ryde Amateur Dramatic Society twenty years ago."

"Do you have a personal relationship?"

"We are actors and it might appear that way, but we are not in a relationship. However, we try to put into our acting the most thoughtful performances. We study the roles and the performances of actors who've performed the roles in public. Now I will explain about Ali, Inspector. Our next public performance, in the autumn, is E. M. Forster's *An Indian Summer*, set in India in 1947. I won't go into the play except to say that I play the lead role of Muninda Ali, an Indian lawyer who works for a British mining company in Bombay. Marion was unsure whether I could play the part authentically. She is directing this play, so she does not want an actor in a poor performance pretending to be an Indian lawyer, so learning that Kaz Ali was unable to attend the school reunion she suggested I attend as him. Having confirmed in an email from Paris saying he was unable to attend, I impersonated him, and I paid the 75 quid, it was by an international money order, and no one detected anything unusual. I was not exposed. I admit I was nervous at the start, but no one suspected me or recognised me and as the day progressed, I was very pleased at my performance. I did not speak to Geoff. I wish I had now, because in some way I believe I could have saved him. Sadly, that afternoon, my brother was murdered, but not by me Inspector, as I believe that is in your mind, or by Marion. Can you understand how devastated we both were when we found out? In the normal course of events we would have considered the afternoon a triumph. Now we feel like murder suspects."

"Did any of the other members of the Ryde Drama Group know about this?"

"No one, it was just Marion and me."

"So, you impersonated Kaz Ali and got away with it? What an incredibly unlucky experience for you that your brother should have been murdered, almost in your presence, and you be unaware of it?"

Bowen was astonished at Harris' revelation, and disappointed that it had taken the wind out of his sails.

"I don't think I have committed a crime, Inspector?"

Andy Bowen didn't confirm or deny that.

"We will come back to that," he said. "Tell me what you saw during the day that could have made you suspicious of anyone?"

"I was too focused on my own performance so I can tell you very little about the day," Harris replied. "When I left Havenstreet at 15.30, I was elated that I'd gotten away with it and I didn't want to stumble at the last, or meet any of the other attendees on my journey. I had phoned a taxi before tea, so as soon as I had finished and said a few goodbyes, not to everyone, I left for Ryde Hovercraft, caught the 16.15 flight to Clarence Pier where a taxi drove me to Portsmouth and Southsea railway station, where I boarded the 17.15 train to Havant, where I had left my car, and drove back to Southampton for my evening conference appointment."

"Why Havant?" said Andy Bowen.

"Havant is on the A27, which becomes the M27, a direct motorway to Southampton. Southampton to Havant is quick – less than 45 minutes."

Andy resisted asking chapter and verse on Havant. The police had tracked him that far and even witnessed him leave Havant Station, having changed from his suit and without make-up, at about 17.40 on 8 June.

"I was back in my hotel a little after 18.30, ready for my evening session."

"Nothing you have said precludes you from killing Geoff Klinker," said Andy.

"I know that, Inspector, and that worries me, but it does not implicate me any more than any other member of the school group. For that whole day I was busy. I couldn't relax for one second. Whereas the murderer, if he is one of the group, could relax until the moment he struck in the Gents' lavatory. It may not have been his ideal choice of venue for the killing, it was just the opportunity that presented itself to him."

"Throughout the day did you spot anything that could help us?"

"Of the school party, Beale and Walters are bachelors, so was Geoff, and Edward the artist. Mullion, the hospital consultant, it seemed, played games with any other willing female, although he was married. Lewis, the chemist was a divorcee, and that leaves the Colonel, Billings the baker and Tennant. Only the last three seemed normal people," observed Harris.

"So, who could the murderer be from that lot?" Andy asked.

"I don't think there is a motive for Geoff's murder, and that is your problem."

"Forget those who are trying to get their hands on the farm. None of them would have dreamt of murdering

Klinker to get their hands on it. Edward the artist lives on a different level. So that leaves Walters, the criminologist," noted Andy.

"Don't you think it's odd, Inspector, that one of ten classmates is killed, leaving nine suspects without motives?"

Andy could not answer that question.

"Who else is there?" said Harris.

"At the moment there is yourself."

"Except you have no evidence, and you won't find any, because there is none. I also have a motive for attending the reunion. What has the university Don said about the murder? At whom has he pointed the finger?"

Andy didn't answer that question because he was finally beginning to understand Bruno's view that Harris would not kill his half-brother. He was, nevertheless, incredibly unfortunate that he practised his acting skills on the occasion his brother was murdered.

Harris had underlined the lack of motive that existed amongst the group, and his conclusion that the murder was committed by someone without motive. It was a valid assessment that Andy would convey to Bruno for his response.

◈

Bruno listened to Andy's report for some confirmation that he'd convinced himself that Harris was the killer. However, in spite of his attempt, he got nowhere near to accusing Harris and was forced to the same conclusion as Bruno – that Harris was not the killer.

Arnold Harris and Marion Hislop had dreamt up this impersonation from an actor's desire to convince an audience, and he succeeded in doing it. However, instead of being able to congratulate themselves on the success of their plan, sadly one of the school group, his brother, was murdered. Suspicions immediately fell on the school party, and Marion Hislop, which Harris believed would make Ali an immediate suspect, but he was nowhere to be found. He had disappeared off the face of the earth, because he had never existed, but a substitute, an impersonator, an actor, did exist, and his identity had not been unveiled until now and instead of well-deserved applause for a very credible performance he was being pursued as a killer.

"So, where do we go from here?" said Bruno.

"We know that Harris attended the reunion and saw nothing unusual with the other members of the group, nothing suspicious that might encourage him to suspect that there was a subtext to the day, which suggests the killing was random. It need not have been Klinker, or have taken place at all. It could have been any of the others in the school party. It was just unfortunate that Klinker put himself in danger, in that place where the killer could kill undetected."

"It's an interesting theory that gets Harris off the hook," said Bruno.

"Harris was performing, watching everybody for a reaction to him, but nobody, during the entire day, gave the slightest indication that Harris was an impostor. During our interviews no member from the group has even mentioned him, but his scrutiny concludes that from amongst his schoolmates no one had a motive to kill for gain, so what else is there? Curiously, Harris points the finger at Walters," said Andy. "Harris thinks the staging could not have been improved by Agatha Christie: a school outing, ten attendees, and one gets murdered. Just her kind of thing."

"Yes, but we'd like a small piece of evidence, not something imagined by a crime writer. Why don't we contact Nigel Woodruff in Oxford and see if he has come up with anything we don't already have about Walters?"

◆

Later that afternoon, in response to Andy Bowen's email to Superintendent Woodruff, Bruno received a telephone call from him, in which he communicated some of what they had in their records about Professor Walters.

During the eight years that he has been a lecturer at the University in Oxford he had helped the police with several incidents of a vicious criminal nature. Although in most of the situations his presence could be explained as he had been invited to give his opinion as a professional Criminologist after the killings.

However, there was one situation in which he was connected, which had remained unsolved, four and half years since. It involved the murder of a twenty-one-year-old hotel waiter named Lee Sharp, who worked in the cocktail bar of the Churchill Hotel in Oxford City centre, just 100 metres from the Randolph Hotel where Andy and Bruno had recently enjoyed a drawn-out lunch with Professor Walters. In 2015 Lee Sharp had been found stabbed to death in the ground floor staff lavatory at the end of his afternoon shift at 18.00. During the afternoon the cocktail bar doubled as a place to enjoy afternoon tea. On the day of Sharp's murder the CCTV camera in the cocktail bar showed Professor Walters arriving alone at about 16.00 for afternoon tea. Lee Sharp served him tea, in a friendly manner, and had chatted to him in a friendly way. When he finished tea just after 17.45, he paid and left with a brief wave to Lee Sharp.

The Police were called to the hotel at 18.05 p.m. by a male member of staff who discovered the body.

"When we arrived at the scene at 18.25 p.m., we discovered Sharp stabbed to death in the staff lavatories. Professor Walters was interviewed at the time, having been one of the last people to speak to Lee Sharp. He said he often visited the hotel for tea, and sometimes in the early evening for a drink, and frequently spoke to Lee Sharp about different things. Lee Sharp had spoken to Walters about his ambition to become a writer, which Walters claimed to have encouraged by advising him to set aside at least one hour every day to write, and that a good time to do that was early in the day, at say 6.00 a.m.

"Sharp had said he sometimes had plenty of time in the afternoons when he would write. He came from Harrogate and had worked in the Churchill for two years, at first in the restaurant, and latterly in the cocktail bar. He was liked, honest and ambitious and lived in one of the staff bedsits in an annexe across the hotel park. He did not mix socially with the other residents who lived in the annexe. His main recreation was cycling, and weather permitting, he would join Oxford Cycling Club members for all-day cycle rides into the Oxfordshire countryside.

"When we searched his room it was tidy. We found a young man's selection of clothes, jeans, T-shirts, sports shoes and various other semi-fashionable items of clothing, stacked in an orderly manner. On a table were notebooks containing a number of stories he had written, a dictionary, a copy of 2012 *Writers' And Artists' Yearbook*, pencils, a thesaurus, dictionaries – all the tools of someone seriously working towards being a writer. In one folder, separately, were a number of stories, each about 10 pages of A4, that had comments written by Professor Walters on the final pages. We considered this unusual because Professor Walters had not mentioned this on our first interview. It was obvious from the comments that he had written at the bottom of each story he had taken time to read them. By and large the comments were demeaning. Not at all encouraging to a young person determined to improve himself beyond being a hotel waiter. These comments all in the same vein were spread over a period of six months, the time it had taken for Sharp to write them. So it clearly showed some kind of relationship between the two."

"What were these stories about?" Bruno asked.

"Mostly people who stayed at the hotel. Lee Sharp had imagined the life of hotel visitors from the brief knowledge he'd gleaned about them from serving them, and the short discussions a waiter might have with a hotel guest. Walters' comments written in ink consisted of a few words with numerous question marks. However, none of these stories were happy tales. They featured crooked, dishonest, evil people, and the most startling short story was about a criminologist who undertook the perfect murder. This story was not found amongst the ten or so on the table, but separately underneath his mattress, and it did not have Walters' unpleasant comments, presumably because Sharp had not shown the story to Walters. But that is how he imagined him."

"Did you question Walters about what Lee Sharp had written?"

"We questioned him at length about his relationship with Sharp but there was no evidence of anything other than their conversations over tea during his afternoon visit. He said he did not know him at all, and he only knew his name from his hotel name badge. All of this seemed perfectly normal. We left the short story about the perfect murder by a criminologist on his file and we have not questioned him about it."

"Why not?"

"Because the detective in charge of the investigation did not want to reveal what might become important evidence."

Bruno decided that if he and Superintendent Woodruff believed Walters was the killer a trap should be set for him. It had to be one that appealed to his ego so he took the bait. Woodruff had neither the appetite, nor the resources, to open a five-year-old unsolved murder case, but agreed to make the Lee Sharp murder file available to Bruno and his investigation team.

Bruno thanked the Superintendent for his co-operation in sharing confidential police information about the Sharp case and promised that once the Island police had progressed their investigation, they would keep him informed. Bruno did not believe in coincidence in any event, so it was his opinion that these two murders were committed by the same person. Also, that Lee Sharp had detected during his brief contact with Walters something sinister. However, there was no evidence or motive to link him with either murder, a point that had been made in the case by Arnold Harris.

The murder of Lee Sharp in Oxford had uncanny similarities to the Klinker murder and the common thread was Walters. Both men were chillingly killed in the same manner, in a men's lavatory. The "on the spot" detectives investigating the Sharp case had not even considered him a suspect because they could not establish a connection between the two persons. Now, the identical circumstances in both of which Walters was present made a compelling case for suspecting the Professor as the murderer. However, there was a glaring lack of evidence in both murders, for which reason Bruno thought it would be a mistake to bring Walters in for further questioning at this time.

Bruno had no experience of finding a serial killer, although he understood many of the psychological traits they possessed.

The answers he needed about Walters would only be discovered from personal contact. Perhaps a closer look at the murder of the prison inmate at Exeter prison where Walters had been a prison visitor, and the telling fact that the prisoner he was visiting had been killed with a knife in the inmate's lavatory made a total of three almost identical killings in which Walters was in some way connected. The contact with Oxford had put their investigation onto a different level.

"These are murders where the killer has a complex psychological make-up. It's not to do with possessions or anger, only the person himself. So that is what we concentrate on?" asked Andy. "What do we know about Walters?"

Bruno replied, "We know a certain amount, but we need to return to his previous lives at his earlier jobs and see if there is a clue. Perhaps we can visit the University, talk to other professors who work there."

Andy added, "We know that he is a single man. We cannot

guess his sexual feelings. He may have girlfriends, or just be absorbed with criminology. It does not appear that he has ever married. Is he a misogynist? The three victims were all male and have been killed in a place where women would not be, which suggests that he has an anti-social trait."

To which Bruno added, "The murders have taken place over a considerable period of time which indicates an addictive element to his behaviour. He is driven to commit the murders after a period of abstinence, creating a state of anxiety that could induce him into making mistakes. We have to discover what those mistakes are."

Andy observed, "His professional status shows that he is a planner. All three murders have required perfect timing and planning. They are not simply off-the-cuff or opportunistic. If they are driven by an addiction, then why is he connected to the victims by association? He could go to a city where he is unknown, and choose a victim at random and vanish until the next time."

"Except that would not satisfy his ego," said Bruno. "He needs to be involved in the investigation and the search for the killer, showing us the blind alleys to explore, which adds to his narcissistic belief in his own cleverness."

"Are we convinced that he is our man?" said Andy.

"Not completely," said Bruno. "Even if he is the killer, as yet we have no evidence."

"Then we need to go back to Oxford and examine the Lee Sharp murder and search for a link with the Klinker murder. The Oxford Constabulary did not have the benefit of comparing two different murders but we do. In fact we have three cases in which we might see patterns of behaviour. Let's go through their file and compare notes, and then we might have something to discuss with Walters. I am sure that he is waiting to send us up another blind alley. Before we rush off to confront him, let's present him with one of our persons of interest who we plan to charge with Klinker's murder. Let's choose Harris, Ali's impersonator, and get him to focus on him and present him as the murderer of Klinker, how he travelled to the reunion together with the intriguing disguise, and his return to Southampton. Let's persuade Walters we think he is the murderer and see what he says. But first let's get to grips with the Lee Sharp killing in Oxford, after which we could be in a position to bring him in."

CHAPTER 28

Friday 13 July

Bruno and Andy arrived at Oxford Police Headquarters by car at 10.00 a.m. to begin their investigation into Lee Sharp's murder, having eaten breakfast locally at a greasy spoon café for students.

Superintendent Woodruff had collected the police records of the Sharp investigation and allocated an interview room for their use, which they interpreted as meaning they might need an overnight stay.

"Gentlemen, if there is anything else you need, ask the desk sergeant and he'll get it for you. If you suspect that a serial killer could be responsible for Lee Sharp's murder, good luck. We did not take that view."

The detectives appointed to the case described the victim's wounds, which were similar to Klinker's. The murder took place in the male staff lavatory. Sharp had been stabbed from behind while using the urinal, never seeing who had dealt him the fatal blows. The SOCOs' report stated that two measured blows with a long narrow-bladed knife had penetrated 7 inches into the heart and liver through the back whilst the victim was relieving his bladder into the urinal. He had slumped forward dying instantly and falling backwards onto the floor with blood gushing from both wounds across the lavatory floor. All fingerprints matched those of male staff members, including Lee Sharp, who used the lavatory during working hours, all of whom had been interviewed by the Oxford Constabulary and regarded as innocent staff colleagues.

"What is the significance of the men's lavatory? Is it sexual?"

"It suggests that because of the location, a men's lavatory, but we've found nothing that indicates these murders have a sexual dimension. I am inclined to think that it is one activity that men do which is uninterruptable, your concentration is totally focused on the job in hand," said Bruno. "The opportunity to kill is unseen, and because the killer is sufficiently knowledgeable of anatomy, his knife thrusts kill the victim instantly."

"We could be reading about Klinker's murder from these records," said Bruno. "But we need to read the Coroner's report and see if the same conclusions were drawn."

◆

The Coroner's report was part of the bundle and confirmed the cause of death, the angle and depth of penetration of the blade, seven inches, and the size of the blade, which corresponded exactly with the Klinker Coroner's report.

Apart from the prints, which matched members of staff, nothing was found by the SOCO team, and after thorough and diligent searches the weapon was not found. From the possessions of Lee Sharp, the police had retained the bunch of short stories written by him, in which consistently after each final paragraph Walters had written highly critical, cruel short comments, which might have had a very demoralising effect on a young student writer. But it seems he was not put off by Walters' comments. Did this suggest that the young writer's imagination had frightened Walters, or that Walters had seen his final short story about a criminologist planning the perfect murder?

The short story read like an extract from *Crime and Punishment*: a meticulously planned murder leaving no clue as to the identity of the killer or a motive for the crime. Its character was a middle-aged man, who targeted young men with aspirations, who offered friendship and promised assistance and guidance, while demonstrating his intellectual superiority to a person he considered beneath him, socially and intellectually, and whose true aim was to suppress and

take revenge at the least glimmer of talent, which the murderer did not possess.

Over several weeks Walters would have acquired an intimate knowledge of the victim and explored every personal
aspect of his life, although he never introduced the subject
of sex or alluded to it in a subliminal way. Gradually the victim feared his arrival for tea or at the bar and saw him as a
towering threat to his existence but he resisted his instincts
to vanish, to leave his job, magnetised by the constant fear of
him encroaching into his domain.

This story is very intuitive and came as a result of discussions with Walters during his visits to the hotel for tea
and drinks when he must have conveyed a sinister aura to
Lee Sharp whose imagination was capable of a prophetic
conclusion.

◈

Bruno expressed his deductions out loud. "With Walters
let's be sure where we want to end up and what facts we have.
We will come back to the prison murder where an inmate
was deemed responsible and concentrate on the murders of
Klinker and Sharp. They were stabbed in an identical fash-
ion, and the signs point to Professor Walters because he was
present at the location of the murders on each occasion. Do
we have anything else? Witnesses, fingerprints, evidence of
a connection, the murder weapon? We have nothing, and
especially no motive in either case so we must rely on our
assessment of his personality.

"He was seen having tea on the CCTV camera in the cocktail bar, and he left the hotel at 17.45, fifteen minutes before
Lee Sharp was found murdered. But there is no camera that
saw him leave the hotel. The fact that the method of killing
is the same for Sharp and Klinker is the only factor between
them and we have nothing that connects him directly with
either murder."

The advantage Bruno had was that Walters would not

know about their contact with the City of Oxford Police. Disclosing that information to him might induce an error or a miscalculation by him and prove to be Bruno's trump card.

They agreed that they needed something specific to set up another meeting with Walters again, so instead of taking the opportunity to visit him whilst in Oxford, they packed up their papers and returned to Portsmouth.

The Lee Sharp murder had changed this murder enquiry dramatically. It was no longer a whodunit!

If, as now seemed likely, Klinker was killed by Professor Walters, their task now was to prove it. The killing of Lee Sharp had produced nothing more than circumstantial evidence, because nothing substantial had connected him with his murderer. The same could be said of the Klinker case, and the Exeter Prison inmate who had been stabbed to death after Walters' visit that afternoon.

Serial killers are profoundly psychologically disturbed and behave in strange and unusual ways as a result of cruelty or indifference they suffered when young or a long time ago. It could also be caused by being denied a longed-for entitlement, which to them became a matter of pride, a long-held grudge that needed lancing like a boil. It could return with a kindling spark of love, leading to a humiliating rejection and living each day under a shroud of yesterdays. This concentrates their mind so that they live eternally in the past, denying that the present or future have meaning for them.

"So, what is it with Walters?" said Andy.

"We will re-examine what we already know about him and when we have accurately mapped his past we'll confront him hoping he will do something that will expose him. Let's start with what we know about his character, personality, interests and what he does when he is not involved in academic work at the University."

"We know nothing," said Andy, staring blankly at Bruno.

"Even though we've seen him over lunch, he let us in on nothing. We don't know where he goes or what he does, what interests him. He didn't mention anything over lunch, not what he is reading, watching on TV, sport, politics, where he goes on holiday for more than half the year. The undergrads at Oxford do three eight-week terms, so he can do almost anything when he's not in Oxford lecturing."

"Perhaps what he does is highly intellectual?" said Andy. "Above our heads."

"These murders appear to be spontaneous but they are timed and planned meticulously, which fits with his acknowledged academic position at this prestigious university. His selection of victims appears to be random, and so far, they have nothing in common. Jack the Ripper targeted prostitutes; Harold Shipman decided when to terminate the lives of his patients. So the key to these murders is in the planning and the similarity of the killing which, successfully executed, gave the killer enormous professional satisfaction. What led him to commit these murders?

"We don't know yet, and to answer that question we will put the facts to a psychoanalyst. It could have been because of something that happened to him as a child, either real abuse, by a parent or guardian, or a stranger, or it could be a dream that has become reality, to him, a fantasy. If we walk in the footsteps of Walters we will identify a pattern to his killings. The violence, although brutal, is just enough to kill.

"His written comments at the end of Lee Sharp's short stories are destructive, cruel and negative. Having read them, I thought they were well written and near to being publishable. It was the behaviour of a person with no empathy, only evil intent."

"Why did he pretend to be helping Lee Sharp?" asked Andy.

"To demonstrate his superiority over him as a teacher."

"Why did Lee Sharp accept the criticism for so long?"

"Because Walters behaved in a charming manner towards him. He was manipulative and he saw Sharp as an object, not as a person. If Walters killed three people, as we believe he has, he has psychopathic traits which are very uncommon and we must stop him from murdering again."

"How can we do that, sir?" said Andy.

"We need a little bit of luck, so let's go through with our plan, which is to ask for his help before we arrest and charge Harris, and see what it brings us."

"Do you think he is dangerous?"

"Walters is very dangerous, and when he thinks we are onto him he could kill both of us, but we will not give him an opportunity. To him it is a game he must win, but it is not personalised. We are just players and any player could be a target."

"So, we are targets?"

"Yes, and if we can gradually play him along until he suspects us and we become targets he will make a mistake."

"So, we are like bait," said Andy.

"We are dealing with a killer whose actions are performed skilfully, and depend on morbid influences and the curious act of stabbing twice with great force on two, possibly three occasions. So far he has had good fortune and an animal instinct for self-preservation.

"Let's begin with a friendly, light-hearted conversation, then we will ask for his help in a serious manner, and let us hope that his ego will see the whole of the Hampshire Constabulary as asking for the help of an eminent Oxford University Professor of Criminology. He has never expressed any sympathy for our victim, a well-regarded hospital consultant and an old school friend, whose life is suddenly snuffed out.

"We'll tell him about Harris and why we are convinced he is our killer, and if we study his responses, he might give us what he sees as his reasons for somebody to kill Klinker.

Make him walk in the murderer's shoes and try to get him to give us his reasons for this evil murder.

"To him we are two provincial police detectives, one a bit old and the other a rookie, new to crime solving, investigating a single murder, not looking for a serial killer, so he doesn't think for a second that we might be on to him."

"When do we open up on that?"

"We don't, not until we have evidence. So far we have nothing that would stand up in court."

◆

They arrived by appointment at Walters' small detached house on the outskirts of the city at 15.00 and were greeted in a friendly manner.

When Andy Bowen called Walters they said they wanted his advice as an expert before making an arrest. Andy suggested lunch, which he declined, blaming work pressures. 15.00 suited the detectives and as planned they presented their case against Harris, in detail, omitting any reference to his acting hobby, implying that the impersonation had been planned in order to murder Klinker. His motive being that he would inherit the estate as his brother's legitimate heir. Walters listened carefully, whilst they presented their case against Harris. When they had finished he sat staring towards the city centre through his front room window.

"Gentlemen you have no tangible evidence that he is your murderer, but everything points to him. There is no other possible reason for his behaviour which, in the circumstances, is incredible. I think you should congratulate yourselves on some superb detective work. When did you first believe that somebody could have impersonated Kaz Ali?"

"We compared his body shape from photographs taken by George Lewis, with his physical appearance at his Newport Council offices, where we photographed him leaving his office. On 8 June, his car was parked in the Havant railway station car park throughout the day of the murder, enabling him to travel to the Island to attend the reunion, murder his brother, in a place he had obviously planned, then return to Havant and drive to Southampton in time for his early evening seminar. You have to admire his courage. He could have been discovered at any time during the course of the day."

"I cannot remember having a conversation with him. I did say hello and I asked how long he was staying; he was very Indian, I thought. What an ingenious plan! He must have planned this murder weeks before, with the belief that Kaz Ali from India would never be suspected, never turn up and the murder would be unsolved. Gentlemen, I think we should celebrate with a drink. I have prepared tea with a chunk of fruitcake fresh this morning, give me a few minutes."

With that he left the detectives alone whilst he boiled a kettle for tea. The room was pleasantly decorated and clean, one would assume that the person of his stature would have a cleaner. A bookcase stood against a wall containing a selection of criminal law books by lawyers and judges and a section of light reading, mainly detective and classic horror stories.

When Walters returned with tea in a large willow teapot, water jug and a round fruitcake, that was obviously home baked, and a bottle of Rémy Martin with three brandy glasses, his mood was relaxed and for the first time since their arrival he smiled, and poured three measures into the glasses.

"We must drink a toast to your success. It was a complicated mystery, so here's to the Isle of Wight murder squad."

Bruno swallowed the brandy to stop himself laughing, and Andy followed suit.

He poured tea and using a long-bladed knife, with a bone handle, cut three large wedge-shaped portions from the fruitcake.

"This cake has been made for me by my next-door neighbour. She is elderly and looks on me as her son, and every two or three weeks she comes in with cake."

"Are they always fruitcakes?" said Andy.

"No, sometimes it's a Victoria sponge or a lemon drizzle, she makes them for the wives' group at the local church. My favourite is the fruitcake."

They all agreed it was a delicious cake and after a second cup of tea while the detectives readied themselves to leave, Walters summed up their meeting, congratulating them on solving the Klinker murder and offering to appear as an expert witness at the trial. He claimed that being present on the school outing his observations would support their murder charge, although he didn't say what those observations were, Bruno believed that he simply wanted to be seen as an eminent criminologist who'd helped solve a murder case.

When they got up to leave, Walters led Bruno out of the lounge. In a flash of a second, without breaking stride, Andy slipped the long-bladed bone handled cake knife into his document folder. After handshakes and promising a phone call with the results of their murder charge, they drove off.

Andy had a hunch. But what would the knife tell them? He also knew that stealing the cake knife would blow this case wide open and Walters would know he was a suspect.

◆

When he told Bruno what he had done, he did not get the bollocking he'd anticipated, instead Bruno said they would submit it to forensics in Portsmouth for analysis on their way home.

"It was a peculiar knife to use to cut a cake," said Bruno, "a long narrow blade with a bone handle. In all it must measure 12 inches."

"What do you think he will do when he finds the knife missing?"

"He will wait, because if it reveals nothing contrary to what you are thinking you might feel like returning it."

"How?" said Andy. "I'm sorry Professor, I accidently stole your knife!"

A smile from Bruno implied they never would admit to stealing it.

"So, do you think it could be the murder weapon?" said Bruno.

"I stared at the knife for several minutes over tea. It was the right size to commit these murders, without looking like a murder weapon. My mother use to have a set of bone-handled knives and the handles often fell off when washing them. She threw them away when she discovered they harboured germs inside the handles. If this is the murder weapon, it's possible that a tiny spec of blood could have remained in the handle which might give us a DNA profile," said Andy.

It's possible, thought Bruno, but a long shot. "Well, let's find out," said Bruno, knowing that if a victim's blood matched it would be Klinker's, as the most recent victim. "Could a kitchen knife used to cut a fruitcake be a murder weapon?"

"Think about it," said Andy. "No weapon has been found at the scene of either crime, so the killer is still in possession of it. He's not going to keep it in the kitchen. Until I stole his knife, he had no idea he was a suspect. The cakes are a gift, so he'd not be equipped with a stand and a cake knife."

"The knife will tell us nothing, or everything. However, if there is just a speck of blood that had seeped into the bone handle, a DNA result could prove our case."

"Do you think he deliberately cut the cake with the murder weapon to satisfy a macabre impulse?"

"Probably, it's a strange sort of joke, and the kind that could backfire," said Bruno.

"Did we get anything from him?"

"Only what we observed around us."

"For a man who must be wealthy there was little evidence of affluence. Here is a man who has earned a good salary for twenty-five years, and lives modestly."

"All academics are like that," said Bruno.

"He is not a drinker or gambler, his wristwatch could not have cost £50, the furniture in his house was dated, and a neighbour bakes him a cake."

"I don't know what that tells us and it doesn't help us solve the case."

CHAPTER 29

Monday 16 July

The Portsmouth Forensic laboratory needed three days to examine the cake knife and a blood sample from the victim.

So far, no call had been received from Walters about the missing knife. He would believe that by now the detectives would have called him to report on the outcome of charging Harris with the murder of Dr Klinker.

"Why don't we call him? Say Harris is away from the Island, and we are waiting for him to return. It will give him an opportunity to respond to our visit and we can sense any change of mood."

"Okay," said Bruno. "Just don't mention the knife."

Andy immediately picked up the office phone and dialled the number in Oxford.

"Hello, Professor Walters? It's Andy Bowen, Isle of Wight Police. Harris is away for a couple of days, off the Island, so we shall have to wait until he comes back tomorrow, or the next day. I thought you might be waiting for an update, and thanks for your help, you helped to clear our minds."

"Glad to be of assistance, any time, just call. And thank you for the update," Walters said, and put the phone down.

Andy turned to Bruno. "If the knife draws a blank we have to rely on the strange method of killing the three victims. Each was using a urinal, standing with their backs to the killer, and was knifed in the same place on the body. What is the significance of that: the surprise, they did not see the face of the killer? Or is there something about a urinal that attracts the murderer? We need to take a close look at the prison murder, and read the report of the investigating officers."

◈

Obtaining a copy of the prison and police archives was a task for Kevin Bell, who was charged with chasing Portsmouth Forensics for the DNA report on the knife.

The Exeter prison murder was fifteen years ago and Bruno knew they'd be lucky if any records still existed. It was a long journey and the prison governor was available to see them the following day.

CHAPTER 30

Tuesday 17 July

They were in luck. Stan Lucas had been the governor of Exeter Prison for twenty years and remembered the murder of Simon Dyer, aged twenty-nine. He pulled the Dyer file out of his archive.

Dyer was serving a life sentence for manslaughter. While driving under the influence he had killed a woman and child on a zebra crossing. He had served nine years and was recommended for parole within three months of seeing a counsellor, who would rubber-stamp the parole board's decision. Sadly, he never made it. Some enemy he had made in prison custody knifed him in the back in the lavatory while he stood at the urinal.

That washed away any doubts the detectives had about Ian Walters being the killer they were searching for. Now they felt more confident than ever.

"Do you have any reference to the counsellor who was assessing Simon Dyer for release?"

"We know that Ian Walters was his prison visitor, or counsellor, and he had visited him on the afternoon of Dyer's murder."

"There isn't anything about his visits to the prison on file?"

Stan Lucas explained, "Fifteen years ago it was easier to move around the prison as an authorised visitor. But I remember the guy clearly. I never worked out who he thought he was, mind you. He never asked me a single question about Dyer, or provided us with any feedback. He made me feel as if I was a prisoner here, and that's how he regarded us all, as if we were all inmates. Dyer was the only prisoner he went near here and after the murder we banned him from the prison. I know the police interviewed him, looked at his notes, but nothing came of that."

"What did the police do?"

"Everyone was banged up for two days whilst the police conducted their investigations, but no one was charged. Most of them don't have access to the relevant floor, and there was no weapon and no evidence that it was a prisoner. It obviously was, but without evidence the police did nothing. Their attitude is that we should keep our own house in order."

"Do you have a Coroner's report?"

"Yes, Dyer was killed with a long thin blade from behind, two stab wounds."

"Can we copy a few pages from your record? There are a few things that interest us, we don't want the whole file."

"You can take it with you, if you give me a signature, and promise to return it," he said. "And share your findings when you return it."

"We might do better than that," said Andy.

Convinced they had enough to charge Walters, Bruno and Andy made their way back to the Newport Police Station.

※

When Bruno called in to his office, Kevin Bell read out the result of the DNA analysis of the bone-handled kitchen knife.

It confirmed a match with Klinker's blood sample which, crucially, confirmed beyond any doubt that Walters was the killer. The nature of the killing at Exeter Prison fifteen years ago, and the DNA match, with a scarcely traceable blood stain beneath the bone handle of the knife that Andy Bowen had taken from Ian Walters; these two discoveries were proof that Walters was their man. However, Bruno knew they needed something more, even a confession, to be certain of obtaining a conviction.

Walters' matter-of-fact response to Andy's phone call suggested that he was waiting for a call, saying they had charged

Harris with Klinker's murder. A delay, for whatever reason, irritated him, and with the disappearance of the murder weapon from his home might have caused him considerable anguish.

◆

When Bruno updated their progress to his boss John Barlow, he was delighted. Barlow warned him against interviewing and charging Walters in Oxford.

"If you do that, they will claim credit for your hard work. Bring him here for cross-examination and I will see that does not happen, and everything positive in finding a serial killer will be credited to us, or you, and not claimed by the Oxford police unit. So you have to bring him to Newport. Can you do that? He has to be charged with Klinker's murder on the Island. What follows, namely the murder in Exeter prison and Lee Sharp's murder in Oxford, you can get to whilst he is on remand, but the DNA blood match from the bone handled knife and Klinker is evidence to charge him with his murder in the Havenstreet Gents' lavatory."

"Thank you, sir," said Bruno. "We will do as you advise."

◆

Getting Walters to make another visit to the Island without a pretext might be a problem, so they needed a reason that would trigger his ego.

"If he thinks we suspect him, he will come to challenge us because he believes he is untouchable."

"At some time, we have suspected several of the school party, including him, but the only evidence he thinks we have leads to Harris. So, it's not a case of Daniel walking into the lion's den; he is king of the jungle, the master listening to his subjects. Why don't we ask him to sit in as an observer whilst we charge Harris in his professional capacity?"

"Trick him, you mean?"

"He will come, sir," said Andy.

"I'm not sure we'll get that past John Barlow."

"But are we not charging Harris?"

It was a task Bruno could not delegate, so he dialled Walters' Oxford home number. The Professor was at home and he listened to Bruno's pitch and agreed to come on Saturday around midday, which gave the police time to prepare the charge documentation.

Andy was not at all surprised that Walters had accepted Bruno's invitation to witness the police charge an innocent man with Klinker's murder.

"His behaviour is consistent with that of a psychopath. Inviting him to attend indicated a total lack of remorse, empathy or emotion for us charging Harris for the murder. He sees Harris as an object to be incarcerated. It is an opportunity for him to display his superior knowledge as an exceptional person."

Bruno did not feel elation at the point they had reached in their investigation into the death of Klinker. A clumsy murder by a suspect who had a viable motive would have satisfied him and confirmed their place as two good solid Isle of Wight detectives. But that their victim, Dr Klinker, had been murdered by a psychopath, a serial killer, a man who sought only malicious satisfaction in the act of murder with no purpose other than committing the act itself, aroused feelings of hatred and disgust, and numbed his senses. And he would have to fight tooth-and-nail to see that he spent the rest of his life behind bars.

The gloom that had enveloped him was suddenly lifted in a call from Maisie Longmore. She had arranged a funeral for her husband, a burial plot in Ryde churchyard and a priest to take the Requiem Mass. All that remained was for the Coroner to release the body. She spoke in a kind, gentle manner that gave him peace of mind that Dr Klinker would be seen off properly. Bruno put her request at the top of his list, but meanwhile he felt there was still something missing with regard to Walters.

During his meetings with him he had never mentioned his parents or his association with Portsmouth. He had lived and worked in the city for four years, during which time he had lived with his parents, and they might be able to shine a light into a dark corner and provide Bruno with the missing piece of the jigsaw. To avoid crowding the couple with two detectives, Bruno choose to visit the Admiral and his wife alone, delegating the task of helping Maisie Longmore obtain the release of Dr Klinker's body to Andy Bowen.

Kevin Bell set up a meeting between Bruno and Admiral Walters through Jim, the concierge at their apartment, who confirmed that they were at home, giving Bruno the immediate opportunity to call.

◈

Surprisingly Admiral Walters did not sound like a very old man in his eighties, and agreed to see Bruno within a couple of hours.

Jim, the concierge, met Bruno in the foyer of the apartment building.

"Detective Inspector, the Admiral is expecting you, sir, and he has asked me to show you up."

As the lift took them to the fifth floor, Bruno became nervous at meeting two octogenarians and unsettling them in their old age.

He was searching for a link, a common thread that ran through the three murders. Something had happened in Walters' home life, or his school life, that had given him a lifelong desire for revenge.

The Admiral's home was a luxuriously decorated apartment on the top floor of a superior apartment building with a magnificent view of the Solent. The relative new-build was within walking distance of Klinker's artist school friend with the same magnificent views of the sea.

The Admiral and his wife of nearly sixty years made an

attractive couple, given they were both eighty-four years of age.

"Good morning, Inspector. You said you wanted to discuss our son, Ian? Have you spoken to Ian?" said the Admiral.

"Several times," said Bruno.

Mrs Walters joined them as the Admiral led Bruno through into a room overlooking the waters, through which all vessels entering Portsmouth harbour would pass before them.

"Is he in any trouble with the police?" Mrs Walters asked.

"We are investigating a murder that took place at Havenstreet Steam Railway on 8 June."

"That weekend was the last time we saw him," she said.

"Are you aware of the school outing that he attended on that day, at which one of his school friends was murdered during that school reunion?"

"Oh, how awful," said Mrs Walters. "Which person was murdered?"

"Dr Klinker, madam. We are speaking to all of the nine attendees, one of whom we think could be the killer. Could you shed some light on his early life? I know he joined Ryde School aged twelve or thirteen, and before that he was at school in Portsmouth."

"Is he a suspect?" she asked.

"Not more than the other eight attendees at the reunion at this stage."

"As a little boy he went to St James's Preparatory School which is in Southsea from the age of six until he went to board in Ryde. Who was murdered?" said Mrs Walters repeating her question and displaying some anxiety, as one might expect in an elderly lady.

"A former pupil who was on the school outing, Dr Klinker, who was a consultant surgeon at a prominent London hospital."

"Oh dear," she said. "And you think our son could have killed him?"

"Anyone who was visiting the Havenstreet Steam Railway that day, well over one hundred visitors and many others, could have committed the crime. Since the killing we have interviewed the school party."

"And how can we help?"

Her tone was aggressively defensive which prompted Bruno to proceed in a direct manner.

"You said that weekend was the last time you saw him, is that correct?"

"Yes," said Admiral Walters. "He arrived, as usual for Ian, out of the blue and said he was visiting the Island on Friday, which would have been 8 June, to go on a school trip."

"He came on Wednesday," interrupted Mrs Walters. "And he went to the Island on Thursday and Friday. He said he wanted to see how long it would take to get to the steam railway. Apparently, it was straightforward. The train from Ryde stops at Havenstreet. Is our son a suspect?" repeated Mrs Walters.

"No one has been ruled out yet," said Bruno.

"So how can we help you?" said the Admiral.

"You've already been very helpful, sir," said Bruno. "We know your son is an eminent criminologist at Oxford University, and he has helped us with his analytical approach. We would like to fill in our profile of him by knowing about his private life."

"He doesn't have one," said Mrs Walters.

"We know nothing about his private life, Inspector," said the Admiral. "When he comes here, he eats our food, drinks our wine, treats this place like a bloody hotel and then buggers off. We think he only comes to check if we are still alive. We never know when he might turn up," she said.

"Does he visit often?"

"Not often," said the Admiral. "But we are always happy to see him."

"You might be," said Mrs Walters. "Inspector, we are ter-rified of him, always have been."

"That is why we sent him to Ryde School," said the Admiral. "We thought he needed a more structured environment. He is a bright lad and now he is an Oxford University Professor, and we are proud of him. But on a personal level he guards his privacy, there has always been a distance between us. I blame that on my job. I was often at sea for months on end, leaving Harriet to look after the boy and they were never close, and when I was home, I wanted her exclusive atten-tion, so I didn't get to know Ian. In the early 1980s, during the Falklands war, I was away most of the time, so I never saw the boy. When he was eighteen, he was gone, up to London to study Law. So, I know very little about him that might be of interest to you, Inspector."

"But he did live with you for four years after he came back from London to work at Portsmouth University?"

"Yes, it was not a happy time. He came to live here because he had no money, all he had done was study, and at the age of thirty Portsmouth University was his only job offer. It was not what we wanted so we offered to rent a small flat for him, but he refused that offer. Instead he just stayed here. We didn't see much of him because he had his meals at the university. When he came home, he'd hide away in his room, watching television. He would use the bathroom and make a noise in the kitchen. We tried to be nice to him and get to know him, but he'd communicate with single words or short sentences, and that went on for four years. During that time, he'd saved up and could afford to rent in Exeter, where he'd secured a senior lecturer's position."

"We are sorry we can't be of more help to you, Inspector," said Mrs Walters, which Bruno read as an instruction to leave, and believing he had obtained everything he could, he brought the meeting to an end by thanking them for their help.

After Bruno had said goodbye to Mrs Walters, the Admiral said, "I will show you out, Inspector. I need to speak to Jim."

They left the flat watched by the sad disapproving eye of Mrs Walters. In the lift to the ground floor the Admiral said, "Inspector, there is something I should tell you because occasionally it troubles me, so I will walk along to where you can best get a taxi and explain. I need to tell you why we chose Ryde School for Ian. We had to find a school away from Portsmouth when he was expelled for fighting from St James's Preparatory School. He attacked a pupil in the school lavatories. Of course Ian denied this and claimed he was attacked first, but the other boy's account of the circumstances was believed, because it was the second occasion that Ian had been involved in a fracas in the lavatories.

"Those incidents have worried us ever since. We thought that when he was at Ryde School it had been just an incident in his growing up, but his behaviour has disturbed Harriet and me for most of our lives, and as she told you, she has always been frightened of him. I thought you should know of this because there is obviously something you have not told us, and I thought it might help."

It did, but Bruno felt under no obligation to tell the Admiral the reason he had sought him out. He would learn the horrible truth soon enough.

In the taxi ride to Clarence Pier he became depressed at the situation he found himself in. Was it the Admiral's sting in the tail, or the entire situation? He didn't know.

He was homing in on the killer. And his visit to Walters' parents had provided the proof he was looking for, which confirmed the Oxford professor was a serial killer.

Exactly what event had taken place in his early life that had turned him into a killer would probably never be discovered, certainly not by the detectives.

However, the Admiral's private admission that a traumatic event in childhood had almost certainly determined how his son had endured and lived his life was the final piece of the jigsaw for Bruno.

◆

Back at Newport Police station Bruno informed Andy and John Barlow of the outcome of his visit to Admiral and Mrs Walters and drafted the charge documentation, which concentrated solely on the murder of Klinker and the weapon that had been used in the murder.

Andy Bowen had spent his morning with Maisie Longmore, or Mrs Geoffrey Klinker, as she was to be identified in the police records at the Coroner's office in Newport. He had not been successful in negotiating a release of the body for burial but had gained a promise that once the police had charged a suspect with murder, the body might be released.

Maisie Longmore confided to Andy that it had never been her wish to remain married, it was his, as he too had promised in their marriage vows to remain married until death "us do part". He would of course have consented if she wanted to divorce, but as a devout Catholic girl, he also knew that she would never have divorced him.

She wished she had kept in touch with him over the years, she said. Perhaps this would never have happened?

Andy had reassured her that she could never have changed the circumstances that had caused his death.

Andy regarded Bruno's visit to Walters' parents as vindication of his belief that in the mind of a psychopath lurks a memory of a traumatic or violent experience endured during childhood.

◆

In preparation for Saturday's visit by their chief suspect Bruno took off to relax and enjoy a Friday fish supper with Janet at their favourite fish restaurant in Newport.

"How do you know he'll turn up tomorrow?" she said. "He must believe you suspect him?"

"That is why he will turn up," said Bruno. "He has to come to find out. I don't know if he believed us when we said we intend to charge Harris, but he will come."

"Why?"

"My guess is he knows what we are up to and with his knowledge of legal procedure he has enough experience of police work to know how we have to operate. However we behave towards him, he will believe that he is untouchable, and even if we were to cobble together evidence to charge him with Klinker's murder, he would convince himself that a jury would not convict him."

"Tell me about the knife," said Janet.

"It's one of those pieces of table cutlery that had a yellow-ish-white bone handle which you might find at a boot sale. The handle slides over the steel shaft of the blade. Within the shaft were identifiable specks of blood that proved a match with Klinker's DNA. Fingerprints were on the handle, which we believe are Walters', although we've not matched those yet. He cut the fruitcake with the knife, so the prints on the handle will be his."

Janet did not see how Bruno could fail to get a conviction with that evidence.

Bruno was tired and needed to switch off so, as was his usual habit, he changed the subject as soon as he was politely able, to talk about gardening and rebuilding a dry-stone wall at the side of their house. He also promised to visit Morrisons for their regular Saturday shop before meeting Ian Walters at lunchtime.

He was now convinced that Ian Walters was the killer of Klinker and at least two other men and he had to be stopped before another person succumbed to a fourth vicious murder. He knew he had one shot at nailing Walters and if he wriggled off the hook for any reason, another person's life would soon be in danger.

In preparation for formally accusing him he had spent

three hours laying his case before the police lawyer. This prosecutor would stand up in court on Monday before the judge and present the evidence in the police case and request a remand in custody until trial. He would be supported by a criminal psychologist who would ask for a remand in custody to obtain psychological evidence.

CHAPTER 31

Saturday 21 July

At noon the following day Professor Ian Walters walked into the reception at Newport Police Station in good spirits anticipating the warm reception his stature as Oxford University Professor of Criminal Jurisprudence merited.

Waiting for him, supporting Bruno and Andy, were two uniformed police officers, several other policemen and women going about their police work, and Superintendent John Barlow. Having signed the visitors' book a Police Constable said: "Detective Inspector Peach is waiting for you, sir, in his office. I'll show you the way."

He led him through the secure part of the station to an interview room that was fitted out with electronic devices, recording the meeting audibly and visually, which could be watched and heard from an adjoining room. Although Bruno did not believe that Walters would attempt to leave the room at any point during their meeting, he'd ensured that he would not be able to exit the station.

"Good morning, Ian, and thank you for making the journey to meet us here."

They shook hands like old friends and sat down on comfortable chairs across a rectangular table.

Walters was in a happy mood having brought a notebook and pencil to record the events of the afternoon in what he believed was the crunch meeting with the suspect.

"Ian, we would like to begin with a brief recap on our investigation which has brought us to our conclusion as to the identity of the killer of Dr Geoffrey Klinker on 8 June. We have interviewed on more than one occasion all of the school friends who attended the reunion, and everyone who had any social or business connection with the victim here

273

on the Island and in London, as well as everyone present at Havenstreet railway station on the day of the murder. A variety of vague, inconclusive motives exist that in certain circumstances might persuade a determined individual to kill but none, except in one case, are other than circumstantial. We have no evidence to support any further investigation."

Bruno then went through those suspects and persons of interest whose motives might be considered as a reason to kill, eliminating each person in turn, avoiding any reference or mention of the Professor who listened carefully making the occasional written note in his book.

"This brings us to the last person on our list of persons of interest, and that is yourself, Professor."

"I have told you everything I know about the murder, and I agreed with your conclusion that Arnold Harris is the killer."

"But that is no longer our conclusion. We now believe we have evidence to charge you with the murder of Dr Klinker."

Walters sat calmly while Bruno began to make his case.

"During our investigation we researched the background of every person involved in our investigation. They have ordinary backgrounds and no one provided us with any substantial reason for murdering someone who was almost a stranger to them."

"And you are saying that I had such a background?"

"Oh yes," said Bruno. "But not one that you would discuss with me."

"Then I don't see how you can charge me with a murder with a reason you are not prepared to put to me. That's absurd, Inspector."

Up until now Walters had remained aloof, as Bruno believed was his normal manner with the police, with whom he had been dealing for a lifetime.

"The secrets of the backgrounds of the school party were

in a few cases unusual, but did not persuade us that they were in anyway capable of, or connected with, this murder. Except for yours, Professor."

"Are you saying that you have invited me here under false pretences?"

"Not at all."

"I understood I was invited to witness the police charging Arnold Harris with this murder?"

"The procedure for charging a suspect with murder can only be done under certain rules and they do not permit us inviting a spectator."

"So, I am here under false pretences?"

"If you like Professor, we prefer to think you are here to assist us with our enquiries and to enable us formally to charge you with the murder of Dr Klinker on 8 June, and to persuade the magistrates to remand you in custody until you appear for trial."

"On what evidence are you proposing to charge me?"

"We shall present our evidence to a judge in court on Monday, until then you will be detained here in a police cell."

Bruno then read out the charge notice given to Professor Walters, as follows:

"On 8 June you murdered Dr Geoffrey Klinker in the public lavatory on Platform A at the Isle of Wight Steam Railway Havenstreet station, by administering two fatal wounds through the liver and the heart, using a seven-inch bladed knife.

"Signed Detective Inspector Bruno Peach.

"Signed Superintendent John Barlow."

"You do not have to say anything, but anything you do say may be used in evidence."

The notice contained his full name, address and date of birth. Bruno confirmed that a qualified defence lawyer would visit him within one hour to advise him during the formal charge procedure, and he would be detained in a police cell until Monday.

Walters said nothing, except for repeating that this was a mistake for which the police would pay.

"How could you treat a man such as me, an Oxford Professor, in this manner? When there is not a scrap of evidence to support a murder charge based on this amateurish investigation and borne out of ignorance. You will be drummed out of the police for this colossal error," said the Professor.

Bruno adhered strictly to the correct procedure they had to follow under the Police and Criminal Evidence Act 1984. They had a short timescale within which the charge had to be made, and clear evidence was needed to convince the judge that Professor Walters was a danger to the public and capable of committing another murder if given bail.

◆

Bruno had recruited Jack Lewinski, a local criminal lawyer who knew the ropes, as Walters' legal representative who would try for bail for Walters if the police case were not perfect, and for it to be perfect would require precise adherence to PACE rules. Lewinski was also clever and would see through Walters.

Based upon the evidence submitted by Bruno, the experienced police lawyer was confident of obtaining a decision from the judge that would detain Walters in a remand centre until the trial.

Also present at Monday's hearing would be a Doctor White, a consultant psychiatrist, who would support the absolute necessity to detain the suspect.

◆

It was little over an hour later when Bruno and Andy showed up back at the Newport Police cells to charge Ian Walters with the murder of Dr Klinker. Jack Lewinski had responded quickly but wanted an extra hour with his client to put him on a solid base and understand his defendant. When he was ready, the two detectives and Superintendent Barlow assembled in the Police Station interview room.

Superintendent Johnny Barlow was confident that his two detectives were well in control of the case. He too was learning, and his presence provided the necessary level of authority to detain the suspect in a Police cell, pending bringing him before a judge in the Magistrates' court on Monday morning, where Police Counsel would ask the judge to place the suspect on remand at a secure prison, namely Winchester, to await trial for the murder of Dr Geoffrey Klinker on the afternoon of 8 June.

Pending the hearing on Monday, Lewinski rather tamely requested that his client should be released to return to Oxford, on his undertaking to attend the court on Monday, which he knew was a pointless request. When he said he needed more time with Walters to understand the detail, Bruno said that he could visit Walters at any time in the Police Station cells before the court hearing. He claimed that from what he had heard from his client, the charges were preposterous and invented by Police, who had failed to find the real killer.

Walters did not speak during the meeting, sitting quietly staring at the police officers in turn, not knowing that his days as a free man were probably over, possibly forever, and if he was found guilty, he would be detained in a high security establishment, determined by the judge based on medical and psychiatric reports, for the rest of his life.

Lewinsky asked Bruno to reveal the police evidence to him. However, Bruno relied on Police procedure not to disclose any evidence until the court proceedings in front of a magistrate on Monday morning, when a Police barrister would present the Police case.

Lewinsky understood the Police powers to detain a suspect for forty-eight hours on suspicion without charging him and that, if necessary, an extension could be granted. On Walters' insistence he tried again, unsuccessfully, to persuade the Police to accept his promise to return for the hearing at the court on Monday. This plea was rejected, and Walters was then returned to a Police cell to wait an appearance before a magistrate at 10.00 a.m. on Monday, conveniently allowing Bruno time before the court hearing to brief the Prosecution Counsel with the evidence he hoped would persuade the Magistrate to remand him in custody to await trial.

Bruno was certain they had the right man, but uneasy about the knife as their key evidence, and suspected Lewinsky would claim or suggest a Police stitch-up. In case Walters denied ownership, he requested from his boss a search warrant of Walters' home in Oxford, which was granted by the local Magistrate after consultation with Johnny Barlow. This enabled him to take Janet on a visit to this wonderful city to spend a few hours visiting its famous sites.

⁂

Bruno, Andy Bowen and a third officer took a tool kit to open the door locks and searched the home of Professor Walters, looking for evidence that might prove conclusively that he was their man. Bruno recognised the interior of a middle-aged bachelor's dwelling, having lived as one for most of his life. Walters was organised, yet ordinary. His wardrobe contained fashionable, up-to-date suits and jackets you'd expect an academic to wear. His shoes were from Barratts. The furnishings were unspectacular, and if one day for some reason you did not return, you would not miss it. It was no more homely than you would experience in a modest hotel, or a rented flat.

Paperwork in his study lay on his table: phone, council tax and other bills of no interest, except for an unopened credit card statement from Barclays for the month of June, which they opened and examined. The itemised transactions showed that Walters had bought a return ticket to Ryde Pier Head on three consecutive days, 6, 7, and 8 June.

Bruno recalled his conversation with Admiral and Mrs Walters who had said their son had arrived at their apartment on Tuesday 5 June and had visited the Island on Wednesday, Thursday and Friday, one and two days before the murder. Could that have been to visit Havenstreet Railway Station to identify a location to commit his crime?

Bruno thought it would be sufficient proof that he'd visited the Island on the days before the murder for it to be used as evidence. What other reason except to plan his murder would he visit the Island the day before the murder? It was compensation for Kevin Bell's failure to identify Walters on the CCTV cameras at Portsmouth or Ryde stations.

The second discovery of major importance was the boxed set of bone-handled cutlery on the china cabinet. There Bruno found what his instinct had driven him in search of – an irrefutable piece of evidence. On a lower shelf lay a polished mahogany wooden canteen containing an eight-piece place setting, a serrated bread knife, serving spoons and a space for a missing bone handled carving knife that almost certainly was for the knife that Andy Bowen had taken with him when they had tea with Walters in his house. Bruno took the decision to remove the canteen of cutlery and credit card statements to place before the judge at Monday's court hearing.

Armed with these crucial pieces of evidence on a beautiful afternoon the three detectives could at last relax, so they joined Janet for afternoon tea. She was waiting for them in the Churchill Hotel, occupying possibly the same table as Ian Walters prior to murdering Lee Sharp. The hotel furnishings looked tired and had remained unchanged for some years, and the young waiter who served tea looked as vulnerable as Lee Sharp would have done four years before.

By the time they had to leave, Bruno's mood had changed.

He had become upbeat and confident that they had their
man, and that the following morning he would be remanded
in custody to await trial as the criminal responsible for three
murders.

CHAPTER 32

Monday 23 July

At 10.00 a.m. on Monday Bruno and Andy met at the court and presented their evidence to Prosecuting Counsel, explaining the who, why and where to Mr Justin McConner, QC. They had arrived at the conclusion that the Oxford Professor, Ian Walters, was a serial killer who had to be detained in custody.

Mr McConner listened and wrote down everything he needed to build the prosecution case, sometimes playing devil's advocate at certain points of their reporting. At the conclusion of his examination of the two detectives he congratulated them on their skilful detective work, and promised a successful outcome in court.

At 9.45 a.m. they were ushered into Court No 1, before His Honour Judge James, a young man in his forties having enjoyed a successful twenty-year career as a QC.

Professor Walters was brought into court with his lawyer, Jack Lewinsky. Walters did not look tired or dishevelled as you might expect after two nights in Police cells. He looked as if he had just showered, put on a clean shirt to prove to the judge that he was not the person presented to him by the Police. Bruno was certain that if these charges went to trial Walters would engage a senior Counsel with a reputation for winning this kind of case, but for now Lewinsky was his man.

Mr McConner's first act in the session was to request a five-minute recess to speak to the judge. This was a usual request for a prosecuting counsel who wanted to share evidence that he did not wish to rely on at the hearing.

During the five minutes Bruno stared continuously at Ian Walters for a sign but received not one glance. He had made every effort to appear unruffled, look professional and worthy of the position he held at the Oxford College where he occupied the Chair of Criminal Jurisprudence, and to which he would never return.

◆

What Mr McConner told Judge James was detail of charges they intended to bring for the murders of Lee Sharp and Simon Dyer, the Exeter Prison inmate, which would involve the Police from Devon and Oxfordshire, where these murders were committed and remained unsolved open cases.

The Police evidence presented by Mr McConner began with a summary of the background to the murder of Dr Klinker by the accused.

Walters sat motionless in disbelief as the two crucial pieces of evidence were presented. It was a short statement by prosecuting counsel, sufficient to convince the judge to remand Walters in custody. Lewinsky's response on behalf of his client was to deny the charges and request that Walters address the judge, which was granted.

"Your Honour, these charges are an outrageous fabrication. My involvement with Isle of Wight Police has been at their request because they have repeatedly failed to find the murderer. My qualifications as an eminent Criminologist led them to seek my advice, which I gave, as to who the suspects were and the possible motives for the murder of a wealthy Island resident. I met the victim once on a school reunion six weeks ago, prior to which I had not seen this man since we left school in 1983. Once I had decided to attend the reunion I did visit the Island on the Wednesday and Thursday before the day of the reunion for nostalgic reasons, and as I had not visited for thirty-five years, to familiarise myself with the travel arrangements for meeting my old school friends. As regards the murder weapon, I can't imagine how the Police arrived at their decision that it was used to kill Dr Klinker. As a professional analyst of the criminal mind I do not connect myself with this crime, and it must stare any fair-minded person in the face, that this is a stitch-up by two failed detectives, which could result in the murderer going free.

"Your Honour, if I may, I'd like to give you examples in cases I examined of how Police detectives tire after exhausting every avenue and then narrow their investigation to who they can pin the crime on, instead of revisiting their work done to find flaws on their deductions. Let me give you an example by drawing your attention to a recent murder enquiry where a wife was accused of murdering her husband."

This was a far as judge James was prepared to allow him to go. Before Walters could begin his lecture, he firmly curtailed his presentation.

"Professor Walters, this is not a university lecture and we are not undergraduates, so I do not want to attend a lecture. Please reserve your statements for your legal representatives, or your trial judge. Professor Walters, on the evidence that has been put before me, I shall remand you in custody until the trial date is set by the Crown Prosecution Service. In view of the seriousness of the charge, I shall officially remand you to HM Prison Winchester, in which city your trial will take place."

With that pronouncement Judge James left the court, and the accused was taken back to the cells.

◈

Bruno first phoned Superintendent Woodruff of the Oxford Constabulary, then spoke on the phone to the Governor of the prison at Exeter, informing them that Professor Walters had been charged with the murder of Dr Klinker and was remanded in custody awaiting trial. He arranged a conference call to discuss their conclusions regarding the unsolved murders in their areas, and Professor Walters' connection with each case.

Superintendent Nigel Woodruff from Oxford was delighted to hear from Bruno and was excited at solving the Lee

Sharp murder. He agreed to visit Newport Police Station the following day. Superintendent Woodruff had considered their failure to find the killer as a personal black mark on a distinguished career, probably the result of not believing the killer could be someone as close as a professor from an Oxford college.

Likewise, Chief Superintendent David Cassidy from Exeter prison agreed to attend the meeting on Tuesday afternoon with Devon Constabulary.

CHAPTER 33

Tuesday 24 July

Bruno began the meeting with the two senior officers from Oxford and Exeter by explaining Dr Klinker's murder, highlighting the killer's method and the similarities between Klinker's killing and that of Lee Sharp in Oxford and Simon Dyer at HM Prison in Exeter.

Bruno produced a drawing showing location, method of killing, and the proximity of Ian Walters to each killing.

Individually each killing did not connect Walters to the victim even though he was almost present on each occasion, at the Churchill Hotel in Oxford, as a prison visitor in Exeter and finally as an attendee at the Ryde School reunion. Altogether the case was overwhelming.

Having not been on the list of suspects in the other constabularies was understandable. Now that everything had changed, based on the information he had given them, Bruno requested they reopen the case and examine their investigations to search for a link between the victims and Walters. Then additional charges could be brought before the judge in the central criminal court in Winchester, where all serious criminals were placed on remand until a trial date.

Both officers congratulated Bruno and his team on their investigation and jointly agreed to prosecute Walters. They promised an immediate response to Bruno's request to support the Island police in their endeavour and to search their records for evidence which knowledge of the identity of the killer might reveal.

Bruno was not as optimistic as the senior police officers congratulating him on his success. He knew that an adept lawyer could render his evidence suspect and inadmissible at trial. Walters would see his trial as an opportunity to show everyone, the judge and jury, the police, the press and the public – in fact the whole world – what a clever criminologist he was.

Bruno had no doubt that Walters was clever, but did that suggest he might set traps with false evidence? Every serial killer displayed traits, they engaged in vendettas against certain types. They never admitted their guilt, or confessed, even after a lifetime of incarceration in a secure prison. They appear devoid of insecurities and doubts that conceal the evil acts that cause them to embark on their individual crusade of heartless evil.

Bruno knew that when the judges set this case down for trial it would take several weeks of preparation. It was eventually set down for 28 November, giving both sides four months to prepare their case.

Superintendent Woodruff had appointed Bob Lord, a detective, to liaise and assist Bruno in any further investigation in Oxford. That began with Bruno's request to visit the college where Walters lectured in Criminology. If possible, Bruno wanted to link his academic work with the three murders, and find out if Walters had some personal knowledge that only a participant in the killing could possess.

Police generally understand that criminology is not concerned with ways of catching criminals; that is for them, assisted by a good supply of information from witnesses and the public. It is an academic discipline, which explains the cause of crime through behaviour that violates and denies basic human rights that are not enshrined in law.

To do this the criminologist develops an insight into other disciplines, such as psychiatry, sociology, psychology and law. Bruno wanted to discover Walters' approach to his subject. To do so, Detective Bob Lord had obtained permission from the College President to enter Walters' rooms at St John's College. These consisted of two comfortably furnished rooms in the North Quadrangle. One, furnished with table and chairs, was used for individual tutorials and a second comfortable lounge study, had a desk and a computer.

The room provided space for books and storage for personal files on undergraduates. It was an insider study teaching environment, in which one could remain without contact with the University life surrounding it, or integrate fully with the college social life. It seemed that Walters fell into the former category as when his name was mentioned to other lecturers, they had no idea of who he was except as a person they occasionally saw in the Senior Common Room, or at lunch in Hall.

They did acknowledge, however, that he gave well-attended lectures on his subject in the St Cross Building lecture theatres during term time.

Bruno had no preconceived idea of what they were looking for, except to re-create the real Walters, and try to understand as much about him as possible.

His behaviour was not dissimilar to the accepted and well understood pattern of a serial killer. Many kept a diary which recorded their reactions to their self-centred, narcissistic deeds. Perhaps somewhere in Walters' files lay an explanation of this kind?

They were fortunate, because amongst his case study files were media reports on serial murder cases, downloaded from the internet. Two of these were Harold Shipman, guilty of murdering two hundred elderly, mostly female patients, and Peter Sutcliffe, the Yorkshire Ripper, who had killed a dozen females on the 1980s.

The newspaper reports on their activities were graphic and Walters had underlined passages that were relevant to a study of serial killers.

Amongst these files three were in the names of Simon Dyer, Lee Sharp and Dr Geoffrey Klinker, suggesting that he had a personal interest in the three deceased as subjects or victims. These were in the same section as Shipman and

Sutcliffe, and suggested a more sinister conclusion. It was as if he were making a specialist study of serial killers, Andy Bowen suggested.

That thought crossed Bruno's mind, but he dismissed it for fear it could shake his belief that Walters was guilty of at least three murders, and for the want of a more concerted report at the time of the killing by the Portsmouth police, possibly a fourth.

But what the separate files contained was sensational, starting with Simon Dyer, the prisoner at Exeter prison who was murdered in the same manner as Lee Sharp and Dr Klinker. He was described as a simple-minded, long serving killer, who had been unlucky to have attracted the attention of an inmate, who was seeking revenge against a person who had abused him in a public lavatory in an earlier part of his life, possibly in his childhood, which suggested that Walters believed that some crimes were justifiable, contrary to the accepted belief amongst criminologists.

Walters avoided describing the manner of the victim's death in detail, as it would have required an explanation and a conclusion, as if he was so familiar with the victim's death that he could not write about it.

Lee Sharp's file contained a description of the young man, his background, his job and his aspirations to become a writer. There were dates of his weekly meetings with Lee Sharp in the Churchill Hotel lounge, where he went for tea, and sometimes early evening for a whisky and soda, before dining, presumably alone at home.

"Strange," remarked Andy, "that he did not socialise in the college bar, with a colleague or undergraduate. It's as if he was searching for a victim?"

Bruno nodded his agreement.

Dates over a period of three months prior to his murder recorded Walters' visits to the Churchill Hotel and his contact with Lee Sharp. One entry recorded: "Lee has ambitions to be a writer. Told him to show me something he had written. A week later he produced a story about the fear of bidding at an auction, quite interesting, revealed his working-class background, promising start, encouraged him to continue."

For the following weeks, Walters recorded comments on short stories that Lee Sharp had shown him during his tea visits. By week five his comments about Sharp's short stories were not complimentary: the stories were biographical and boring. Walters could have been describing himself as a person with undesirable personality traits: obsessive, with difficulty in expressing emotions and low self-esteem.

By week nine Walters comment was contained in a one-word comment: "Rubbish."

"In three months, Lee Sharp had gone in Walters mind from 'promising' to 'rubbish'," said Bruno. "How can that be? And how could Lee Sharp have read Walters so well as to have hidden his final story from him? In which he revealed his fear that he might be a murderer?" Bruno recalled their view of it in the Lee Sharp file at Oxford police station.

"He served him afternoon tea once too often," said Andy.

Walters' next entry read: "Stopped showing me his written work. Must have become confused with the advice I've given him."

"Walters was the one who was confused," said Bruno. "And then he decides to kill him. The Lee Sharp murder is like the prison murder. He gets to know the victim, and after a short time he becomes transfigured into the person of his own demon, then he takes what he thinks is his justifiable revenge which exorcises the demon, but only until the next time."

"The murder satisfies his hedonistic desire to exercise power and control."

The third file on the front page contained a computer printed biography of Dr Geoffrey Klinker that was dated six months before the school reunion on 8 June.

On 1 February Walters had attended an appointment at Dr Klinker's clinic in Harley Street for a consultation on his prostate, which, after a physical examination, proved to be in order. However, he was not convinced about the negative diagnosis and it worried him continuously.

What irritated him about his consultation was that Klinker did not recognise him as his old school chum.

"So, it seems he could have had a motive for killing Dr Klinker?" said Andy.

Bruno wasn't sure. "We'll leave that for the experts," he said, meaning Dr White, the police psychiatrist.

His next entry on the Klinker file was dated 5 June: "Visit Island, stay with the Admiral Tuesday, Wednesday, Thursday and Friday."

"No mention of his mother?" said Andy.

"They hated each other," said Bruno. "And I suspect she saw his evil side."

"Reunion Friday 10.30 a.m. at Havenstreet Steam Railway."

"Saturday 9 June: School reunion went very well – no problem with Klinker."

This was followed by a series of entries concerning meetings with Bruno and Andy. The entries revealed an impatience with the police investigation and were derogatory towards Bruno and Andy, particularly Andy's failure to charge Arnold Harris with Klinker's murder, which Bruno had planned only to put Walters on the back foot.

Walters' conclusion was: "They will never find out who killed Klinker."

As a police officer, Bruno accepted he was not qualified to analyse the contents of Walters' files, but they contained enough to enable Dr David White, the court-appointed psychiatrist, to establish Walters' guilt, perhaps even to obtain a confession from him.

The files were the only items of interest in Walters'

University rooms, but Bruno requested from Oxford Police copies of Lee Sharp's essays as some of Walters' comments to Lee Sharp were revealingly contradictory.

One of the mysteries that they did not clear up from examining Walters' office was the time between Simon Dyer's murder in Exeter Prison and Lee Sharp's murder in Oxford, a period of about ten years. Bruno did not find leads to other crimes or murders committed by Walters in between.

Stan Lucas had provided his file on Dyer's murder, but the accompanying notes added nothing. The Devonshire Constabulary could add nothing of interest, which left only Nigel Woodruff in Oxford, where the murder had long since faded from the memory of officers still at the station who remembered the case.

For Bruno it was time to focus on a new case, and leave the structuring of the Crown's case against Walters to the lawyers. He felt they'd exhausted all lines of enquiry and could move on leaving him with the question that would remain with him: why did Walters choose to kill Dr Klinker? Was it simply what he thought was a put-down at his private hospital consultation?

By the time the case reached court in late November, Bruno and Andy had moved on to a mysterious death of a fisherman in Cowes.

The Crown lawyers did not stop at obtaining a conviction for Klinker's murder. By relating the identical physical characteristics of the three killings and Walters' physical presence in the near vicinity of the killings, he was convicted of all three killings and sentenced to a whole life term, without release, in a secure psychiatric prison, as a serial killer.